Sing A New Song

Sing A New Song

Michelle Lindo-Rice

www.urbanchristianonline.com

Urban Books, LLC
78 East Industry Court
Deer Park, NY 11729

ISBN 13: 978-1-60162-748-3
ISBN 10: 1-60162-748-3

First Printing February 2013
Printed in the United States of America

10 9 8 7 6 5 4 3 2 1

Distributed by Kensington Corp.
Submit Wholesale Orders to:
Kensington Publishing Corp.
C/O Penguin Group (USA) Inc.
Attention: Order Processing
405 Murray Hill Parkway
East Rutherford, NJ 07073-2316
Phone: 1-800-526-0275
Fax: 1-800-227-9604

Sing A New Song

Michelle Lindo-Rice

A Note to My Readers

Sing A New Song has a sensitive subject matter that may be hard to digest. However, my aim is to deliver the content tastefully, and with artistry, which I could do only through the direct leading of the Holy Spirit.

Sing A New Song introduces you to characters with difficult and life-changing situations. It is my hope that you will read this work of fiction but see truth. Jesus said, "I am the way, the truth, and the life. . . ."

It is my distinct pleasure that after reading *Sing A New Song,* you will be inspired to "love your neighbor as thyself" and perhaps be a little less judgmental, and realize that everything that happens in your life and others' happens for a reason.

Every single one of our life experiences sets us on a path intending to lead us to accepting the gift of salvation from our Lord Jesus Christ. My father, Pastor Clive Lindo, often says, "Nothing just happens," and Romans 8:28 sums it up well: "And, we know all things work together for good to them that love Him, to them that are called according to His purpose. . . ."

You will not be reading *Sing A New Song* by chance. Thank you, and I hope you enjoy. Above all, I truly hope it inspires you. May God bless you always.

Sincerely,
Michelle Lindo-Rice

Acknowledgments

I did not get here by myself! After years of rejections, rewrites, and revamping, I am here.

Countless thoughts and prayers and a lot of encouragement followed me each step of the way. I cannot begin to name them all. The good news is that if I missed you, forgive me. I will have other books for which you will have top billing. LOL.

Thank you, Lord. You gave me this gift. I sought to use it for my gain, but, Lord, now I use it to bring you glory, and I am content.

My sons, Eric Michael and Jordan Elijah: Hard work does pay off! I love you both and hope you will come to know and accept Jesus in your life. Let Him direct your path.

I'd like to acknowledge my parents, Clive and Pauline. My dad is not perfect, but he is perfect for me. And my sisters Zara Anderson and Christine Lindo, and my brothers, Mark Lindo (my twin), Ronald Lindo, and Sean Anderson.

I would like to give a special shout-out to Arielle, Erika, Erin, Katherine, Lisa, and Angela (Choo-Choo).

Kisses and hugs to my first fan readers and unpaid editors. Special thanks to Sobi-Dee Ophelia Lindo, my little sister and biggest fan; Glenda Momrelle-Clark, the first to read *Sing A New Song* way back when; Nicole Fox, for keeping me concise and in the active voice; Sandy Ward, my walking partner; Jane Adams,

Acknowledgments

punctuation/grammar guru; Colette Jeffries-Alexander, who has that weird kind of gift to catch the tiny inconsistencies that would have driven you nuts; and Bridgette Murray, who listened to me while I bounced story ideas/concepts. Thank you for consistently encouraging me and for keeping me going.

Thank you to my church brethren at Agape Church of God Seventh Day—including Missionary Velma Thompson.

To "Grandma" Lucille Adams, who has taught me the importance of attending conferences and networking.

To LaToya Haley, hairdresser and avid reader, who has read some of my earlier work and told me she wanted to see my book on the shelves.

To my numerous cousins and family members who support me. Some special mention goes to Arlene Murdock (Dolly), Patricia Walker (Precious), Karlene Summerall (June), Andrea Saunders, and Abbey Resilus.

I have to mention Annemarie Maynard, Linda Apple, and Karen Owens and all the staff in the ESE office. Hey, Peace River Elementary!

To established and awesome writers and women of faith who built my confidence when they told me I *can* write at the 2011 Faith and Fiction Retreat—Tiffany L. Warren, Victoria Christopher Murray, Pat Simmons, and ReShonda Tate Billingsley. To Cherise Fisher, the amazing editor who helped me stay focused and develop the story into what it is.

Finally, I give a heartfelt thanks to Joylynn Jossel-Ross, author and acquisitions editor at Urban Books, who gave content-editing tips to make me a better writer and to make *Sing A New Song* pop and jump off the page. Thank you.

Dedicated to . . .

My sister Sobi-Dee Ophelia Lindo. Stick around to live your life and your dreams to the fullest.

My aunt Dawna, and my cousin Pauline, who are cancer survivors, and my aunt Flavia, who took care of them. One day at a time.

♪ Chapter One

"I'm sorry, Tiffany. We've done all that we can do."
Dr. Ettelman spoke those words with great dread.

Tiffany Knightly leaned back in the plush black chair
across from Dr. Ettelman's wide mahogany desk. The
sun beamed on her honey-blond curls and heightened
her hazel-colored eyes. From her vantage point of three
floors up, she could look out the window behind him
and make out the business-clad people scurrying like
ants to keep appointments.

Tiffany blinked in slow motion. How could the world
go on when she had just received the most devastating
news of her life?

Dr. Ettelman must have moved from behind his
chair, though Tiffany did not recall seeing him move.
But the next thing she felt were his hands gently
squeezing her shoulders. Instinctively she shrank away
from him. He was the monster at that moment.

"Whoosh." Tiffany finally exhaled the breath she had
been holding. Vehemently, she shook her head. "No,
Dr. Ettelman, I must not have heard you correctly,"
she croaked in a voice she hardly even recognized. She
panted hard, feeling as if she was about to pass out
from the magnitude of emotions hitting her all at once.

Dr. Ettelman's face reflected empathy. He was still
talking about something. What was he even saying?

"We've done all that we could do, Ms. Knightly. Is
there someone that you can call?" She heard the hope-

ful inquiry but robotically shook her head. She needed some alone time to process the news she'd just received, and did not feel like calling anyone.

Tiffany opened her mouth, but it just hung open. Words were stuck in her throat. Vestiges of all coherent thought left her body. It was as if her mind had disintegrated, leaving her powerless to stop the feeling of losing sanity. She screamed on the inside to regain some semblance of control.

Tiffany could barely process the doctor's words, but he had said it. He had said that she was dying.

No. He must be mistaken—he was talking about someone else.

Tiffany frantically looked around the room, scarcely seeing the pictures on the wall. Her eyes rested on his medical degree prominently displaying his specialty. Her eyes zoomed in on the calendar behind her. Today was March 17 . . . March 17 . . . March 17. . . . March 17 was the day she received her death sentence.

Almost subconsciously, Tiffany picked up a picture frame on his desk. There was a girl smiling back at her. In slow motion, she replaced the silver-encrusted frame before finally looking into Dr. Ettelman's sympathetic face. Her tall, lithe frame drooped, and she sank even lower in her chair.

She could not be . . . No, she could not be dying. Tiffany absolutely refused to accept that, emphatically shaking her head in abject denial. Death was too . . . final.

She looked to Dr. Ettelman to provide some measure of comfort. In her heyday, she had been a national icon, but at this moment, Tiffany Knightly was just a patient, like any other who was the recipient of terrible news. "In my twenty-odd years of practice, it has never gotten any easier to tell any of my patients such devastating news, but I cannot give false hope. I have to tell the truth." Tiffany's initial shock turned into disbelief, and an unmistakable anger started to form. She keenly listened as he spoke.

"You are wrong," Tiffany shouted. Her long curly hair slapped across her face as she sprung to her feet. Tiffany's hazel-green eyes looked almost red with her palpitating fury. She had finally found her voice, and it reverberated like a crescendo off the walls. She bent her five-foot-nine frame over the doctor's desk and demanded, "You did something wrong. Test it again."

Dr. Ettelman remained calm and professional. Her demand was one he faced almost daily, and it was expected. He quickly assured her. "I have tested and retested the specimen carefully, Ms. Knightly. I would not give you this kind of news if I were not absolutely certain. However, you can get a second opinion—if you would like. I know someone I can recommend."

As if they were a lifeline, Tiffany zeroed in on his comments. Slowly, the reality of his words registered. Rationale was returning. She was dying. She had lung cancer, and the worst part was Tiffany did not even know how she had developed the disease. It wasn't like she was a smoker.

The symptoms had been inconsequential at first. Tiffany had been on tour and had started coughing a little. The coughing made her voice hoarse, but she was not overly concerned. Then, before she knew it, her little cough had escalated into bronchitis and eventually pneumonia. Just when she thought that she was well, the coughing returned suddenly and with a vengeance.

That was when Dr. Ettelman had checked for the possibility of lung cancer. He had found the lump on her lungs, had biopsied it, and had begun chemotherapy almost immediately. Tiffany had not been a viable candidate for surgery because of where the tumor was growing. Even removing the small specimen for testing had been a serious undertaking.

Evidently, all the treatments had been to no avail. Tiffany grappled with that thought. The chemotherapy had not proven an effective remedy. All the radiation, losing most of her hair, and feeling ghastly sick had all been in vain. The cancer had returned and had spread rapidly through her body. She did not know how long she had before the pain and agony would set in or before she looked sick and frail.

Dr. Ettelman prescribed some strong painkillers for her, but they made her feel nauseous or they put her to sleep, and radiation was not an option. She needed to have all her strength because her life was going to get increasingly difficult, and she had to be able to withstand it to the very end.

Time was all she had left.

Tiffany placed her hands in her hair, feeling the extensions she had put in to blend with her own natural curls—her immediate cure for hair loss. It was time to take them out, she mused.

Swallowing deeply, Tiffany gathered her courage and asked the question uppermost on her mind. "How long do I have?"

Her heart hammered so loudly in her chest that she could hear the beats resound like a drum. It felt like her heart was literally about to explode and splatter across the room. Unabashed, Tiffany allowed the tears welling in her eyes to fall. She felt a moment of helplessness and utter defeat.

With gritted teeth, Dr. Ettelman handed Tiffany a box of tissues, which she gratefully accepted with a resigned look on her face.

"I do not know for sure. It could be months. The human body has been known to show resilience that remains a miracle and a mystery. But from my experience, I would say about no more than a year. Do you need to talk to someone?" Dr. Ettelman offered.

"No," Tiffany assured him. "I will be all right."

Dr. Ettelman refrained from responding, but they both knew that was a lie. She was not going to be all right. She was going to be six feet under. Under the ground, not breathing, not seeing the sunshine. What was death like? How could anybody know?

Dazed, Tiffany stood to her feet, found her balance, and walked out of the doctor's office. When she got to the elevator, she vaguely heard someone calling her name.

Tiffany stopped and turned around with stiff, controlled movements. It was Dr. Ettelman's nurse, and it took everything in Tiffany's willpower to listen to what the nurse was telling her.

"Your purse," the nurse huffed, slightly out of breath. She extended the purse toward Tiffany. "You left it in Dr. Ettelman's office."

"Thank you," Tiffany politely responded and took the bag out of the waiting hands. She entered the elevator and gave a slight wave, but she did not want to be so civilized. She wanted to scream or yell like a banshee. Yet here she was, exchanging mere pleasantries about a bag that she could replace with hundreds more.

Tiffany let out a huge breath of air and knew she had to get out of the doctor's office. She needed some alone time to vent.

Just let everything out.

Her driver, Marlon, opened the town car door when he saw her exit the building, but Tiffany shook her head. She needed to walk and clear her head.

As Tiffany walked, she reflected on her life.

She had unfinished business to take care of before she . . .

Tiffany gulped, unable to complete that thought. She needed to make sure Karlie would be all right once she was . . . gone.

Karlie.

How was Tiffany going to tell her daughter she was dying?

Buzz . . . buzz . . .

Tiffany felt the vibration against her hip, and her brain slowly registered that it was a call from her cell phone. One she needed to answer.

Tiffany dug into her purse and grabbed the device, cringing when she saw who was calling. "Hi, Winona."

"Marlon called."

Winona Franks was a woman of few words. Highly efficient to a fault, she had been Tiffany's manager from the days of her "one-hit wonders" from her six albums. Tiffany met Winona by accident when she was preparing to do a spread with *Cosmopolitan*. With her long blond tresses, svelte shape, and sparkly blue eyes, Winona, then Winona Young, had been on her way to becoming a highly sought-after fashion model. When the two met, they became fast friends. The only problem was that Winona hated modeling. She wanted to use her brains and not her body to get ahead. Using her earnings, Winona dropped from the modeling scene and went to the NYU Stern School of Business. Tiffany later became her top client.

With her business acumen and expertise, Winona had amassed such a huge fortune for Tiffany that she could live quite comfortably for two, even three lifetimes. Throughout Tiffany's cancer nightmare, Winona had been a rock and a fortress to her. There was only one other person who Tiffany could rely on—a special friend—who not even Winona knew about, but she was not ready to call just yet.

"The news isn't . . . ," Tiffany trailed off.

"Tiffany? Are you saying what I think you're saying? Tiffany, please answer me." Winona's worry screamed through the phone. Winona knew about Tiffany's appointment with Dr. Ettelman and had waited anxiously for Tiffany to tell her she now had a clean bill of health.

Tiffany exhaled, hearing Winona breathing deeply on the other line. "I just needed a minute." Actually, she needed a lifetime to come to grips with her imminent death. Tiffany shuddered but continued. "I—I—I have a year, Winona. One measly year to . . . How am I going to tell Karlie?"

"Get in the car and go home, Tiffany. I am coming," Winona directed.

Tiffany belatedly realized that Marlon was creeping alongside her. She could see the worry etched across his face as his head turned back and forth from the road to where she was now standing.

Tiffany swung her bag back and forth in her arms like a pendulum while she debated. She felt like just running off into the sunset and disappearing for parts unknown.

"Tiffany," Winona called out, her urgency evident through the line. "Please I am thousands of miles away. Please just get—"

"I'm going." Tiffany dragged her feet toward her car. Marlon put on the hazard lights and quickly got out and opened the rear door for her. Like a dutiful child, Tiffany entered the car. She told Winona, "Don't come. I'll be in touch," then ended the call.

As they drove toward her huge L.A. mansion, Tiffany took in the sights before her. Was it just her imagination or did the world suddenly seem brighter? The water from the beach sparkled and shone brightly. The leaves on the trees appeared greener. The sun beamed with unequaled brilliance.

"I can't look anymore," Tiffany whispered before closing her eyes and leaning back into the comfortable leather seats.

"Did you say something, miss?" Marlon asked.

"No," Tiffany replied and turned her head away from his piercing eyes. Tears rolled down her face. Silently they fell. Tiffany placed her fist in her mouth to keep from crying aloud. There was so much she had to do, and how much time she had to do it, only God knew.

♪ Chapter Two

How could she tell Karlie she was dying? How could she not? Tiffany asked herself.

A week had passed since her devastating news, and Tiffany had been ensconced in her room in a self-imposed exile. She still had not generated a good lead-in for telling her daughter the cancer had returned.

Winona had called several times, but Tiffany had needed space. She sent a terse text message to Winona, telling her to book her round-trip passage to New York.

When Tiffany got up this morning, she knew she could not let another day pass without telling her daughter the truth. Today, March 24, was the day she would tell her daughter that she was dying. Karlie had given her space, assuming she had a cold or something and was simply recuperating. Now Tiffany was about to shatter that thought.

Tiffany paced back and forth, trying to compose the right words. That had been about a half hour ago, and Tiffany was still hemming and hawing. Her living room, decorated in varying shades of yellow, was sunny and cheerful. Tiffany would read in this room and look out the window to view the spacious backyard, which housed the pool and a man-made pond complete with ducks and fish. But the brightness of the room couldn't make what she had to tell Karlie any better.

"Mom," Karlie said softly. "You're going to wear a hole in the rug. Just tell me what's going on."

Instinctively, Tiffany lifted her heel to peek. Her Prada shoes did look a little worn. She shrugged. There was a closet full of replacements.

Tiffany stopped pacing and finally looked into the face so like her own. Karlie had the same skin tone, hair, and body type. She was a mini-replica of Tiffany herself, except for her honey-brown eyes and slightly fuller lips. Tiffany could see Karlie preparing herself, instinctively knowing that whatever it was, she would not like it.

My own gift from heaven—so beautiful and so precious, Tiffany thought. A single tear pricked her eye and ran down the side of her face.

The antithesis of Tiffany at that age, Karlie was smart as a whip and never gave an ounce of trouble. Her teachers doted on her. Tiffany knew that she had lucked out when it came to Karlie.

She just had to do it.

Tiffany steeled herself and collected her thoughts. "Okay, there is no easy way to say this." She had to give Karlie the straight facts. Wiping her hands on her cream-colored linen slacks, Tiffany sat down and took her daughter's hands in hers. Karlie trembled beneath her touch.

"Karlie," Tiffany began, "you know how for the past couple of years I have been fighting this cancer. You know all about the chemo and everything."

Karlie nodded her head. Fear slowly crept up her spine and chilled her to the core. Karlie broke into tears.

Tiffany started crying at the sight of her daughter's pain. She hugged her daughter tightly and whispered in her hair, "I am sorry, honey. The doctors tried. They've done all they could—"

"No!" Karlie wailed. "You cannot be dying. Do not leave me, Mommy. What did I do to deserve this?" She grabbed her mother, crumpling her linen shirt. "I'm not going to let you go, Mom."

Tiffany wailed in earnest then. She cried and cried. This was the worst pain she could inflict on a fifteen-year-old. However, Tiffany knew she had to be forthright with her daughter. She needed to prepare Karlie somehow for her impending death.

Karlie pulled out of her mother's arms and ran into her bedroom. Tiffany let her daughter go, knowing that she herself needed time. She had some tough decisions to make and some dirty linens to dredge up.

Tiffany pulled out her cell phone and quickly speed dialed the one person she knew she could call. When she heard the voice on the other end, Tiffany's composure cracked. "I need to see you."

♪ Chapter Three

"Five months?" Winona's mouth sprung open with disbelief. "You expect me to settle your affairs and your vast estate and share holdings in merely five months?"

Tiffany nodded.

"Impossible." Winona dragged her hands through her hair. "Tiffany, forgive me, but this is just too much. I'm telling you right now it's not doable. I can't get this all done by September."

"Make it happen," Tiffany shot back. "I don't have time. Time is one luxury I do not have. I have to get my affairs in order in an extraordinarily short amount of time. Winona, I need you to be on this, like, yesterday. I need to be settled here in New York by the end of August, early September."

Leaving Karlie behind while she made this trip had been painful because her daughter was still in the throes of coming to grips with losing her mother. But Tiffany had no choice. She had flown to New York to meet with up with Winona. Winona had moved to New York when she met and married her third husband, Harvey Franks. The distance had not affected Winona's capability or their relationship.

Tiffany also had another discreet matter that necessitated her trip to New York, but first things first.

"Winona, I've thought long and hard about this, and I have to liquidate my assets. It makes sense to me. Karlie is way too young to handle the magnitude of my estate. You know that."

"Yeah." Winona's eyes glazed over. "I'm not even sure that I can handle the task, Tiffany, because I refuse to give your properties and stocks away for pennies. Are you sure you don't want Arnold in on this?"

Arnold Truitt was Winona's second husband and Tiffany's legal attorney. Somehow, after their parting, Winona and Arnold had remained amicable and even lunched together as old friends. *Kudos to her,* Tiffany thought. Her mind wandered to her own ex-husband, Thomas. She hadn't spoken to him in years. That was about to change now, too.

Tiffany realized Winona was waiting with a pen and notepad on one leg and her iPad on the other. Tiffany said, "No. At least not yet. I can't think past six months' time, Winona. I might not be here."

"You will be." Winona scribbled furiously on her notepad before pulling up the calendar on her iPad.

Tiffany sat while Winona finished her notes. She looked around the room, taking in the understated elegance of Winona's loft, which doubled as her office. Winona had purchased the loft as her temporary home, refusing to live with Harvey until they were married. The rich browns and burgundies were soothing, especially since outside did not feel like spring. It was the end of March, but outside it was a whopping forty degrees.

"What about the house?" Tiffany asked. She could not refer to the place in question as her home, though she had lived there for most of her childhood.

"It is being gutted and renovations have been made, as per your directions," Winona replied. She removed her trendy shades to peer into Tiffany's eyes. "I still don't get why you're planning to move there."

Tiffany did not expect Winona to understand why she would leave her elegant million-dollar home to take on anonymity and move back to Hempstead, New York. "Because I am dying, Winona. I want to go home. Correction, I *need* to go home. I am doing this for Karlie. Believe me, if it weren't for her, I would not step another foot into that place. When can I go take a look at it?"

Instead of answering Tiffany's question, Winona asked another. "Did you tell Karlie about the move yet?"

"No. I plan to do that when I get home." Tiffany arched her eyebrow, indicating she wanted an answer to her original question.

Winona lowered her head to glance at the delicate diamond-encrusted timepiece on her slender wrist. "The workers assured me that you can go over there late tomorrow afternoon. Did you need me to come with you?"

"No."

Winona's head popped up at Tiffany's abrupt response.

Taking a deep breath, Tiffany softened her tone. "No, I mean, that is something I have to do on my own." Tiffany swallowed after her blatant lie, but she could not bring Winona with her.

Winona got up and walked around her desk to sit next to Tiffany on the small couch. She hugged the younger woman. "Tiffany, I have been with you through chemotherapy and radiation. I have seen you at your best and at your worst. You are more than a client to me. You know that. You know you could stay here with me until . . . that time came," Winona gently assured her.

"I know." Tiffany nodded and pulled out of the embrace to look at Winona. "Winona, you have been good to me. You have stood by me through it all. But Karlie needs family—someone who will be her guardian and take care of her. Winona, Karlie needs her father."

"Thomas?" Winona sputtered. "Is he the reason you are going home? Even if you're dying, I do not think a reunion is the answer."

Tiffany chuckled. Winona was not one to mince her words. "Let's just say Thomas is a part of the reason." Tiffany knew she was deliberately being vague, but she was about to delve into a topic that left a sour taste in her mouth.

Winona's eyebrow arched with inquiry. Tiffany's subtle remarks did not suit a woman of her disposition. Patience was not her strong point, and brutal honesty was her trademark. "Hit the nail on the head, Tiffany. Quit hedging."

"I plan to visit my mother," Tiffany began. Winona prodded her on, knowing that Tiffany had more to share. "Winona, I need the name of a good private detective."

Winona's eyes widened as her active imagination took over. She lowered her voice to a conspiratorial whisper. "I know the perfect person—Edison Sniles—a retired detective who's fast, reliable, and discreet. Tiffany, what are you planning to do? Are you going to plot your revenge on Thomas after all these years?"

"Nothing of the sort," Tiffany quickly assured her. "I just need to conduct a little . . . ah . . . research . . . to determine who is best suited to become Karlie's guardian." *Father,* Tiffany corrected inwardly. Actually, she first had to find out *who* Karlie's father was.

Tiffany fretted. She had done a dirty deed and now was going to pay. Not once had she thought she was going to have to reveal her most shameful secret—that she, Tiffany Knightly, had married Thomas knowing that there was a strong possibility that he might not be

Karlie's father. Tiffany turned away from Winona for a moment and closed her eyes. Why had she done it? She exhaled. Why had she gone on a promiscuous rampage and slept with four men? At that time in her life, she thought it was for revenge. But now that she was a little older and wiser, Tiffany admitted that she had only exacerbated a situation that was going to disrupt quite a few lives. Should she just perpetuate the lie? After all, no one would know if she only kept her mouth shut. No, Tiffany reasoned, it was time to come clean. She turned to face Winona again, who had been watching her with a puzzled expression on her face.

"I have to do this, Winona," she said desperately. That was all she could say without saying too much. "I just have to," she whispered with tightly clenched fists.

Winona pointed to the goose bumps popping up on her flesh. "I knew there was more going on than you're telling me. Tiffany, what aren't you telling me?" she asked with quiet concern.

Gathering her dignity, Tiffany facetiously replied, "Ask me no question, I tell you no lie."

♫ Chapter Four

"Never say never," Tiffany chided herself bitterly. She tossed herself on the king-size bed in the expansive guest quarters of Winona's majestic Park Avenue apartment.

Tiffany held on to her head with both her hands. The demons of her past attacked and whipped her with guilt. Her mind raced about a hundred miles per hour as she contemplated the magnitude of the task before her.

The past she had to revisit.

Tiffany mulled over other alternatives for Karlie and her estate. Sadly, the truth twisted within her being, pushing her to belch it out. She needed to dig up ancient history because Karlie needed family.

Family.

There was always Tiffany's mother—Merle Peterson.

Tiffany rented an Escalade equipped with GPS to drive to her mother's home in Baldwin. She had dutifully purchased the home but had never paid a visit. She knew if she ever set foot in her mother's house, she would regret it, but now she had to.

Merle was blood.

Tiffany hoped her mother would look beyond the past and see that. She purposely went alone because with Merle, well, one could never know what to expect, and it could not be expected that Winona would remain cool when faced with Merle's rancor.

The traffic was light, and approximately forty-five minutes later, Tiffany pulled up to the curb outside her mother's house. She sat in her car and studied the two-story structure for several minutes.

Tiffany dreaded this moment. Her palms felt sweaty as she gripped the steering wheel. Exactly two weeks after learning about her imminent death, she was about to break the news to her mother. A woman who couldn't care less if she ever rested eyes on her again.

Her knuckles were taut and white. Perspiration soaked her Armani blouse. She had not seen her mother face-to-face in over fifteen years. Not that it would matter to Merle. Knowing her, Tiffany anticipated she would not be there long. Taking a deep breath, Tiffany whipped her sunglasses on her face, opened the car door, and stepped out. Her sleek high heels crunched on the gravel as she walked toward the sidewalk.

The kids in the neighborhood stopped playing to stare at the lovely woman. Tiffany was not worried that they would not recognize her. She had been before their time.

Gathering her courage, Tiffany sped up the three steps and rang her mother's doorbell. Almost immediately, Merle opened the door and stood in the doorway.

"What do you want?"

Tiffany's demeanor changed with her mother's abrupt question. "You haven't seen me in almost sixteen years, and this is how you greet me?"

Merle did not answer. She frowned and gave Tiffany the once-over, which left no doubt how she felt.

Tiffany knew she was the last person her mother wanted to lay eyes on, but this was a matter of life and death. "May I come in?" she pointedly asked, since her mother had not made any motion to invite her into her home. The home she'd bought. Tiffany tried to swallow the bitter thought.

Merle reached into her pocket, took out a pack of gum, and pulled out a piece. She opened the wrapper and stuck the piece of gum in her mouth. She stared Tiffany up and down once more before she begrudgingly stepped aside.

Tiffany bit her tongue to refrain from saying something nasty and entered her mother's house. She walked into the living room and sat on the edge of the sofa. Painted a soft buttercup yellow with green trimmings, the living room was warm and inviting, opposite to her mother's temperament. The sofa and love seat were color coordinated, and the decor was impeccable.

Merle sat down and gave Tiffany a look of utter unconcealed disgust.

Tiffany took a deep breath before spitting out her news. "Mama, I thought it best to let you know in person that I am dying." Tiffany nervously wiped her hands on her dark crimson jeans. She wore a thick black sweater with a matching jean jacket, but the coldness in the room chilled her very core.

Merle remained unresponsive, and her face mirrored no emotion. In fact, she gave no indication that Tiffany had even spoken.

Tiffany sat in suspense as she waited for her mother to cry, say something, or provide some sort of human feedback. Merle displayed none of those reactions. She remained stoic, unaffected as she popped her gum. Then she bit out, "So what did you expect me to do about that?"

"Wow." This time Tiffany did not hold her tongue. "I tell you that I am dying, and this is how you react? Have you no feelings for me whatsoever?" Tiffany's chest heaved. Overcome with pent-up anger and hurt, she resisted the urge to rant or pummel her mother with her fists. Tiffany chose instead to dig her heels into the plush carpet to prevent herself from ripping Merle's eyes from the sockets.

Warring with that emotion, Tiffany sat silently, unconsciously willing her mother to care. She desperately needed her mother to comfort her, but instead she was faced with a cold, aloof, uncaring shell of a human being.

Merle declined to answer Tiffany's question but asked another instead. "What do you plan to do with the girl?"

Her tenuous rein on her self-control snapped. Her eyes bulged, and she got right into her mother's face. "You are unbelievable. How can you be so heartless?"

"Heartless? I have got no respect for whores," Merle hurled back while giving Tiffany a look of sheer contempt. Merle was just as slender as Tiffany and an inch taller. She had once been beautiful, but bitterness had left lines and marks that changed her entire countenance. Her hair and nails were well tended, though, thanks to Tiffany's generous monthly checks.

"You might see me as a whore, but I am still your daughter, and the girl you are talking about is your granddaughter," Tiffany passionately shot back.

Though she yelled, Tiffany felt a deep, unfathomable hurt. All the old pain and anger returned with full force. To Tiffany, it felt like it was yesterday instead of fifteen years later. She did not know why she had expected any warm sentiment from her mother.

Merle had never cared about her welfare when it truly mattered. Her actions had consistently demonstrated that. Tiffany had been insane to expect an entirely different response.

Merle scoffed at her daughter's remark. "You are nothing to me." She enunciated the words loudly to drive the point home.

"Oh, but my money's good enough, isn't it?" Her mother religiously cashed the monthly checks.

Merle merely rolled her eyes and sucked her teeth.

Tiffany watched as her mother stood up, wiped her hands on her pants, and walked to the door.

Merle opened her front door, signaling their impromptu meeting was officially over. "I think you've overstayed your welcome and it's time for you to leave."

Tiffany picked up her purse and keys and walked out of her mother's house without a backward glance. She would not allow her mother to see how affected she was by her cold, callous behavior. As she drove off, Tiffany finally let the tears fall. Her vision blurred, so she pulled over at the next block and cried her eyes out, intensely regretting her decision to seek her mother's help. Seeing her mother had served only to exhume all the past hurt and pain she had so carefully buried.

If only her mother had offered to take Karlie. But Merle didn't care to know her only grandchild; she was more interested in calling Tiffany a whore.

"Why did I go there?" Tiffany opened the glove compartment, haphazardly searching for some tissues. "Why did I let her get to me, again?" Tiffany cried, knowing deep down inside that what her mother had said was true. She was a whore.

♫ Chapter Five

Tiffany exited the elevator that led into the Franks' apartment. Her eyes were puffy and red, and her nose stuffy.

"Winona?" Her voice echoed. Winona and Harvey must have been out to dinner, she surmised. Tiffany felt glad she would not need to make excuses, for she was not hungry and was in no mood for company. She was drained and tired after her run-in with her mother. Tiffany called Karlie to check on her, but her nerves were too frayed for any lengthy conversation. Instead, she got into bed fully dressed and closed her eyes, falling into a restless sleep. She tossed and turned as memories assailed her from so many years ago.

Tiffany ran out the gate to meet Myra Crumb, who impatiently tapped her foot. "Where you been, girl? Let's get a move on, or we're going to be late." The two girls wore matching summer outfits and just knew they looked too cute for words. Thomas Knightly and Neil Jameson caught up with them. Both girls giggled, feeling good about walking to school with their men.

Excitement filled their veins. "We got to get the prom tickets before school," Myra imperiously demanded, "or the line during lunch and after school is going to be ridiculous." Myra looked at her watch. "We should just make it."

Tiffany and the boys shook their head and readily agreed. They knew better than to argue with Myra when she was in a tizzy.

"Did you bring your money for later?" Myra asked, double-checking with Tiffany. They planned to go to the mall and find dresses and all the accessories they would need to get all decked out for prom. Both girls felt so grown up to take public transportation to the mall instead of relying on Myra's mom to drive them.

"Yep," Tiffany replied. She patted the money sling she wore underneath her shirt. "I have more than enough right here. What about you?" Tiffany looked at Myra. "My parents gave me their credit card."

To Tiffany, Myra sounded like a real adult since she would sign a credit card. "Awesome."

"Yeah, I know." Myra grabbed her hand giddily.

The two girls shopped for hours to find the accessories. Myra even generously purchased a pair of shoes for Tiffany that she felt Tiffany "just had to have" to match her dress.

The night of the prom, Tiffany left the house, feeling like a fairy-tale princess. Actually, she felt like a woman. Thomas's eyes bulged when he saw her, and Tiffany glowed with pleasure. They went to the prom with Myra and Neil, and then the two couples ventured to an after party at one of the football players' house. Tiffany and Myra were nervous because they had both decided prom was the night they were going to do "it."

They had held hands and prayed. Yes, they had prayed about committing fornication. With stars in her eyes, Tiffany made up her mind to give herself to Thomas, knowing in her heart that she loved him.

Thomas was eager and awkward but was too young to know exactly what to do. After fumbling around in the dark, Tiffany swallowed her disappointment but lovingly suggested, "How about we wait to make our first time really special? We should go all out and book

*a hotel room or something, instead of here where any-
body can just walk in on us."*

*Tiffany felt since they were in love, there was no
reason they could not wait. Thomas agreed with it
with an eloquent "Um, okay, yeah," because he needed
to get some advice from his friends—and protection.*

*Tiffany could still see him with his hands poked into
his pockets, looking boyish and unsure.*

*It was four thirty in the morning when Tiffany en-
tered her house after the prom and the after party.
Her mother was a nurse and worked the graveyard
shift, so Tiffany had not cared when she got home. As
long as she got in before her mother got home at 7:30
A.M., she was satisfied.*

*But her stepfather, Clifford Peterson, was still up.
It was obvious he had been waiting for her. Clifford
Peterson was an imposing man. He was only a couple
inches shorter than her five feet nine inches, but he
was broad and thick. He had a gut from drinking too
much beer. His eyes were his greatest feature, for
they were a golden shade, which must have drawn
her mother in, but to Tiffany, they were like the devil's
spawn.*

*Tiffany bid him a hasty good night and retreated to
her room, as far away from Clifford Peterson as she
could get. She didn't know if it was just pure instinct
on her part or a woman's intuition.*

*Merle had married Clifford when Tiffany was
about eight or nine, and he had adopted her. Tiffany
had never known her real father, and Merle had never
mentioned him, so Clifford was the only father she'd
ever known. But for some reason Tiffany never quite
warmed up to him. She did not know why. She just did
not like the way he looked at her, and never stayed in
the house alone with him when her mother was not
around.*

Tiffany raced into her room, intending to be fully asleep by the time Merle returned. She had barely undressed before Clifford boldly opened the door and entered her room.

"What!" Tiffany exclaimed. Had she forgotten to lock her door?

He closed the door behind him with a decisive click.

Oh, no. Her eyes fell on the key he was pocketing in his jeans. He was shirtless. Gross. "You have a key to my room?"

"Yeah," Clifford's gravelly voice answered. "And it isn't your room. You don't pay the bills in here. I do."

He belched loudly. Tiffany could smell the alcohol and covered her mouth to keep from gagging at the stench. Feeling closed in, Tiffany moved into a corner of her room to put as much space between them as possible. She wished he would just leave, but Clifford blocked the door. Clifford walked over until his putrid breath hit her face. He ground his body against hers and called her a tease and a taunt.

"What are you doing?" Scared, Tiffany pushed against his frame. With the element of surprise in her favor, Clifford's body gave and she bolted for the door, but Clifford was too quick for her. He grabbed her and unceremoniously tossed her onto the bed.

Clifford pounced on top of her and touched her intimately. Tiffany squealed aloud, wondering what time it was and when her mother would come home. "Mommy! Mommy!" Tiffany yelled and fought back. She pushed, but he was like a brick wall, so she bit down into his arm.

Clifford yelped, grabbed her hair, and twisted it. "You little . . ." He stopped and looked at her menacingly. A wicked gleam entered his eyes. "I see how you like it," Clifford whispered. He gripped her mouth with his hands before removing her underwear.

Tiffany cried. Tears rolled down her face. She bucked her body to get him off, but her strength failed. Clifford entered her without thought or concern. Tiffany cried out in agony as she felt her insides being ripped asunder. "Stop! Stop!"

She thrashed her body to get him off, but her efforts only served to entice him, as the lunatic cackled, "Yes, yes, yes." *Still she fought. Her hands dug into his skin, drawing blood.* "Feisty little thing, aren't you?"

"Please, Clifford, please stop," *Tiffany begged. She felt suffocated and helpless against the torturous assault on her body.* "Please, Daddy."

Clifford was past the point of hearing her pleas. He continued continued his assault, and to Tiffany it felt like days, but he would not stop not until he was done. Tiffany cried uncontrollably while she secretly plotted his murder. She was going to castrate Clifford Peterson for doing this to her.

She heard a crack in the door. "Mama."

Clifford jumped off the top of Tiffany.

Thank God. Her mother would put Clifford out on his butt.

"What is . . . going on . . . here?" *Merle placed both hands on her hips, and her face twisted with disgust. She whipped her head from one to the other and waited for an answer.*

Sober, Clifford buttoned his pants and backed away from the bed. "Merle, honey," *he huffed,* "this isn't what it looks like." *He vainly tried to capture his breath.* "She"—*Clifford pointed at Tiffany with contempt*—"she did this. Tiffany enticed me, Merle."

Tiffany released an odd-sounding laugh, fully expecting her mother to kick Clifford out and pummel him for what he had done. To her surprise, her mother rounded on her.

"You whore! Harlot! What did I do to deserve this from my own daughter?"

"I'm sorry, baby." Clifford now sat in the corner. The very corner he'd had Tiffany sequestered in earlier.

Ignoring her soiled linens and torn gown, Tiffany shot out of bed. She ached and hurt in places she shouldn't have. "Mom, he raped me! He raped me. Even when I called him Daddy, he still raped me."

"I was drunk, Merle." Clifford balled like a baby. "I didn't know what I was doing."

"He's lying, Mama." Tiffany choked on her tears. Beseechingly, she looked toward her mother and held her hands out.

"Mama. Mama . . ." Tiffany woke up out of her sleep with her arms outstretched. Tears soaked the silk pillow on which her head lay. Tiffany realized she was in Winona's apartment and not her old home in Hempstead. She got up off the bed to grab some tissues, wiped her face, and sat on the ottoman placed at the edge of the bed. It had been years since this had happened. Seeing her mother must have triggered the old nightmares.

Fully alert, Tiffany remembered how Merle had walked right past her daughter and over to Clifford. He also had had his hands outstretched.

Merle had chosen.

Behind Merle's back, Clifford had given Tiffany a look of triumph and had had the gall to lick his lips.

At that moment, Tiffany did not know what else to do. She felt hopeless and utterly alone. So she ran.

♬ Chapter Six

Neil pulled his car in front of Tiffany's house in Hempstead. He got out of his car and walked over to where Tiffany sat waiting on her stoop. She'd park her truck in the driveway. "Tiffany Knightly," he called and extended his arms.

Tiffany took a moment to study the man before her. Time had been good to him. He looked the same, except for the fact that he had more muscles on his six-foot-three-inch frame and a mustache and slightly peppered sideburns. Neil was the delicious color of dark molasses. Idris Elba had some serious competition. She felt herself drawn into a tight embrace. Hugging Neil was like coming home.

"I've missed you," Tiffany said in a tone filled with warmth and affection.

Neil released her and touched her cheek fondly. "I nearly keeled over when I got your phone call that you were moving back here."

"I know I was a bit dramatic," Tiffany confessed. She splayed her hands toward her house. "But I couldn't come back to this house on my own. Truthfully, I only bought it because of Ben—my special tree. I never thought I would actually ever set foot in this house again."

Neil nodded, fully understanding. "I am glad you called me. I know you couldn't do this on your own." He looked at his watch. "Come on. Let's go inside."

"I feel fortunate your job gave you the time to come."

"Tiffany, I took the time. Now, quit stalling." Neil took the keys from her hands. The two remained silent as they opened the gate.

Tiffany was pleased at how clean the house was. Winona had carried out her wishes to the fullest. The caretakers had mowed the lawn and installed new siding, along with a fresh coat of paint. She must have hired gardeners, because there were all sorts of flowers planted along the edges of the lawn. It was breathtaking.

"Nice," Neil commented. "I wondered what was going on when I saw all the commotion going down over here." His house was at the end of a cul-de-sac. Tiffany lived at the other end of the block, right across the street.

"Yes, they did a good job," Tiffany whispered. "The only thing left is the decorating. I'm having a few pieces shipped from my house in L.A., but otherwise everything will be brand new."

Neil looked at Tiffany. Her hazel eyes looked hollow and sad. He kissed her on both cheeks. "I am so sorry, honey."

Tears flooded her eyes, and Tiffany nodded, knowing he was referring to her diagnosis. "Thanks, but I'm even more sorry for Karlie."

Tiffany walked over and sat on the third step. "Neil, do you think all this is happening because of—"

"No," Neil cut in. "Tiffany, don't even go there. All that stuff with Clifford went down a long time ago."

"Yes, but you told me, warned me even, to tell the truth."

"Tiffany, Clifford raped you. You can be excused for your temporary . . . ah . . . insanity."

All those years ago, after seeing how her mother had blatantly chosen her rapist over her, Tiffany had raced outside to her tree. She had really wanted to run away, but she had no job, no money, and nowhere to go. For days, she had cried and cried, pleading with her mother to believe her. Yet the more she'd pleaded, the more Merle had closed her mind and heart toward her daughter. Merle had treated her like scum around the toilet or something on the bottom of her shoe.

Distraught, Tiffany had become a shell of her former self. She'd even dropped Thomas and avoided Myra's calls. Normally, Myra would have been at her door, demanding an explanation but she was preparing to go visit her grandparents for a month in Florida. But something else happened to Tiffany during that time. Neil.

Neil Jameson. The two had forged a secret friendship that no one was privy to, not even Neil's wife and Tiffany's best friend, Myra. They knew that Myra wouldn't understand or appreciate their close friendship.

Tiffany looked at him with a self-deprecating smile. "Insanity? That's a cute euphemism for my past peccadilloes."

Neil sat next to her on the step and scooted his huge frame closer to her. "Tiffany, you have to forgive yourself for your past. It has been sixteen years. God has already thrown that in the sea of forgetfulness. Believe me."

Tiffany leaned into his strong shoulders, soaking up his strength. Neil had such faith in her. He was her staunch defender to the end.

"I saw my mother."

Neil tensed. "Why did you even waste your time visiting that cantankerous spawn of Satan? That explains your renewed bout with self-recrimination."

Tiffany beseechingly held his arm and pleaded for him to understand. "She's my mother, Neil. I felt she had a right to know."

"Well, did she welcome you with open arms?"

His sarcasm grated on her fragile ego, and Tiffany burst into tears. "No. She called me a slut."

Neil expended a deep breath. "I didn't mean to make you cry, love. That is the last thing I meant to do." Neil reached into his suit pocket to pull out a handkerchief. He gently wiped her face. "Don't let Merle Peterson get to you now. Not after all you have accomplished in your life. Not after everything you have been through."

Tiffany nodded. She got up and faced the rest of the stairs. "I cannot avoid it any longer," she whispered. "I have to go up."

Neil followed suit. "Lead the way."

They walked into what had been her parents' old room. "This will be my room." The only way she had been able to move in here was knowing Clifford Peterson was six feet under and he had taken his dastardly deeds with him to the grave.

Her temperature rose every time she thought about that . . . monster. That was why she had done all in her power to ensure that every remnant of him and her childhood here was removed. Gone were the tattered curtains and grungy furnishings. They would be replaced by the best money could buy.

By mutual consent, Tiffany and Neil visited the bedroom down the hall, near the scene of the crime. "This will be my workout room."

Neil only nodded. He was more concerned about Tiffany's mental state than the physical structure. "Let's go to your old room."

"Karlie's new bedroom," Tiffany announced. She entered, and goose bumps rose on her flesh.

Neil hugged her close. "How do you feel?"

Tiffany laughed. "Relieved. Wow, what a difference a can of paint makes."

"Well, I think it was more than that."

Tiffany agreed. "Karlie is going to love it here."

"Does she know about the move yet? Have you told her your true reasons for moving?"

"No to both questions."

"How do you think she is going to react?"

"Like the typical teen. She's going to scream bloody murder about the move. And I think she's going to hate me once she finds out that the man she grew up thinking was her father might not be," Tiffany said, predicting her daughter's reaction.

Neil exhaled. "You can always change your mind about all of it, you know. I mean, I don't understand why you insisted on holding on to this house. You could've had your choice of houses to buy with today's market." Neil couldn't fathom why Tiffany would hold on to the place where she had experienced the greatest hurt of her life.

Tiffany looked Neil in the eyes to communicate the depth of what she had to say. "Honestly, Neil, I don't know why I held on to the house, especially since my mother wanted to move. I haven't examined my motives that deeply. But I think I owe it to Karlie to tell her the sordid truth. But you're here, Neil. You're here."

♪ Chapter Seven

"I'm not leaving. You can't make me."

"Karlie, it's what is best," Tiffany replied, eyeing the poked-out lip of her sulking fifteen- year-old daughter. She dug her hands through her curls with extreme frustration. She was jet-lagged and could barely stand on her two feet. But Tiffany knew she had to let Karlie know they would be moving by the end of summer, God willing.

"All my stuff is here. All my friends are here. You can't expect me to just up and leave," Karlie screamed.

"Who is this?" Tiffany asked. "And what have you done with my precious, agreeable daughter?"

"I'm still me, Mom," Karlie countered. She dropped her voice a few notches as the waterworks began. "I know you're dying . . . and I am trying to deal with that." Karlie hiccupped. "But now we have to move? It's just too much."

Tiffany took her daughter's hands and led her to the very couch where she had spilled the news about her impending death.

"I hate this couch," Karlie cried.

"I'll get rid of it," Tiffany promised. "Karlie, I know it is a lot to uproot you from everything you hold dear, especially now. But . . . I have to, Karlie. You have to get to know your . . . your father."

"My father?" Karlie's brown eyes filled with tears. "I don't even know him, Mom. I only know that his name is Thomas Knightly, and he never comes around, and I can count on one hand the amount of times I've actually spoken to him."

Tiffany felt guilt swarm around her belly at the half-truths she had fed her daughter over the years. She continued gently, "You still have to get to know your father, because I won't be around much longer, and I have to make sure you're okay." That was the truth, she told herself.

Karlie leaned in until her head rested on her mother's lap. Tiffany smoothed her curls and wiped the tears with the edge of her shirt.

"Life is just so unfair," Karlie moaned. "I don't want to lose you, Mommy." Karlie reverted to calling Tiffany "Mommy" when she was truly upset. "Why did this happen?"

"I don't know," Tiffany whispered and gently stroked her daughter's hair. "I don't know what else to do, Karlie. That's why I am selling everything and moving to my old home in Hempstead."

Karlie sat up. Her face was red and splotchy from crying. "Paula and Lorna are not going to believe this." Paula Style and Lorna Persimmon were Karlie's best friends from childhood.

Tiffany knew they were not going to take Karlie's departure well. She sighed. "I'm sorry, honey. Truly sorry."

"I know, but this sucks."

"How about a shopping spree?"

Karlie perked up. "Shopping?"

"Yeah." Tiffany had thrown out that ace to change the mood. "Invite Paula and Lorna, and I will give you carte blanche with my card. You guys can have the ultimate girls' night out. No limits."

"Seriously? Mom, you are the best." Karlie rushed out to call her friends and make some plans to hit the road for a shopping spree. Lorna had her license and drove a Range Rover, so Tiffany wasn't overly concerned.

Tiffany smiled but knew she had manipulated her daughter's cooperation with bribery. It left a slightly bad taste in her mouth. But she knew this was only the first of many briberies to come.

It was mid-September before Tiffany and Karlie finally made the move. True to form, Winona had turned most of Tiffany's assets into cold, hard cash, the majority of which now sat in a trust fund for Karlie. Some Tiffany would spend as she pleased, some she had already donated to several charities, and the rest would be for Karlie's father. He would receive a significant sum for Karlie's care. Tiffany had decided against selling her L.A. mansion, so instead she left Winona as the trustee for its upkeep until Karlie was capable of taking over its care.

Before she knew it, Tiffany was driving from the airport back to her childhood home in the brand-new red Escalade Winona had purchased for her. She slowly parked in front of the house and turned the ignition off. "Here we are," Tiffany said with a bright tone she did not feel. She pointed past Karlie to the house.

"This is where you grew up, Mommy?" Karlie asked, making conversation as she undid her seat belt. She looked out her window at the house. "It's nice," she said in a polite but noncommittal tone.

"Yes, it is," Tiffany answered, wryly noting the significant lack of enthusiasm. "I know it's a far cry from what you're used to, but hopefully, you'll find it charming." With that, Tiffany opened her door, and Karlie proceeded to do the same. Tiffany walked around the car to where Karlie stood waiting with some apprehension.

Holding hands, the two of them walked up the stairs to the entrance.

Tiffany inserted the key in the lock, feeling hopeful. She was not disappointed when she stepped inside. Both she and Karlie gushed and prattled on at their surroundings. The designer had outdone herself, for the place was impeccable and immaculate. The furnishings complimented the structure and the colors of the house. Tiffany liked the overall ambiance immensely. In short, the house was now absolutely nothing like the place where she had grown up. The house exuded so much warmth that Tiffany knew that she could finally call it home.

"I guess it's okay, Mom," Karlie admitted. "But our home in L.A. is five times the size of this one."

Tiffany decided to ignore that comment and led Karlie upstairs to her room.

"I love it." Karlie spontaneously hugged her mom upon entering her room. "It's not as big as my other room, but it is cozy." The room's decor featured purple and pink hues, along with carefully selected pieces of Hello Kitty memorabilia, which Karlie adored. She saw a plush life-size Hello Kitty couch, and she lunged into it. "This couch is off the chain."

"High praises. I'm glad your room passed inspection."

Tiffany left Karlie basking in her new quarters and went down the hall to her room. This would do for her. Both of their bags had been sent ahead, had arrived, and had been unpacked, so there wasn't much to do.

Tiffany sat on the bed and sighed. She hoped coming back here was the best move. Tiffany spotted a photo. She went closer and saw that it was one of her holding one of the three Grammys that she had won a lifetime ago.

Karlie would inherit those treasures and other paraphernalia from her singing career over ten years ago. That was one decision she had made with the other obligatory preparations that came with dying. Winona had them in safekeeping, as Tiffany could not see bringing them here.

Tiffany overheard Karlie's giggling and loud chatter from her phone conversation. "Karlie, keep it down, or at least shut your door. I can hear your yammering all the way down here," Tiffany hollered, but smiled when she heard the lock click. She marveled at how kids adapted so much easier in a case like this. Once she had gotten over her initial rant, Karlie had been a trouper.

Tiffany looked out the window. She thought of Myra—her best friend in the entire world way back when—and Neil's wife.

A few doors down, Neil sat in his study, deep in thought. He was thinking about Tiffany and how they had become friends—well, actually they were closer than most friends were. Their friendship had been forged sixteen years ago, on one of the worse nights of his life—the night right after prom. Neil leaned his head back into the chair. If he closed his eyes, he could picture and remember everything about that night.

His parents had broken the news that they were getting a divorce. Evidently, they had judiciously waited a month after his graduating before breaking his heart. His father was packed and ready to go like an expectant mother.

A hot, muggy July night meant the mosquitoes were out in full force. Neil swatted at the annoying pests but refused to go home for the bug spray. "They're eating me alive." He walked the short blocks to Myra's house. She was in one of her moods, and after a heated exchange, he left before telling her his devastating news.

He was walking past Tiffany's house when he spotted her sitting underneath the big tree in the backyard. Neil ignored the heavy squeak of her gate and went to see what she was doing. Neil was surprised to see her in tears.

It took some doing, but Tiffany finally confessed, "I'm pregnant."

"Whoa." Neil dropped beside her. He had no inkling that Thomas had even gotten past first base. The rumor was that they broke up after prom, but he was the only likely candidate. "Does Thomas know? And didn't you two break up?"

"Yes and no. I did break up with him, but I went out with him to . . . you know." Tiffany gulped. "And, no, I haven't told him about the pregnancy."

"But you have to. If it were me, I would want to know."

"It's a little more complicated than that."

Dumbfounded, Neil held her in his arms.

Her own face tear-streaked, Tiffany noticed Neil's face and asked, "Have you been crying?"

"My parents are getting divorced—yes, divorced— and my dad is moving tonight, as we speak," Neil cried.

Tiffany offered him some of the tissues from the almost empty box and listened as he poured out the pain of his heart. Maybe it was because he had opened up to her, but Tiffany revealed her deepest secret. "Neil, I don't know who the father is."

"What?" Neil's eyes bulged, and he looked at Tiffany.

Tiffany told him about Clifford. "You need to tell the police," Neil urged. "I will go with you."

"No. It's been, like, forever already," Tiffany said. "No one will believe me, anyway. My own mother doesn't believe me. I just want to get out of here."

"Well, is the baby his?" Neil inquired.

"No," Tiffany said, passionately denying the possibility. But second-guessing herself, she added, "well, I don't know whose it is, but I refuse to accept that this baby is Clifford's. Neil, please don't hate me, but I slept with Thomas and . . . three other boys."

"Three? I feel very inexperienced compared to you now. Wow. Do I know them?"

"You know two of them, Pierce and Darnell from the football team. And the other one, Ryan, is actually a college student I met at a club."

"You went to a club?" This was so unlike Tiffany. Neil was out of his element. He wondered if this was how sexual abuse could affect the victims.

Tiffany hung her head in shame. "Yeah, I bribed my way in, partied, got drunk, I think, and I ended up going with this guy, Ryan. I've never done anything like that before. I think I was just trying to erase all thoughts of Clifford inside me. Neil, my mother blamed me. I slept with those boys to get back at her. She said I was a whore, so I decided to prove her right."

"But how is that getting back at her? You're damaging yourself, Tiffany. You're too beautiful and too special to let any of these boys use you like that. Plus, weren't you worried about diseases?" Neil pleaded. "You need to put that pain and hurt to better use."

"I felt lucky, ou know, like I wouldn't catch any-thing, and that was dumb, I know. I just wasn't think-ing. And the only thing that helped besides that was singing."

"You sing?"

"Yes," Tiffany said.

Neil urged her to sing for him. After much urging, Tiffany complied. When she was done, he said, "That's what you need to be doing. You need to be singing. You also need to tell Thomas the truth."

"No."

Neil urged her to confess and tell the truth but was unable to sway her mind. Instead, Tiffany somehow persuaded Thomas to marry her; then they both took off for L.A. That had been her curtain call following one crazy summer.

Now Tiffany had come full circle and was about to stir up some serious sugar.

Older and wiser, Neil wished he had reported Clifford and confronted Merle on Tiffany's behalf. But he had been a kid himself. What had he known about dealing with a victim of sexual abuse?

Neil also had another weapon. He had God. Neil had given his life to the Lord seven years ago, and he had come to rely on God's guidance and strength. He got on his knees. "Lord, You are in charge of the world, and nothing happens without Your consent. I place Tiffany before You, Lord. I ask, Heavenly Father, that You will place her on the right path. I pray that You will help her settle her affairs and that the truth will now free her. But, Father, I also pray that You will draw her closer to You and that she will discover Your healing and Your divine love. I ask these mercies in Jesus' name. Amen."

♪ Chapter Eight

She needed to stop doing this, Myra Jameson told herself. She stood at the mirror with a pillow shoved under her housedress. Imagining, pretending, she carried Neil's child, but she just could not help hoping. A dreamy smile filled her face, making her appear somewhat ethereal. Try as she might to understand and accept the Lord's will, Myra yearned for children, whom she had yet to bear.

"Why, God? Why?" Myra tortuously whispered the words aloud. Her face reflected savage pain. Speaking in hushed tones, she shook her head. "I just can't understand it."

Of course, as usual, there was no response. *Ugh.* Disgusted with God and His deafening silence, Myra curled her fists and, in a move reminiscent of ardent club goers, pumped her hands in the air as she looked up at the ceiling. "Why won't you give me a child? So many other people out there are throwing their babies away. Why won't you give me one when you know I deserve it?"

Like a child engaged in a temper tantrum, she slapped her tummy. "Right here, God, right here."

Spent and sweaty, Myra clutched her stomach and fell to her knees. Her round-shaped face quivered, and her eyes filled with tears. Angrily, she swiped at them, refusing to cry anymore. She was not going to cry. "I'm so tired of praying and asking, Lord, so tired." She pressed both her lips together as she sought to bring her torment under wraps.

"I should've gone into work today, because I'm driving myself nuts thinking about this stuff," she muttered. In one rapid fluid movement, Myra jumped to her feet and wrestled the pillow from underneath her blouse. Irate, she threw it on the bed while cursing her stupid, pointless wishful thoughts.

Myra laughed at the irony. Umpteen years ago, she'd anxiously stood before another, similar mirror, praying she was not pregnant. Now she was standing in front of this one, pleading for something that appeared to be impossible.

Leaving the room, she slammed the door with such force that the windows rattled. Myra stomped down the stairs to her kitchen. Blatantly ignoring the strong encouragement to pray or meditate, Myra decided to bake. In her haste, she stumbled down the last two steps and banged her little toe. Instinctively, Myra grabbed her toe and jumped around, trying to keep her balance.

Sadly, she stumbled and her bottom hit the floor. Her toe throbbed so hard, she could feel her heartbeat. Myra squelched her outcry but automatically looked around to see if anybody else had witnessed her little accident. She chuckled at her idiocy because she was alone in the house. Myra instantly sobered, feeling sorry again.

She was alone. Empty.

From where she was standing near the front door, she saw the small table with the Bible and various junk mail. Childishly cutting her eyes at the good book, Myra stomped into the kitchen, limping.

Baking seemed to be doing more to soothe her than the words in her Bible. She did not want to read about waiting or divine providence. Myra wanted a baby—yesterday.

Since she was alone, Myra had no problem transferring her frustration to her pots and pans. Her clamoring vibrated through the whole house.

She opened the cupboard doors. *Bang.*

She put the tins out. *Bang.*

She shut the refrigerator door. *Bang.*

She gathered the items and plopped them on her counter with such force that there was flour dust all over. Her housedress and face were slightly covered.

Whatever. Myra did not care. She would clean it later. It was not as if she had any children to take care of or anything.

Calming down as she mixed and blended the necessary ingredients, Myra baked enough cookies so the neighborhood children could have some. The children were the main reason she stayed in the neighborhood. Their parents were often too busy overdosing on drugs to pay them any real attention. Myra was more than happy to provide a brief escape for the children. Her eyes shone as she thought about their messy mouths and chocolate-covered hands. Then her eyes dimmed at the old adage. "Those who had them did not want them. Those who wanted them could not have them." That was life. Well, it was the story of hers, anyway.

Myra hissed, making her displeasure known to God.

The smell of chocolate chip cookies wafted up her nostrils. Her mouth watered. Myra swallowed in anticipation. Washing her hands, then wiping them on her apron, Myra was ready to eat them. She would savor every bite.

To pass the time, Myra drifted into the front parlor and peeped out the windows. *Is that a vehicle parked in the driveway of the Petersons' house?* "Nobody has lived in that house for so long. I wonder who finally bought it." Myra spoke the words aloud, though nobody was there to answer. She figured it was okay to talk to herself—just as long as she didn't answer. Sometimes the house was too still.

Hearing the timer go off, Myra went to retrieve the cookies from the oven, even while thoughts about her new neighbor filled her mind. She knew exactly what she would do. She would give her neighbor the cookies instead of eating them. Her size fourteen made her look even bigger on her five-foot-three-inch frame.

One well-shaped eyebrow arched in thought, and her lips poked out. She prayed her new neighbor was a working professional. There were a few middle-income families moving on the block, and thankfully, most of the lowlifes were moving out or facing eviction.

Myra knew the better way, but people were not trying to hear about God. Apparently—and she must have missed the memo—God was now out of style. He was not trending right now. Everybody was just all about making a dollar. People were hardly interested in hearing about their soul. Time and time again, they consistently chose the quick buck over getting an education.

When she was a kid, she had made a conscious decision not to cave to the lull of easy money. Although to be fair, Myra reflected, she had the privilege of both her parents, who were saved and Holy Ghost filled. They had made sure that Myra was actively involved with the church since she could walk.

Myra's chest puffed. When she accepted Jesus and got baptized, she prided herself on being a living example. That was why she stuck around here, even when Neil wanted to move. Well, she amended, that was what she had voiced aloud. Secretly, Myra wouldn't mind moving to a more upscale town. Between her and

Neil, they could more than afford to, since she was a teacher and he a computer analyst.

However, her parents hadn't raised a fool. This house was a bought and paid in full hand-me-down from her parents before they retired and moved to Florida. Practically speaking, there was no reason to move, unless they had a child. Myra wanted one badly. She snagged a cookie, thinking some more about her "baby" dilemma. Sitting on a stool, she put her head on the countertop while eating, giving the impression that she was praying.

She knew that with God, all things were possible, but after years with no success, Myra, who suffered from endometriosis, was seriously considering the option of in vitro fertilization. The procedure was costly and intrusive, and some folks believed God did not need that kind of help.

Still deep in thought, Myra raised her head and glanced up at the ceiling. A few church people, with that backward mentality, came to mind. She and Neil believed that God increased knowledge so that the doctors could do their "magic." They subscribed to the notion that God was behind it all. He was the physician, and the doctors were merely his tools.

In autopilot mode, Myra bit into her fifth cookie. She had set out two full plates of cookies, but Myra had no idea just how much she'd eaten. What did I do to deserve infertility? she thought. Myra was genuinely perplexed and vexed about it. She knew God was a just God, but she did not do anything to displease Him, so God had no reason to keep her womb closed.

Guilt plagued her so much that she could barely look Neil in the eyes sometimes. He could not have a child because of her. On second thought, she was not at fault, either. Life was God's decision. He gave it, and He took it away. "So, in essence, it's on you, God, all on you," Myra shouted freely, not worrying or even caring if Neil came in and overheard her tirade.

Myra bit into a few more cookies before realizing she had lost count. Now she felt disgusted with herself for eating away her frustrations, and she had only a paltry serving left. "Yeah, yeah, I know I need to trust you, God," Myra belted out. "But where is trust getting me? Answer me that, God. I pay my tithes, help the children, go to church, all of that. I call the main line, I call Jesus up, but I guess He's way too busy for me." Bitterness washed her insides, whirled around, darkening her very countenance.

Myra saw she was holding a cookie as her microphone. Well, she might as well finish it since she had already started eating it. That mentality was the devil's doing, and it would gain her twenty pounds. It was hard to believe that she was once a size two and the head of the cheerleading squad in high school.

Myra stood up, defiantly tossing the half-eaten cookie in the garbage. She went into her bedroom and headed straight for the mirror. She studied herself before slowly turning sideways, imagining her womb swelled with child.

The cookies had not filled her. Unless she had a child, nothing would.

Surreptitiously, she confessed, not even God.

Later that evening, Myra decided to work on a recipe for key lime pie. She had tasted the treat when she and Neil visited her parents in Key West. Her doorbell rang, but Myra was too engrossed in her task to answer the door. Sometimes the neighborhood kids got a kick out of ringing the doorbells and running off.

The second chime told Myra she needed to heed the call. Wiping her hands on her apron, Myra walked over and opened the front door, forgetting to use the peephole as a precaution. Her mouth dropped open, as if she had seen a ghost.

"Tiffany! Tiffany Knightly!" Myra squealed and hugged her old friend close. After a few seconds, she released her hold and just looked. "What're you doing here? I thought you were living it up in the big L.A."

"I know," Tiffany agreed as she entered Myra's home. She knew Neil would not tell Myra about her moving back until she was ready. She knew Myra had no clue just what close friends she and Neil were and that they had maintained contact over the years. Looking around, Tiffany experienced the same warm sensation she used to feel every time she entered this house. "Gosh, this house feels the same as when I used to come here."

Myra laughed and keenly studied Tiffany's facial reactions. Myra was not going to let her question slide. Tiffany was going to answer her question. "So, girl, what're you doing here?" She followed Tiffany into the kitchen and took a seat at the round table.

"I have moved back into my old house."

Since Tiffany declined her coffee offer, Myra joined her. She had kept herself abreast of the latest news and knew Tiffany had retired from showbiz. She had also heard about the lung cancer. "I'm sorry about . . . you know . . . your situation," Myra said, fumbling the words, not quite knowing how to express her sympathy.

Tiffany waved her hands, dismissing Myra's concern. She responded with a glib comment. "I have officially come home to die."

Myra did not know how to respond to that. She took the inferred hint that Tiffany did not want to get too sentimental, but she could not let that comment pass. "Don't say that. You never know what could happen. I serve a miraculous God, who specializes in things that seem impossible." Myra squelched her own betraying thought about her empty womb and the apparent lack of a miracle.

Tiffany wisely let the comment slide. Her impending death was something she did not want to talk about right now. She was sick and tired of talking about it and worrying about it. Tiffany did not want to hear about God, either. If she had any contact with God, it would be to ask Him if He had forgotten she had a daughter, who, because of her death, would have no one to care for her. Tiffany did not relish getting into any discussion about God with Myra. She changed subjects without batting an eye over her bald-faced lie. She knew all about their lives because Neil updated her whenever they spoke. "I did not know you would still be here. I just took a chance. How come you're still here?" she said.

"Where was I going to go?" Myra responded, biting the bait. "My parents left me this home when they moved to Florida, so I stayed."

"Oh, I see you are married." Tiffany noted the rings on Myra's left hand.

Instinctively, Myra touched them and smiled, "Yeah, it's been about seven years now. I married Neil."

"I never would have guessed you two would have gotten married and would still be together after all these years." The lie spilled off Tiffany's tongue like honey. She deserved an Academy Award for this performance. She could play dumb like nobody's business. But she knew that if Myra had any inkling that she and

Neil had kept in touch, there would no convincing her that there was nothing going on and that they were truly just friends.

Myra blushed. "Well, we did, and we are still together."

"So what do you do? You already know what I do—excuse me, *used* to do—for a living," Tiffany quipped.

"I'm a fourth grade teacher at Smith Street School in Uniondale," Myra replied. She then launched into a more detailed job description. Myra's love for her job was apparent as she spoke with suppressed excitement about her daily tasks. She regaled Tiffany with funny tales of things her students had done or said. Myra informed Tiffany that when she was not teaching, she was playing an active role in the church.

"Being a schoolteacher sounds extremely entertaining and interesting," Tiffany commented, purposely not addressing the religious aspects of Myra's life. "So how come you're not at work today?"

Myra stumbled over her words. "I don't know really. I think I just haven't accepted that summer is over, and Mondays are so hard to get back to work." Myra laughed awkwardly. "Besides, I have so many days in my sick-leave bank that this one day won't even make a dent."

"I hear you," Tiffany said.

Then, just as quickly, the air between the two women intensified. Astute, Tiffany knew why.

Myra did too.

Tiffany deduced Myra wanted to know why she never kept in touch when she ran away from home all those years ago. "Myra," Tiffany began, "I am sorry. I know I did not do you justice as a friend when I left like that. But there was a lot going on, and it was a confusing time in my life. Not that it justifies anything, but I was a little messed up."

Myra's shoulders relaxed at Tiffany's perceptiveness. She had to admit that was the sixty-four-thousand-dollar question going through her head. She did not want to appear selfish to Tiffany by asking, so she was deeply relieved that Tiffany had broached the subject. "Why did you leave?" Myra asked, quietly. "I mean, you did not even say good-bye or anything to me, your friend since kindergarten. You just up and disappeared. I went to see my grandparents and came back to learn that you were just . . . gone." She made no attempt to disguise the pain in her voice. She wanted Tiffany to know how much her rash move hurt, even after all these years.

Tiffany hunched her shoulders with shame. She could not answer Myra's question without full disclosure so she simply reiterated. "Myra, I was going through a lot at the time, and I did some things I was not proud of . Then one day it became too much, and I just left."

Myra quelled her inquisitiveness. She knew now was not the time to push for more information. She had to accept Tiffany's sincere apology and move on. That was what God would want her to do as a good Christian woman. Tiffany was dying, and Myra did not want to hold on to old grudges. God's Word said that we have to love and forgive others as Christ forgave us, so Myra graciously accepted her friend's apology.

"I love you, Tiffany. We were such good friends and I want to rekindle our friendship," Myra said, reaching out to hold Tiffany's hands.

"I am going to need it, believe me," Tiffany stressed. "But just for the record, I want you to know that it's not because I am dying that I am here now. I have got a lot I have to do before my time and a lot of demons I have to face."

Myra looked at her friend, silently asking her to explain.

Tiffany let out a huge sigh, before saying, "I have to . . . I just thought it would make things easier for Karlie if I returned home." It was too soon for a tell-all.

"Karlie? That's your daughter, right? I knew you had a daughter, but you kept her under the radar," Myra said.

"Well, certain things in my life I've kept very private, and Karlie is one of them. She is fifteen now."

"Fifteen . . . I thought she was younger than that." Myra did the math in her head. Realization struck. "So you were pregnant around the time when you left?"

"Yes," Tiffany answered. "Yes, I was."

"Oh," Myra said. She mulled that over for a few seconds before asking, "So where is Karlie? You should've brought her here with you."

"Karlie started Hempstead High School today. I tried to get her in before the year started, but I couldn't. But it's only a week, so I'm confident she'll catch up."

"You sent her to public school?" Myra's eyes depicted her shock.

"Yeah," Tiffany answered dryly. "Karlie pleaded and pleaded to go to public school, even though she'd gone to private school all her life. It took some serious thinking on my part before I hesitantly agreed. I am waiting on pins and needles for her to get home so I can hear all about her first day. I hate the fact that school has already started, but it couldn't be helped."

"Well, I imagine it will be an eye-opening experience," Myra returned.

"Karlie is a tough cookie. I think she will be just fine," Tiffany said with a confidence she didn't feel.

♫ Chapter Nine

Even though it was mid-September, it was ninety-six degrees, and everyone moaned about going to school on such a picture-perfect beach day. Karlie walked through the halls of Hempstead High School, which featured student artwork on display. Some of the kids here were truly talented.

She was enrolled in Hempstead High's College Preparatory Academy for Music and Art, but she still had core requirements to fulfill. Her heart was pounding so loudly that Karlie splayed her hands across her chest. She had convinced her mom to send her here instead of to a private school or to a tutor. Karlie had assured her mother she would be just fine. "It would be a piece of cake," she'd said.

However, that was all before Karlie heard the click of her shoes as she meandered down a long hallway. Suddenly the bell rang, and she was whirled around by kids rushing in different directions. "Ow!" Karlie screeched and grabbed her long braid. Someone had tugged her hair. Karlie reached her hands to her head to soothe her tender scalp. Lucky for him, or her, the culprit was long gone.

She knew she stuck out like a sore thumb. With her designer clothes from Beverly Hills, Karlie knew she did not blend in with the Sean Johns and Timberlands crowd. But she wouldn't let that stop her. Resolute, Karlie marched to her next class. "I will not be intimidated." A girl rushing by ran smack into her. "Ooh, I'm sorry," Karlie said instinctively, then thought, Why did I just apologize? Great. Now she felt like a punk.

"Watch where you are going," the girl yelled before continuing on her way.

"What's the big rush?" Karlie asked to no one in particular.

"Lost?" a boy asked.

Startled that she had an audience, Karlie turned toward the voice and saw a tall, lanky boy looking at her. Leaning against his locker, he seemed in no apparent hurry to get to his class. Karlie felt grateful. Now, this was someone who seemed to be more her speed.

The late bell rang.

"Yeah," Karlie said, panicked. She did not want to be the late new girl to class. "I am trying to find Ms. Alexander's class."

"I'll show you," the boy offered and walked over to where Karlie was standing. He slung his arm around her shoulders with the casual ease of someone who was used to getting his own way. Karlie's muscles tensed. She did not feel comfortable with the intimate gesture but did not want to spurn the help of the only person inclined to help her. She remained silent as he led the way down the hall to the last door on the right.

"Um, thanks," she told him.

When Karlie entered the class, quite a few eyes bulged out when they saw who accompanied her. She creased her brows, confused as to why everyone was staring at him with such intensity. The teacher rushed through introductions and went on with the lesson, so Karlie did not think to ask what the big deal was.

She should have asked. She would later learn that her Good Samaritan was none other than Jamaal Weathers, basketball star and boyfriend of Cheyenne

Elliott, head cheerleader. Apparently, Hempstead High had an efficient grapevine and news spread like wildfire. Karlie had just exited Ms. Alexander's class and was navigating her way to her next class when she felt a sharp nudge on her right shoulder.

"What the . . ." Rubbing her shoulder, Karlie turn around to see who the perpetrator was. The other students gave a wide berth, minding their own business. Even the teachers standing in the hallway ignored them.

Karlie saw a petite, light-skinned girl wearing a leopard-print shirt, a broad waist belt, and black tights giving her the evil eye. The girl stood there popping gum for a few seconds before Karlie asked, "Did you just push me?"

"Yes, I did. I am Cheyenne Elliott, Jamaal's girlfriend," she replied haughtily, as if that should be explanation enough for her rudeness.

"Okay, so?" Karlie shook her head, still not understanding. She saw two other girls walk up to stand next to Cheyenne. They were also gum poppers and were staring her down. Karlie's chest heaved. She wasn't about to let these girls punk her out. No way.

Cheyenne marched up into Karlie's space. She became bolder now that her two friends flanked her sides. "So you'd better get to know my name real fast. Jamaal is my boyfriend, and you'd best stay away from him."

"I don't even know who Jamaal is," Karlie replied, still not putting two and two together.

"Oh, now she's playing dumb," one of the other girls said. "I saw her with my own two eyes, Cheyenne."

"Look," Cheyenne said in a threatening manner and pointed her finger at Karlie. "I don't know who you are, and I do not care. Just leave my boyfriend alone, and stay out of my way."

Karlie watched as Cheyenne and the girls stomped off as they giggled among themselves and pointed in her direction, making it obvious she was the topic of their conversation. Karlie's temperature rose, but she was outnumbered.

"Do not let those dry-headed girls get to you."

Karlie swiveled around and made sure that the comment had been directed at her. She didn't want to look stupid. She saw a tall, dark-skinned girl make her way over to where she still stood. "I'm trying not to, but I do not know who this Jamaal is that that Cheyenne girl wants me to stay away from."

"He is the school's basketball star," the girl explained. "And you should stay away from him. Jamaal Weathers is no good. At least that is what I heard."

"My name is Karlie Knightly," Karlie offered.

"And I'm Tanya McAdams. Let me see your schedule," Tanya said, holding out her hand. She quickly skimmed the slightly wrinkled paper. "Good. We've got the same history class. Come with me. Mr. Battle is cool, and you'll like him." She inclined her head, indicating that Karlie should follow.

Karlie smiled, relieved. She had just made her first friend.

♫ Chapter Ten

Tiffany is not getting away that easy, Myra said to herself. It had been two days since Tiffany had shown up on her doorstep, and Myra was curious to catch up on more of Tiffany's life.

Cake in hand, she walked the short distance to Tiffany's house. She rang the doorbell several times, to no avail. "Where is she? Her car is here." She tilted her head, hearing a painful outcry coming from the backyard. Myra's stubby legs hurried toward the sound. She huffed from the effort of running. She really needed to get in shape and do away with the spandex and oversize shirts. Her small frame could not hold the weight of a size fourteen.

"Tiffany!" Myra exclaimed, dropping the cake to take Tiffany in her arms and offer consolation. She assumed the tears were because of her imminent death. Just for a moment, Myra felt Tiffany curve into her arms, taking comfort, before pulling away. Not caring about snot or other fluids, Myra used her shirt and tenderly wiped her friend's face. Her foot accidentally kicked a box that was by Tiffany's feet.

Curious, Myra asked, "What's this?"

"My secret box," Tiffany said and hiccupped. "I just dug it up. I buried it here, underneath Ben."

"Ben?"

"Yeah," Tiffany explained. "You know Ben. My tree? I used to spend so much time here when I needed to get away. Don't you remember?"

Myra didn't, but she nodded her head in the affirmative. "Can I look?"

She saw Tiffany nod her assent.

Myra picked up a piece of underwear, not knowing what it was. She had it between her thumb and forefinger for several seconds before the realization hit. She dropped the undergarment back into the box as if it were the bubonic plague. "Ugh. Is that what I think it is?" Myra wiped her hands on the grass and spat several times. Spotting the cake, her stomach turned. It was going right into the trash.

Tiffany grabbed her hands. "I kept that for a reason."

"Why on earth would you feel the need to do that?" Myra felt like she was about to heave. Yet out of some sort of sick fascination, she desperately wanted to know.

"That was evidence. Proof that my stepfather raped me."

Myra's mouth hung open in shock. She was not sure she had heard right. Had Tiffany revealed that Mr. Peterson had raped her? No, she must have heard wrong. She closed her mouth only because drool had gathered.

"I can see you don't believe a single word coming out of my mouth," Tiffany said with major attitude. "I am already sorry I told you."

"No," Myra said, denying the charge. "I do. It is just that Mr. Peterson seemed so nice. He was always giving us candy or money to buy stuff. I cannot imagine him doing something like that."

"Yeah, well, my mother did not believe me, either—even though she saw him violating me with her own two eyes and even though I showed her my proof. She said I was lying, but why would I lie about something like that? Clifford Peterson did take me against my consent." Her passionate words hung in the air between them.

"Why didn't you ever tell me?" Myra asked. She felt bad for Tiffany, and maybe if she had known . . .

Seeing Tiffany's raised eyebrows until Myra answered her own question. "You didn't think I would believe you."

"You were going away, and I didn't think anybody would believe me," Tiffany defended. "My mother was the first person I told, and she did nothing about it. Instead, she turned around and accused me of being a slut. She whipped me good too and stuck by him. So if my own mother did not believe me, I figured it would be hopeless for me to tell anybody else. I tried to hang in there, but as soon as I graduated, I left." Tiffany ended the last statement with a bitter tone.

"So is Karlie his child?" Myra's stomach churned from the thought of Karlie being the product of such a violent act. Myra shivered as she waited for Tiffany's response.

"No," Tiffany bellowed. She lowered her voice, but the venom remained. "I hate that man, and in my heart of hearts, I know Karlie—my precious pearl—is not his. I hate him for what he did to me. A child so priceless and full of love could never be the product of something so demeaning and inhumane." Her acute pain returned, for Clifford's assault went beyond her physical body. Her self-worth had suffered.

"How long did this go on?" Myra asked, dreading the answer.

"He never came near me again. I think it was because he saw how much I hated him and I kept a butcher knife under my pillow."

"Thank God, it only happened once." Myra exhaled with an involuntary shudder.

"But once was one too many. It should not have happened at all," Tiffany countered.

Myra was silent for several moments before she said, "How could you . . . not tell? I just don't . . ." Myra's words trailed off, for she knew she sounded judgmental, but Tiffany's revelation had torched Myra's mundane existence. Myra's rose-colored glasses had been smashed to pieces, and she needed some process time to recoup.

"I just did not care at the time," Tiffany explained. "Put yourself in my shoes, Myra. What would you have done?"

"Tell the cops, tell my friends, tell anyone," Myra countered without hesitation. Her voice grated with self-righteous censure. "I certainly would not have continued on and pretended nothing happened."

"Like I said, now you know why I never told you certain things. Not everybody was as lucky as you were, Myra. Not everybody had parents from *The Cosby Show*." Tiffany got up and picked up her box. It was time for her to go, because Myra's thoughtless comments grated on her last nerves. She looked Myra in the eyes and whispered bitterly, "Everybody didn't grow up feeling loved and treasured as you did. But you know how that made you, Myra. It made you judgmental and a know-it-all. Well, guess what? You don't have a clue. If you did, you would have known that all I needed right now was a friend. For some unfathomable reason, I imagined you would understand now, after all these years. But I was wrong," Tiffany snarled. "You are still the same perfect, narrow-minded person I left all those years ago."

Stunned, Myra watched as Tiffany stomped off and whispered to herself, "What right does she have to judge me? She doesn't know a thing about me."

Myra picked up the remnants of the cake and held them in her hands. She was never going to darken Tiffany's doorstep again.

♪ Chapter Eleven

Neil dreaded coming home. He acknowledged this as he waited for the garage opener to activate the door that would give him access to his garage. Neil never knew what mood Myra would be in once he put his foot through the door. Sometimes she would be jovial, and Neil would breathe a sigh of relief, silently thanking God. But 99 percent of the time, Myra would be looking sad and depressed, and Neil was at a loss as to what to do. Myra was miserable, and as a result, she was making him miserable.

Neil groaned, "Lord, I am so fed up. I do not want to get out of this car." His confession was one that was difficult for him to admit. He usually pretended everything was okay, but his misery bubbled up and overflowed sometimes, to the point where he had to be honest—at least with himself.

It wasn't that Neil didn't want a baby, but he just was not obsessed about having one—as Myra seemed to be. He figured that Myra must think about babies all day, because it was all she ever seemed to talk about. *Baby this, baby that. I want a girl. No, maybe a boy.* Neil heard Myra's voice drone on in his head.

"I can't take much more of this," he whispered in the car. His torture was apparent in his whole body stance. Five minutes had passed. Neil reckoned he needed to get inside, and he undid his seat belt but only settled back into the cushy leather seat, content to dwell on his thoughts.

He had tried to convince Myra that he was truly okay if they did not have a child, but she did not believe him. Slapping his hands on his forehead, Neil shut his eyes. He was so sick of fertility monitors—when they should do it, how they should do it. All of her drilling—"No, do it this way, but do it that way"—was just wearing him down. It was getting to the point where he could hardly perform because everything felt so contrived.

Neil felt used. God said to be fruitful and multiply, but He never would have designed the female body with certain pleasure spots if its only purpose was for multiplication. Was it too much to ask that he just make love with his wife for a change? Neil craved spontaneous, mind-boggling, earth-shaking intercourse—and he was not shy about mentioning that when he hit knee city. "I just want to make love to my wife, Lord," Neil said, voicing his thoughts, knowing God could hear him.

He punched his hands on the steering wheel. "Ouch." That stung. Instinctively rubbing his palms, Neil turned the ignition to roll the windows down. "I'd better get out before she comes looking for me." Neil reached into the backseat and retrieved his work folders. His muscles bulged from the exertion, as he worked out daily to keep his body in shape. He had to, as he was now Myra's own "robotman" and "on-demand" man—that was him.

Bringing work home with him served two purposes: it was a good get-out-of-sex ticket and he got a lot done, which was bringing him a lot of positive attention in his company. His boss had even complimented him on his devotion to the job and had revealed that Neil was

in line for a promotion. "You're our man, Neil," Gary
Sneads had said. Neil had laughed along with Gary, but
he knew his success had nothing to do with devotion
and everything to do with getting out of sex with his
wife. Making love would be another thing. Neil wanted
to make sweet love to his wife until the sun came up.

He walked from the garage into the back of the house
with the steps of a man approaching a guillotine. In his
study, Neil dropped his briefcase and undid his shirt
and tie.

Myra used to be so carefree and abandoned, until
they decided to start trying to have a child. Neil smiled,
remembering some of her crazy antics and ideas. She
had been . . . *whew*, but now Myra was the fertility police. A firm man of God, Neil was not about to engage
in an extramarital affair, so he occupied his time with
safer exploits. By escaping sex, his spiritual life had also
grown by leaps and bounds. Church provided a safe,
healthy retreat. Pastor Johnston had even broached
the possibility of getting Neil ordained as a deacon.

Neil laughed with a touch of self-recrimination. He
welcomed the opportunity to work for God, but his increased motivation stemmed from the fact that he was
sexually suppressed and frustrated. Neil was not even
100 percent certain God had accepted his offering, but
he figured it was better to put his efforts into God's
work—better than getting caught up with the devil's
distractions.

Neil wandered into the kitchen, searching for Myra.
"Might as well get this over with," he grunted. He
stopped when he saw Myra sitting at the table. He
could tell that she had been waiting for him.

Taking a deep breath, Neil furtively scanned the
calendar to see if it was "blue star" time. Myra put blue
stars on the calendar to mark her fertile times. Neil

knew he was "on duty" then. He actually prayed for some red stars.

"Hey." Neil cautiously tried to ascertain her mood. He bent over to kiss the top of her head. He inhaled appreciatively. Myra's hair smelled like roses.

"Hi."

A one-word answer. Highly unusual. "What's the matter?" Neil asked, concerned. Myra was uncharacteristically subdued. Normally, she would have rattled off her list of "honey do" things by now.

"Am I a selfish person?" She crooked her head up at him inquisitively.

He noted her creased brow and questioning eyes and cautioned himself to tread carefully. *Yes*, Neil thought to himself. Myra could be very, very selfish. In her defense, she was not that way purposely, but Neil knew better than to say that aloud. Her facial expression showed that something had her bothered. "No, I do not think so," Neil said, "Why are you asking?"

"Because Tiffany Knightly pretty much called me that today," Myra sputtered. She poked her lips out, in an obvious funk.

"Tiffany moved back home?"

"Yes," Myra confirmed. "She's back and terminal from lung cancer."

Neil paused. "Wow."

"Yeah," Myra went on. "And listen to this. Her daughter is fifteen. Fifteen. You know what that means?" Myra didn't give any wait time. "She was pregnant when she left. Oh, and apparently, Mr. Peterson sexually abused her all those years ago." Her arms flailed in a sweeping motion to emphasize her point.

"Wow," Neil remarked. "Poor Tiffany."

He must not have provided the desired response, because Myra asked, "That is all you have to say?"

"Yeah, I feel for her," Neil replied. "She was pretty shaken up that her mother didn't believe her." *Uh-oh. I goofed. Maybe she won't catch on.*

"How do you know that? I didn't say anything about her mother. I mean, Tiffany didn't even go into all that with me," Myra quizzed

Neil licked his lips to gather his thoughts. "I saw her the night she and Thomas ran off together," he explained.

"You never told me," Myra said accusingly.

"If I recall correctly, you were not speaking to me, because I tried to make a move on you," Neil returned cheekily. He reached over and affectionately chucked her under the chin. "Just like I am getting ready to do right now."

Neil moved over to Myra and held her hands. *Ah.* He felt Myra lean into him and curve her body into his just the way he liked. Over her head, a tender look crossed his face.

Neil shifted to look his wife in the eyes and saw her speculative gleam. He knew that look meant Myra was in the mood. He bent over to kiss her, and she opened her mouth to give him free access. Feeling his passion rise, Neil groaned and intensified the kiss. He reached under Myra's shirt to touch her.

Myra broke the contact and placed her hands on his chest to hold him at bay. "We—we can't," Myra urged. "It's not the right time."

No, she isn't, Neil thought. Myra could not possibly be trying to press the brakes on him like this. He stepped back. "Lord, give me patience. What do you mean, it's not the right time?" Frustrated, Neil demanded, "It's not like we have any kids running around here to stop us. We can do it anytime we want." Neil forced her back into his arms.

Myra pulled away until she was firmly out of his grasp. "Well, that is precisely why it's not the right time. We do not have any children, and we are trying to remedy that."

Neil bit down on his lower lip to keep from spouting an angry retort. Myra was getting on his last nerves with this baby obsession. Fuming, he stomped out of the house to take a walk and cool off. He just wanted to make nasty, hot, scandalous . . .

"Déjà vu."

Neil stopped and turned around, recognizing that voice. He must have walked right past Tiffany's house, so miffed that he had not seen her.

"Hi, Tiffany." Neil's voice gentled and his anger dissipated.

"Hey, Neil," Tiffany said. He saw her get up off her stoop and walk over to him.

Neil met her at the fence. The two greeted each other with a friendly, loose hug. "So, are you all settled in?" he asked, initiating conversation.

"Yeah," Tiffany returned, trying to be nonchalant about the whole thing. "Myra told you about our little tête-à-tête earlier?"

Neil gave a rueful grin. "Yes."

Tiffany scoffed. "Figured as much. Myra could never keep anything to herself. That is why I didn't feel comfortable telling her certain things. I don't know why I thought today would be the exception."

"Sorry about that. At least you had me to confide those 'certain' things."

"I see you kept them too, because Myra was clueless. I guess you never told her about our midnight talks."

"No," Neil confirmed, a little tense. "I never did. I did not think she would understand, you know? Myra, being Myra, would have read more into it. Besides, we were both going through a rough time, and Myra was away for most of the summer, so I was glad you were there. You were a good listener. Still are, actually."

"I feel the same, Neil. That night you saved me in more ways than one."

"You helped me too," Neil pointed out. "My parents were splitting up, and I was crying—which is something I never do. By the way, you are still the only woman besides my mother who ever saw me cry like that. I hope you kept that information to yourself."

"I have," Tiffany said with a grin. "And though I know I have said it all before, thank you for being there for me."

Neil changed tactics. "So I lived to see something I told you come true."

"What's that?" Tiffany wondered.

"I told you to tell the truth, instead of running off with Thomas Knightly."

"You did, and I should have listened. Now I have to rip off the Band-Aid, so to speak."

"I do not envy you."

"Yeah." Tiffany sighed and touched her head. She felt a headache forming. "It's a good thing I paid him well not to ever give interviews or write a book about me, or I would be in some deep dog doo right now."

Neil shook his head in commiseration. "How're you feeling?"

"I am okay most days. Some mornings, though . . . you know . . ." Tiffany trailed off, but she noticed that she no longer held Neil's attention. *What is he looking at?* Tiffany wondered. She followed Neil's gaze and, seeing Karlie at the door, beckoned for her to come outside.

Bang . . . creak . . . went the screen door in protest.

"Neil, this is my daughter, Karlie."

Neil looked at the young woman who had come out of the house to greet him. "Hi, Karlie, or should I say Little Tiffany?"

Tiffany beamed with motherly pride. "Yeah, that is what everybody says." She looked over at Karlie. "Karlie, this is Neil Jameson, one of my childhood friends. He lives right up the block."

"Hi, Mr. Jameson," Karlie responded shyly.

Aw. He liked her instantly. Her manners were a true indication that Tiffany was doing a good job with her. "Please call me Neil."

"Okay." Karlie stood for a moment before she waved and made her way back inside.

"She seems great."

"Yeah. I hate what I am doing to her. Karlie didn't ask for any of this."

"If there is anything I can do, let me know. I will be praying for you." Neil's sincere behavior was the antithesis of Myra's supercilious attitude.

Tiffany noted that. "Thanks, Neil," she said. "I am okay for now, but I'll let you know."

As Neil returned home, he knew his visit with Tiffany had put everything in its proper perspective. He and Myra did not have any real problems they could not work out. God favored them with divine blessings, so if He chose not to give them a child, then they should not complain. The good outweighed the bad too much for them to be sad. As the saying goes, they really were "too blessed to be stressed."

A renewed vigor permeated his entire being, beseeching him to endure the rough patch in his marriage. Neil enjoyed the encouraging thoughts filling his mind as he returned home. After all, he was leaning on God's everlasting arms, and he was safely sheltered under God's wings.

Neil went into his study to pray and rejoice. Then he played Yolanda Adams, allowing her voice to soothe him. He listened to her song while turning to I Samuel 17. He scanned David's great speech to the Philistine, Goliath, until he reached verse forty-seven. King David was so right. The battle was not his or Myra's, but it was the Lord's.

♫ Chapter Twelve

Four.

Tiffany sat on top of the toilet with her eyes closed. That number rocked her world. She put her head back against the wall. Images from the past clouded her mind. Tiffany could not believe that she had slept with four men in one month. Who did that?

You were young and stupid, she told herself. Tiffany shook her head. There was no excuse for her past actions. She had been only a couple years or so older than Karlie at the time. "Ugh." Tiffany felt the old disgust stir within her belly. Well, it felt like disgust, but she was sick. Tiffany had wheezed and coughed all through the night, shivering despite the warm temperature. Feeling mucus rise, she quickly jumped off the toilet and got on her knees to cough up the contents into the bowl.

"I can't do it," Tiffany whispered. "I can't stir up the past." She flushed the toilet and washed her hands. If only the past was that easy to wash away.

Tiffany looked at herself in the mirror. "You slept with four men." There, she had faced herself and had said it aloud. "Not one, not two, not even three, but four men." She could barely stand her truth.

It was ugly.

It was raw.

It was real.

True to her word, Winona had referred her to Detective Edison Sniles. Eddie, as he preferred to be called, had gotten her all the pertinent information on each of the men. She expected the package later in the day.

Tiffany decided to lie down to get some rest. It took some mental work, but she finally settled down. Not even ten minutes later, the doorbell rang. "Ugh, great. Isn't that what always happens? Just when you get all comfortable . . ." Tiffany compelled herself to get up out of the bed and answer the door. The last three steps felt insurmountable, but she labored on. Sure enough, the UPS truck driver stood outside her door. Eager, Tiffany opened the door and signed for the package.

Seeing the package gave Tiffany a burst of newfound energy. She ripped it open with a strength she did not know she still possessed. Slowly, she pulled the papers out. They held information on three of the men. She had not requested information on her ex-husband, Thomas, since she knew all there was to know about him.

Tiffany quickly glanced through the papers and photographs before going into her kitchen to read. She still wore her red plaid Anne Klein pajamas but walked barefoot.

Pierce Willis. A former captain of the wrestling team in high school, Pierce was now a mechanic. He owned a local auto body shop in Uniondale and, by the look of things, was knee- deep in debt.

Tiffany wrinkled her nose and scrunched her lips in displeasure. "Pierce is probably going to jump on the offer of being Tiffany Knightly's baby daddy. Money would be his motivation." She read on. He was currently dating a beautician by the name of Elyse. "Typical. Let me guess. They have six kids and live with her mother in the basement apartment."

She was wrong. They had four children and lived in a two-bedroom apartment. "Let's see if you have a rap sheet. Surprisingly, Pierce had not spent any time in jail or done any drugs. The only strike against him was his impending bankruptcy, and Tiffany figured that could be due to a few bad choices or investments. "Thank you, Lord, for small favors."

The next name on the list was Ryan Oakes. "Now, he seems like a good potential candidate," Tiffany said aloud. Ryan was healthy, brilliant, and successful. He owned several businesses and was married to a neurosurgeon. Ryan and his wife, Patricia, lived in Garden City with their only child, Brian. If she recalled correctly, Brian should be about two years older than Karlie.

Tiffany suddenly remembered something. When they first met in the bar, Ryan had spoken about Patricia and his son. Apparently, they had had a big fight because Ryan wanted to get married and be the sole provider for the "love of his life." Patricia had had her own grandiose plans of finishing her residency. It took some serious flirting for Tiffany to coax Ryan into taking her to his dorm. They had done the deed, but Ryan had not been into it. Truthfully, neither had she.

Tiffany continued her perusal. It seemed this Brian had been kicked out of several private boarding schools, and he was on his way to becoming a delinquent. What was up with that? Tiffany peeked at Ryan's itinerary. He was always traveling and followed a hectic schedule. Judging by the information she was reading, Tiffany psychoanalyzed that Brian was acting out because his father was never home. *So you are a licensed psychologist now, eh?*

"Now, I know I am in no position to throw stones, but I don't know how I would feel if Ryan Oakes were

Karlie's father," Tiffany said out loud. Tiffany figured with Brian for a brother, Karlie might get on the wrong track, or Ryan might be too busy to give Karlie the attention she needed. Anything could happen to her. Most importantly, what would happen if Ryan's wife, Patricia, refused to accept Karlie? Patricia could make Karlie's life a living torment.

Tiffany sighed loudly, feeling a tension headache threatening. "I have to stop the what-ifs, or I am going to drive myself nuts. How did I get myself into this mess? Better yet, how am I going to get myself out?"

Tiffany went to get a much-needed glass of water. Never one for praying, Tiffany declared, "I'm afraid, afraid to call these men and mess up their lives." She returned to the kitchen table. From what she read, Ryan did not seem as if he would appreciate the news, and Pierce seemed as if he would be happy to get a money ticket.

Tiffany took a huge gulp of water and placed both hands over her eyes. She wished she were drinking something strong. Suddenly, Tiffany slapped her legs with determination. She was dying, so there was no reason why she should not.

With a quick mood change, Tiffany bounced to her feet. "Since I'm dying, I can drink if I want to, drink if I want to. You'd drink too, if it happened to you." Tiffany rocked her head and sang the words while she searched the cupboards for a wine bottle. Her friends would faint if they heard Tiffany singing so raunchily about her death. Tiffany snickered as a cheeky thought occurred to her. She should sing this jig the next time Myra was present, just to see her reaction. Myra would probably douse her with some olive oil and pray some sense into her.

But another memory gave Tiffany pause. She vividly recalled her "Karlie, if you ever in your life see me drink, then you're free to as well" speech. Tiffany changed her mind about the wine, choosing instead to pour a small glass of grape juice, and sat down to read the last piece of data.

When she was finished, Tiffany was smiling and hopeful. She had just found the father of her dreams for Karlie. "Darnell King." Tiffany liked the sound of his name on her lips. "Now, Darnell King is perfect." Darnell was a single father of two young girls, April, age four, and Amber, age six. His wife had died in a fatal car crash, and since then Darnell had tended to his children with a little help from his mother, Leona. *How sad for those children,* Tiffany thought.

Darnell was now the football coach for Hempstead High School. In high school, Darnell had been an all-star champion and the captain of the football and the track team. From his dossier, Tiffany gleaned Darnell was well respected and well liked. She had only one question. Was he as fine as she remembered? She closed her eyes and remembered the boy climbing into her room sixteen years ago. Then she dug through the pictures to see what he looked like now. "Hmmm. Lord, if you were going to give me any favors, this would be the one." She touched both her temples. "I need a massage."

Tiffany gave herself a pep talk. "Tiffany Knightly, you cannot let fear keep you from your goal." Yes, Tiffany told herself, she would break the news to all three men and set appointments for paternity tests. "Darnell King . . . I will save the best for last." Tiffany singsonged the words in her highest falsetto voice and ended with some runs and rips.

Tiffany knew who had to be first. Thomas. Her ex-husband.

♪ Chapter Thirteen

It smells like dog's feet in here or something close to it, Thomas Knightly acknowledged. He really needed to get this place cleaned and get some semblance of order. He was in his workroom back at his mother's house. He had a huge house of his own, but when it came to work, Thomas could not concentrate unless he was in his old spot.

The telephone rang. Typically, he would ignore it, but for some reason his mother did not answer. Tripping over paint cans, empty food containers, and other art supplies, Thomas grabbed the phone and answered it.

"Hi, Thomas," the caller said.

"Tiffany?" Thomas almost dropped the phone from shock when he heard who was on the other end. "Is that you?"

"Yes, yes, it is."

"Is Karlie all right?" Thomas asked the chief question on his mind. He could not think of any other reason why she would be calling *him.*

"Yes, she is."

"So what's up?" Thomas asked. His mind was already on his artwork. A card company had commissioned him to do several paintings, and Thomas wanted to keep working while he was feeling the momentum, and right now he was on a roll.

"I need to see you."

"Well, I do not know when I can fly out," Thomas replied, attempting to end the conversation.

"Actually, I am here in Hempstead," Tiffany informed him.

"Oh." Now curious, he set the paintbrush on the easel. "You are back at the old house?"

"Yeah," Tiffany replied, but she remained tight-lipped.

Something was definitely going on. Thomas flicked his tongue at the roof of his mouth, which was something he did when he was deep in thought. Intrigued, he agreed to meet Tiffany the next day, then hung up the phone.

Seeing his mother standing in the doorway, unabashedly eavesdropping, Thomas resisted the urge to call her on it. He did not feel like having this conversation, but here it came, anyway, in five . . . four . . . three . . .

"What did Tiffany want?"

Didn't even make it to one, Thomas chortled internally. He should have known Wilhelmina Knightly, known to her friends as Willie, wouldn't let it rest. "She wants to meet with me," Thomas replied. He had to get back to work. Thomas picked up his brush, signaling to his mother that the conversation was over, but she ignored the transparent hint.

"I knew this day would come," she said, raising her hands in a gesture of praise and thanksgiving.

"Mother," Thomas cautioned, "it's not what you think. Tiffany is not trying to get back with me."

"Why else would she be calling?" Willie continued in that stubborn tone Thomas knew well. "She wants you back. She has finally come to her senses and decided to forgive you."

"Listen, it's been almost thirteen years. I am quite sure Tiffany is way past all that now."

Agitated, Thomas silently begged for strength, patience, world peace, and all that good stuff. He was not in the mood to rehash all the past drama of his life right now. His mother just needed to leave well enough alone. Thomas remained mute until his mother shrugged her shoulders, capitulating, and left the room. He was glad that she had finally got the picture and had left him in peace. For the moment, anyway.

Drat. Now he was too disturbed to work. Thomas had lost his flow. With consternation, he threw the paintbrush back on the easel and sat down to think. Unbidden memories flooded his mind. Thomas's eyes squinted as he remembered when he and Tiffany ran off together. He smiled. What did they know about anything back then? They had been two hopeful teenagers who were young and in love. Well, truthfully, Thomas amended, he had been more in love than she was.

Thomas recollected the first time he laid eyes on Tiffany Peterson. He and his mother had moved to Hempstead from Queens mid-year. He saw her in the school cafeteria and thought Tiffany was beautiful.

Tiffany was superfine.

Her eyes were what originally drew him to her. They were so full of life and energy that they pulled him into their depth and evident passion. "Girl, those hazel eyes could make me do anything," he would say time and time again. "And I do mean anything for you."

Thomas and Tiffany quickly became an item, inseparable. The T&T Production. He had coined that moniker himself—he, the artist, with Tiffany, the singer.

"A match made in heaven," Tiffany would sing. She often sat, contented to watch him paint for hours on end without complaining. Thomas would return the favor by listening to her sing. He could listen to her endlessly. Her voice had an airy quality that transcended her age. Tiffany was also the most selfless person he knew. She never cared that he did not have a new car or enough money for dates. Her conscientiousness impressed Thomas so much that it motivated him to seek employment at the gas station to make some money.

Thomas earned enough to take her to the prom in style. He shook his head, remembering his nervousness that night. Prom night, he and Tiffany were supposed to do it. Only his nervousness had botched things up. That spooked an already extremely skittish Tiffany, so they decided to wait. For some reason everything changed after that night.

Thomas never knew what happened. Tiffany dumped him the next day for no apparent reason and moved on. He had been heartbroken and had moped around the house for almost two weeks. He was equally bewildered when just as suddenly after graduation Tiffany resurfaced, wanting to pick up where they had left off.

Young and hearty, Thomas willingly complied. Then Tiffany suggested, "Let's blow this town. We can make it big in L.A. I know we should probably try our luck in the city, but I want to get out of New York. I'm ready to go." Thomas was so exhilarated, he never second-guessed anything. Thomas saw stars and dollar signs and eagerly went along with the plan.

Hopping on the first available train, they left, pursuing their dreams. Thomas insisted they get married, though, so they eloped. He must have had some powerful swimmers, because before he knew it, he heard, "Thomas, we're having a baby." In love, he did all sorts of little jobs until Karlie was born.

Then Tiffany started performing in the local night-clubs. Thomas and Karlie would wait for her in the background and watch out for any men making a move on his wife. He loved proclaiming Tiffany as his, saying such things as "I was telling my wife . . . ," "My wife was saying . . . ," and "Let me see what my wife thinks."

Blah, blah, blah.

They were a perfect team until Tiffany landed a singing contract and started gaining notoriety. It all went downhill from there.

Thomas realized now that he was actually stupidly jealous of his wife's sudden success. He let it get to him and started doubting his manhood. He began feeling as if he was less than a man and made the biggest mistake of his life.

Tiffany was out promoting the album, and he was at home with Karlie. She was especially fussy one night. "Calm down, Karlie," he begged. "What's the matter, baby?" Karlie wouldn't stop crying. His head pounded. He wanted to shake her—she was driving him crazy. Thomas moaned, "I don't know what to do." He plunked her in the crib. "Karlie, stop crying," he bellowed. Frustrated, his temperature rising, Thomas grabbed a sweater and walked out of the house, leaving Karlie alone in her crib. He just needed air, to forget for a moment his daughter, his wife—everything.

Thomas wandered the streets, cold and wet from the rain. He sought refuge in a bar, a seedy hole-in-the-wall. He ended up picking up some random woman whose name he could not even remember and whose face he would never be able to recall. Thomas enticed her to come home with him, convinced Karlie would be asleep by now. Rip-roaring drunk, the two entered the small apartment, laughing over what he couldn't even remember.

Unfortunately, Tiffany was already there. She had come home early that night and had found Karlie alone. Thomas could paint on demand the revulsion etched clearly on her face when she saw him. He had sobered instantly, and the woman had scurried off, with an "I don't want no drama." That marked the beginning of the end.

Tiffany had caught him red-handed, with his pants down, so to speak. All his "I'm sorry. Give me another chance. It won't happen again" speeches fell on deaf ears. Tiffany sent him packing, no explanations needed or required.

Thomas went home back to New York with his tail between his legs, feeling miserable and ashamed. He was young and immature, yes, but what he did was unforgivable. He confessed to Wilhelmina about Tiffany catching him with the other woman. Thomas never mentioned his leaving his only child unattended. His mother would have beheaded him if she knew that. That was why Thomas knew Tiffany would never forgive him. He could barely forgive himself. Thomas barely kept in touch after that. He felt he did not deserve to see Karlie or to be a father. Thomas made sure he never had another child too, but Thomas never got over Tiffany.

Sadly, right after Tiffany kicked him to the curb, her career literally exploded. Tiffany's records began selling like hotcakes. Thomas could have kicked his own rear end for his stupid, thoughtless act.

His only consolation was that his pain echoed through his art. Offers began pouring in. "I connect with your pain," people said. "It jumps at me."

Thomas knew Tiffany had used her influence to get him recognized. That was yet another reason why his guilt constantly overwhelmed him. Tiffany still looked out for him. She even gave him a great settlement, more than he deserved, and a house to call his own. Thomas only had to agree never to talk about her or write about her to the press. That was easy. There was nothing for him to say.

Thomas got up and went back to his painting. He was definitely eager to meet Tiffany. Thomas only hoped Karlie would not be around. He could not bear to look his daughter in the eyes.

♫ Chapter Fourteen

When Tiffany got off the phone with Thomas, she felt a piercing pang of regret. She knew Thomas still felt guilty after all these years for what he had done. She could hear it in his voice. She knew he would feel justified once he learned the sorry truth. Her conscience kicked up a notch. Tiffany was truly sorry she had kept all this hidden, because this skeleton was coming out of the closet to bite her on the rear end. She tried to think of what she could say. "I am sorry," did not seem sufficient. Tiffany would only be lucky if Thomas did not come after her with all he had. She may not be around if he did.

Tiffany felt another wave of nausea assault her senses. She quickly ran to the bathroom to empty the entire contents of her stomach in the bowl. The medication she was taking was nothing but a placebo. It did nothing to stem the cancer eating away at her body. Tiffany made an executive decision. "No more, no more."

She went into her medicine chest and in one swoop emptied all the pills into the toilet and flushed them down the drain. What was the point of taking them when the side effects felt worse than the cancer did at times? She was going to let nature take its course.

Tiffany slid her body down to the floor and sat with one hand on the bowl.

The doorbell rang. Sighing, she said aloud, "Who is that? I am not in the mood." Tiffany sucked her teeth as the bell continued to ring throughout the house. "Some people can't take a hint," Tiffany grumbled, got on her feet, and went to answer the door, muttering all the way. "If you don't answer the door, that means you're not here or you don't want to be bothered."

She looked through the tiny peephole. It was Myra. *Not today, Myra,* she thought. Tiffany was not in the right frame of mind to deal with her persnickety friend. Having just finished puking her brains out, Tiffany wanted to be left alone. She did not want to deal with Myra's self-righteous attitude. Nevertheless her upbringing prevailed, and she reluctantly opened the door. "Hi, Myra." At the moment, Tiffany did not care if she sounded surly.

Myra held up what looked like an apple pie.

Tiffany was a sucker for pies and promptly shifted her body to allow Myra to enter.

Myra smirked, knowing some things had not changed. "I see you still have a fondness for pies," Myra stated as she entered and placed the pie on the counter.

"Yes, I do." Tiffany knew she sounded formal, but she still had not gotten past Myra's comments from the other night. She had been offensive.

"Tiffany," Myra began, "I am sorry about the other day. I was way out of line."

Tiffany studied Myra's face, searching for sincerity. She saw that the other woman meant what she said. "Okay." Tiffany watched as Myra's mouth hung open with disbelief.

"Okay? Is that all you are going to say? I was ready for a big showdown, and I had a speech all planned."

"Well, when you are dying, you learn how to let things go, you know?" Tiffany's attempt at humor failed.

"Oh, goodness, Tiffany. Please forgive me. I was way past insensitive—"

Tiffany made a swooping gesture with her hands to drive her point home and to stem Myra's apology. "Listen, I do *not* want this. People walking on eggshells around me, afraid to be themselves and speak their mind. Dying is not something I think about all the time, and you do not want me to censure—" *Oh, no.* Tiffany felt the tears surface. She tried to hold them at bay, but they refused to heed her command. She did not think she had any tears left to cry, but they were coming. She could feel them.

One drop . . .

Became more . . .

Like a dam breaking, Tiffany's face cracked, and she burst into tears.

Myra fought to temper her own tears. She did not know what to do at first. Then she hugged her friend tightly. Following the leading of the Holy Spirit, Myra prayed a short, earnest prayer for Tiffany.

Tiffany felt Myra's words move from her ear to her heart and into her very being. It soothed her and tempered her quivering emotions. At the end of the prayer, Tiffany cried a little bit more before pulling away. "Thank you," she hiccupped. "Sometimes I just cannot handle it."

"There's no need to thank me," Myra told her. "What else are friends for?"

Tiffany smiled through her tears. Myra grabbed a box of tissues and gently wiped Tiffany's face. Tiffany swallowed the tears rising from her simple act of love. She didn't get that often. Despite her ways, Myra was her friend. She did have a friend, and it felt good.

Myra glanced at her watch before springing to her feet. Neil was due home, and she still had not finished cooking her steak and potatoes. "Would you and Karlie like to come by for dinner?" Myra offered.

"No," Tiffany said, declining the invitation. "I think I better stay closer to home. Karlie introduced me to a friend of hers, and I gave her permission to go down the block until sundown."

"Okay," Myra said, stifling her disappointment. She really wanted to lay eyes on Karlie. She had yet to meet Tiffany's daughter. Myra went through the door and walked to her house. Her hands squeezed her midriff, as if to hold in the pain. She had really wanted to ask Tiffany what it was like to carry and deliver a child, but she would have sounded too pitiful. Extremely self-conscious about her infertility, Myra had withheld, not wanting Tiffany to discern her secret torment. As she walked through the garage and opened the side door, Myra bit her lip to keep from crying out from the sheer torture of unfulfilled wishes. She had just prayed for Tiffany, but she could not seem to find that comfort for herself.

♫ Chapter Fifteen

Her first black eye, during her first week of school. What a way to bring in the weekend! "Mom's going to hit the roof," Karlie muttered. She stealthily entered the house and went right into her room. If her mother saw her black eye, she was going to lose her mind. Snuggling under her fluffy comforters, Karlie took a moment to savor the fresh scent of fabric softener before picking up her telephone to dial Tanya's number.

Tanya answered on the second ring. "Are your parents upset?" Karlie asked.

"No," Tanya said, "Well, not once I explained everything. My mother wanted to rush over to Cheyenne's house and sock her a good one, but my father held her back."

Karlie cracked up at Tanya's comment. Her family was hilarious. Karlie had met them the night before, when her mother finally gave her permission to go over to Tanya's house. It was only on the next block, but her mother was worried about her welfare and urged Karlie to be home before dark. Karlie had a lot of fun. Tanya's parents were young like her mother, and their enthusiasm for life was infectious. They made Karlie feel at home and did not treat her differently because her mother used to be famous. Karlie had to help with the dishes, too.

But today the new best friends were on the way home from school when Cheyenne and three of her friends came at them. Karlie and Tanya held their own, even though Karlie ended up nursing a black eye. One of the other girls had elbowed her in the face during the scuffle.

Karlie smiled. She had her revenge lying at the bottom of her backpack. It was a huge chunk out of Cheyenne's hair. "My consolation prize," Karlie boasted and bobbed her head, feeling intense satisfaction at her conquest. Karlie felt assured that after their confrontation today, there would be no more problems. Chuckling to herself, Karlie knew she had surprised the other girls, because they had assumed from her designer clothes that she did not know how to fight. "Well, you thought wrong," Karlie uttered.

Hearing a knock on the door, Karlie quickly got off the telephone. She did not want Tanya hearing her mother ranting and raving.

Tiffany entered Karlie's room with a big smile, which promptly transformed into potent disbelief. "What the . . ." Tiffany rushed over to Karlie and scooped her in her arms before loudly demanding, "What happened? Who did this to your face?"

Karlie shrank against her mother's evident, understandable outrage. Her mother literally foamed at the mouth, which indicated an upcoming explosion. Karlie started talking fast. "Well, I met this guy, Jamaal, and—"

"Jamaal," Tiffany interrupted. "Who's he? Why is this the first time I'm hearing of him? Is he responsible for this?"

"Mommy," Karlie said and gently put one hand over her mother's lips. In a purposely calm tone, Karlie continued, "Mom, you have to give me a chance to explain." She saw her mother nod and removed her hand. "Jamaal is just some guy who showed me where one of my classes was. Anyway, he has a girlfriend, Cheyenne, who's head cheerleader. She stepped to me before telling me to stay away from him." She saw her mom's mouth open, so she held her hands up. "Please, Mom, let me finish."

"Okay . . . okay." Tiffany complied.

Seeing the impatience written on her pursed lips and hearing the telltale tapping feet, Karlie knew she could keep her mother at bay only for a short time. It was time to get to the meat of the story. "So today Cheyenne and two of her friends started major drama with me and Tanya. I mean, she thinks that because I'm from L.A., I must be a pushover and just decks me in the eye. After she hit me, I went crazy, Mom. I even pulled her weave out."

"You did?"

"Yup," Karlie said and reached into her backpack to proudly display the chunk of hair.

"I'm glad you defended yourself, Karlie," Tiffany stated, "but you shouldn't have to. I am going down to the school tomorrow to pull you out of school. As a matter of fact, I think I need to have a talk with Cheyenne." A thought occurred to her. "Weren't there any teachers around?"

"That's 'cause it happened near the bus loop and no one saw," Karlie explained. "But, Mom, I'm fine, and you don't need to pull me out of school. I like it there. I have a friend, and after today I don't think I'll have to worry about Cheyenne again."

"Hmmm." Tiffany was unconvinced.

Karlie turned on the waterworks. "Mom, it would be seriously humiliating if you came down to my school. I mean, I handled it. I am not a baby. You have to trust me. I'll be okay. I promise. Just don't pull me out of school."

Tiffany relented. "We'll see. In the meantime let me get you a piece of steak for that eye."

Karlie almost barfed at the idea of raw steak on her eye, but she knew when to argue and when not to argue. She heard her mother muttering on her way down the stairs to the kitchen and on her way back up the stairs. She handed Karlie the steak on a plate and hovered like a grizzly bear. She would have stayed there if the doorbell hadn't saved the day. Her mother had no choice but to go answer the door. She barked a terse "Stay in bed" before leaving.

Karlie felt like an invalid, when all she wanted to do was a victory dance for whipping Cheyenne's tail. Sadly, though, she had to play the helpless victim.

A few minutes later, Tiffany entered the room. "You have a guest who is most insistent that he see you. He looks a little . . . different." Her mother sounded mildly concerned.

"Who is it?" Karlie eagerly got out of bed, put the steak on her end table, and went to the top of the stairs. Tilting her body forward, she bent to see who was waiting. It was Jamaal. She had on a pair of huge fuzzy slippers, so she navigated the narrow steps carefully. The last thing Karlie wanted or needed was to take a misstep and go plummeting down the stairs, before landing in a heap at his feet. That would be so embarrassing.

"Jamaal?" Karlie asked. "What're you doing here?"

"I heard about the fight and came by to check on you," Jamaal explained. "I am so sorry this happened to you. I know you are new to town and everything. Anyway, I dumped Cheyenne because she is crazy. I didn't know Tiffany Knightly was your mother." Jamaal rambled on, not allowing Karlie a word in edgewise.

Karlie walked farther into the living room, over to where Jamaal was standing. Her mother went into the kitchen, presumably to get some tea. But Karlie was glad for some measure of privacy. "It's not something I talk about, and not many people our age know her," Karlie replied. "I do not understand why your girl-friend came at me like that. This is my first week in this school, and now my mother is threatening to pull me out because of all this drama."

"It's because—" Jamaal stopped. Karlie noticed a huge blush across his cheeks.

"What?" Karlie wanted an explanation.

"Well, she heard from somebody that I liked you, and she got jealous," Jamaal blurted.

Karlie paused, letting that new disclosure sink in. Then she smiled. "You like me?"

"Yeah," Jamaal breathed out nervously. He was still blushing, but against his mocha skin, the rosiness took on a purplish hue.

"But you do not even know me," Karlie said, flattered and unsure of what else to say. Like, this was a crazy moment for her right now. It was definitely surreal to have one of the most popular and good-looking boys in school standing in her house, confessing his feelings

"Well, we could be friends," Jamaal suggested.

"Listen, Jamaal," Karlie said, "I am not the kind of girl you are used to. I am a regular fifteen-year-old."

"Huh?" Jamaal sounded confused.

"I don't do certain things," Karlie stressed. She looked behind her to make sure her mother was not in the vicinity.

"Oh," Jamaal said. He blushed again, thinking California girls must be unusually blunt. "That's okay. So you wanna go out?"

"I do not think my mother will let me date so young," Karlie said. She hated disappointing him, but her mother could be old-fashioned when it came to certain things, and dating was one of those things.

"Then maybe I can come over sometime. You think your mother would mind?" Jamaal asked. He did not intend to give up that easily.

"I don't think she would mind. At least, I hope not. See you Monday."

Karlie went over to Jamaal and reached up to place a light kiss on his cheek. Jamaal raised his eyebrows in alarm. Then wide-eyed, he looked to see where her mother was. Karlie chuckled and walked Jamaal to the door. Once he had left, she leaned against the door and smiled. She definitely liked it here, and she already had a new best friend and, apparently, a soon to be boyfriend. "He is so cute," Karlie squealed. "I'm going out with the head of the basketball team." Excited, Karlie ran up the stairs to call Tanya and fill her in on all the juicy details of her thrilling encounter with Jamaal Weathers.

Tiffany leaned away from the wall where she had been discreetly listening to her daughter's conversation. Karlie was confident and unafraid of speaking her mind. Tiffany was so proud of her, although the verdict was still out on Jamaal. He seemed respectful enough, like he came from a good home, but one could never be too sure.

Tiffany's eyes watered. Her baby girl was growing up. "I'm going to miss it all." Tiffany wished she could be around to see Karlie blossom into full womanhood. The tears flowed from her eyes as she uttered, "I won't get to see Karlie get married or have children—none of it. I won't be here, and there is nothing I can do to change that." Tiffany felt the weight burden her shoulders, knowing that she would miss all of Karlie's important milestones and she was leaving her daughter alone to fend for herself.

Life was funny. Most parents lived long enough to watch their children grow up, but they did not have the resources or money to help them. Yet Karlie was already wealthy, and she was going to lose the only parent she had. She was going to be a poor little rich kid unless Tiffany found Karlie's father. Hopefully, he would accept and give Karlie the love and guidance she needed to become a viable contributor to society. "I'll find him, Karlie," Tiffany vowed. "I will find your father . . . your real father."

♪ Chapter Sixteen

"Lord, there is nothing you cannot do. You specialize in things that seem impossible. There is nothing too big for you, Lord." Neil prayed for about five more minutes before getting into bed. He tried to be quiet, as Myra was already fast asleep.

Propped up against his pillows, his head on his hands, Neil stared at the ceiling in contemplation. He looked over at his wife. Compared to his larger frame, she looked small and helpless. Neil felt his heart stir. He was concerned because it was only October and she was already taking personal days off from work. This was her third personal day in weeks. That was so not like her.

When he had asked why, Myra had given him a noncommittal answer, saying, "I'm okay. I just needed a 'me' day." However, her "me" day was actually two days of moping and moaning around the house. Neil was worried that Myra was actually suffering from clinical depression. Some older church folks did not fathom or agree with the notion of a Christian suffering from depression. "God's people cannot be depressed. Why else would God tell us to cast all our cares on Him?"

Myra was a faithful believer, and she rejoiced and praised God at church. She helped with various women's committees, hospitalities, and missionary outreach work. But she was a different person at home.

Depression was the only word Neil could use to describe her current state of mind.

Neil got up. He needed some air. He grabbed his jacket to put over his pajamas, pushed his feet into a pair of worn slippers, and walked outside his house. Ever since he gave his life to God, Neil had quit smoking cold turkey. Nevertheless, there were still times he felt the old temptation, so whenever he felt the urge arise, Neil walked. He'd promised God and Myra he would never put another butt in his mouth, and he'd meant it.

Neil knew better than to renege on a promise to God. There was no escaping God. Even if he went to hell, God would find him there. He passed by Tiffany's house and noticed there was a light flickering in the backyard. He decided to go back and investigate. He was not surprised to see Tiffany out by her tree.

"Hi," Neil greeted her. "I saw a light flickering back here and came to make sure everything was all right." He saw the huge flashlight bouncing off Tiffany's lap and chuckled. "Oh, that explains it." Neil noticed soiled tissues tossed haphazardly at her feet and used the back of his hand to move them delicately out of the way before he sat next to her. "What's wrong?" he asked.

"I just . . ." Tiffany hiccupped. "I wish I was going to be alive to see my daughter grow up. This is just not fair. I never smoked a day in my life. I just do not understand how I could have gotten lung cancer."

Neil felt his heart constrict with grief. He did not know what to say. Wordlessly, he enfolded Tiffany in his arms and allowed her to cry freely. "Go ahead and cry," Neil whispered in her ear, along with other soothing sentiments, but Tiffany was inconsolable. She was crying nonstop, and all he could do was hold on to his friend.

It felt so good just being held like this by someone who cared, Tiffany thought. Her mother did not do this. But Neil was strong and encouraging. Tiffany knew she could just let go without fear of him taking advantage. Neil was just not that kind of a man. Even though Myra had been her best friend, Neil and Tiffany had forged a bond all those years ago, when they each were facing a difficult time in their lives.

Neil eyed a crumpled tissue box by Tiffany's hip and pulled out a few tissues to wipe Tiffany's tears. "There, there," he said as he patted her shoulders just as a father would a child. His heart went out to this lonely, rich woman. When Tiffany found success in the music world, he was so glad for her and prayed she would finally be happy. Life had dealt her a harsh hand. He wished he knew why Tiffany kept getting such a raw deal. It was just so sad.

After a few moments, Tiffany composed herself. The two of them sat silently under the tree, both caught up in their own thoughts. Finally, Neil looked at his watch. "It's been over an hour since I got here." He had to get home before Myra woke up to find him gone. Her mind was too suspicious for his liking. She was apt to read more into his visit with Tiffany than the actual truth. Neil was not ready for that headache. "I'd better go, but I'll be praying," he said, making his excuses.

"I know," Tiffany responded, looking up at him. "You had better go before Myra gets the wrong impression."

She had echoed his thoughts exactly.

Tiffany watched Neil walk out of her backyard to head back home. He was such a compassionate and caring man. He was for real. Tiffany truly appreciated having him in her life, especially now. Neil was her rock, her fortress. Tiffany could only hope Myra realized what she had. Sighing, Tiffany shifted her thoughts toward Thomas, who had promised to drop by her house. Tiffany wondered if she was wise in letting Thomas visit her here alone. He was a big man, and if he lost his temper . . . "I'd better give him a call."

Tiffany jumped to her feet and brushed the dirt and leaves off her bottom. She went inside the house to get her address book. Quickly, she punched in the numbers to Thomas's cell phone. Thomas kept eclectic hours, so she knew he was generally up until the wee hours of the morning.

"Hi," Thomas greeted affectionately. "Calling about tomorrow?"

"Yeah," Tiffany said, twirling the cord on the landline. "I was hoping we could meet at the Carle Place instead."

"Ah, okay. Sounds cool to me." He hung up the phone without saying good-bye.

Tiffany glanced at the phone in her hand, listening to the dial tone. "Some things never change." He had always hung up without really saying good-bye. It used to drive her nuts, but that was Thomas.

Tiffany went to the refrigerator to get bottled water. The refrigerator temperature was set so cold that if she put the bottled waters on the top shelf, they would semi-freeze. "Ahh. Nothing quenches like water." She gulped the water so fast that it leaked out of the side of her mouth and down her shirt. Tiffany didn't bother to wipe it up.

Aimlessly, she wandered through the house, feeling listless. Nights like these made her feel incredibly lonely. She had been an idol to many men, and yet there was not even one to warm her bed tonight. Tiffany just missed the smell and feel of a man.

Tiffany walked up the stairs and gently opened Karlie's door to check on her. Finding her sound asleep, Tiffany closed the door and went into her bedroom, saying, "Another night in this big bed on my own." She hoped for a good night's sleep.

Tomorrow would be the day.

♪ Chapter Seventeen

Thomas took his time getting dressed. He wanted to look his best when he met with Tiffany. He looked in the mirror to appraise himself. "I look good," he said. "Tiffany ain't ready for all of this." He patted his freshly trimmed hair. He then dabbed some cologne on the crucial spots, just in case. "Hey, a man can always still hope."

Promptly at eleven, Thomas walked into the diner. Tiffany was already there. He noticed there was an excitement in the air. He knew some of the patrons recognized her from back in the day. Thomas puffed out his shoulders, feeling like a million bucks. He knew everybody was looking at him with speculation. Thomas literally bit his tongue to stop himself from proclaiming that Tiffany was his wife—er, ex-wife.

Thomas watched Tiffany eyeing his approach. He noticed her eyes scan him with interest and exaggerated his manly stride. Thomas knew he looked the same from high school and he was still fit. With a lot of swagger, he gave Tiffany a kiss on the cheek. Well, he headed for the lips since he had an audience, but Tiffany quickly sideswiped him and turned her cheek. It was worth a try.

An anxious waiter approached before Thomas's behind even hit the chair. "Are you ready to order?"

Thomas noticed that as he asked the question, the waiter kept his eyes pinned on Tiffany. The waiter appeared to be in his mid-thirties, so he would have recognized Tiffany Knightly. Thomas harrumphed loudly, feeling like Mr. Tiffany again.

Tiffany smiled pleasantly at the waiter and said, "Give us a few minutes, please."

The waiter enthusiastically nodded his head and rushed off without even a glance in Thomas's direction. He supposed the waiter was on the sidelines, waiting for his chance to approach their table again.

Making small talk, they caught up on what was new in their lives. It was not until after they had eaten their meal that Tiffany divulged the reason she needed to see him.

"Thomas, I have to tell you something, and I have no idea how to even begin."

Moved, Thomas grabbed her hands. She was actually shaking. "Tiffany, what is it? I promise you, it cannot be as bad as you imagine. Just say it out loud."

"I—I can't," Tiffany replied, hedging. Her breath caught.

"Just go ahead."

His gentle tone seemed to upset her even more. Thomas saw tears streak down her face. She bit her lips before looking him square in the eyes. "Thomas, I'm sorry. So sorry."

"Tiffany, you're alarming me now. Please, honey, just tell me, because the reality cannot be worse than what I am thinking." Thomas picked up a napkin and wiped the sweat off his face. Tiffany was really scaring him. He had never seen her behave like this.

"I'm afraid it is," Tiffany confessed. She grabbed his hands and finally spoke the words. "Thomas, I lied to you. I lied all those years ago, and our marriage was all based on a lie."

Thomas gave her a couple of tissues to wipe her face. His thoughtfulness made Tiffany utter, "Thomas, it doesn't help my conscience that you are being so nice to me now, especially since I do not deserve it."

"Tiffany, I am in no position to throw stones," Thomas countered. "Remember what I did?"

Tiffany closed her eyes and nodded, remembering the terror she had felt when she had entered their apartment to find Karlie all alone. "Yes, I remember being scared out of my mind. I couldn't fathom why you had done that."

"Tiffany, I just want to apologize all over again. Believe me, I have never forgiven myself for what I did. And I don't even know why."

"Stop, Thomas," Tiffany insisted. "That's not why I wanted to meet. It is not about rehashing the past—well, not your past. I need to come clean."

She had his undivided attention. Thomas's heartbeat escalated, and his body tensed. "Well, let's hear it."

"Thomas, I was not totally honest with you. I—I am not sure you are Karlie's father."

"What?" Thomas grabbed on to his chair. "What do you mean?"

Tiffany licked her lips and took another sip of water. "You weren't the only one I had been with that summer. I had slept with three other guys, so I'm not sure if you are Karlie's father. In my heart, you are, though."

Thomas watched her glossy, full lying lips, willing himself not to put his hands on her. "Why? What?"

"Thomas, I'm dying, and I need you to take a paternity test. I need to make sure you're truly Karlie's father."

Did she really have the nerve to ask if he would be willing to take a paternity test? Was she out of her cotton-picking mind? Thomas wondered. He saw Tiffany's expectant, anxious expression as she waited for his response. Thomas blinked. He sat in his chair and just looked at her as his mind processed everything she had told him. He could feel his blood boiling but resisted the urge to slam his fists on the table. "Now I know why you wanted to meet in public."

She was smart, because if they had been alone . . .

Tiffany sat and watched the different emotions cross her ex-husband's face. She wanted to remain stoic, but she was a basket case. She could only imagine what Thomas was thinking.

"You mean to tell me all these years I have been walking around, feeling like the biggest deadbeat that abandoned his only child, when Karlie might not even be mine?" Thomas growled the question between gritted teeth.

His growl made her insides quake with fear. She released small pent-up breaths, and her body trembled uncontrollably. Tiffany had tried to prepare herself for his certain anger, but what she saw before her surpassed her expectations. Nothing could have prepared her for this. She could feel the force of his wrath hit her body like shock waves. Her mouth felt parched, goose bumps rose on her flesh, and her teeth chattered.

Thomas was at boiling point and made a concerted effort to keep his temper in check.

Realizing she had yet to answer his question, Tiffany nodded her head, for she could not find the voice to answer him aloud. She could see the table rattling because of her shaking legs.

"No," Thomas spat. "There's your answer. No. I am not doing it."

"Thomas, please keep your voice down," Tiffany begged. She looked around, and fortunately, the other diners were busy with their meals.

Thomas did not care, and he looked at Tiffany with utter contempt. "You are not the woman I thought you were. Do you know that it is because of that guilt that I never moved on or had more children? Because I did not think I deserved to be a father. And you let me live my life with this big burden on my back without ever telling me the truth. You never would have told me the truth if you were not dying, would you?"

Tiffany knew she had to be honest. "No, because honestly, I consider you her father. To me, you are Karlie's father."

"Please," Thomas returned. He splayed his hands dramatically. "I am not buying that one at all. This explains why you made me sign those papers promising never to talk about you to the press. You were so conniving. I cannot believe I never saw just how much."

Tiffany felt the tears prick her eyes. She grabbed a tissue before pleading with Thomas. "Please, Thomas, I know you have every right to be angry, but think of Karlie. When I die, she won't have anybody but her father." Tiffany whispered her plea passionately.

Thomas got up and threw his napkin onto the table. Then he spun around and left without another word. His look of disgust said everything.

Tiffany sat there for about fifteen minutes, hoping Thomas would return, but he did not. Holding back the tears, she quickly settled her tab, left a generous tip, and drove to her home. Tiffany was a wreck. She had to get it together before Karlie came home. "I messed up," Tiffany admitted. "I went about it all wrong."

Tiffany threw herself on her bed, feeling extremely disappointed. She knew Thomas would be angry but had counted on him agreeing to take the paternity test. If he turned out to be the biological father, that would spare her from having to place three other calls and interrupt three other lives. But after today she knew she needed to make those calls. She would determine if Thomas was the father using the process of elimination.

A bad feeling came over her. Tiffany quickly raced to the bathroom. She barely made it before she released the soup and crackers she had eaten for lunch into the bowl. Tiffany heaved and heaved until she was exhausted. Sinking to the bathroom floor, she rested her head against the bowl. A few minutes later, she felt another set of cramps assail her and vomited again. This time there was a tiny pool of blood in the bowl. Seeing the blood made dying real to her, because it meant that her condition was worsening.

Spent, Tiffany got up and leaned against the wall of the bathroom. She pulled her body upward until she stood against the sink. Then she washed her hands and brushed her teeth. She looked at herself in the mirror. She saw the gaunt face reflecting her illness but said, "I have to go on for Karlie's sake. I have got to see this nightmare through."

Tiffany regretted throwing the pills out. She would request another prescription on her next scheduled visit. The pills made her feel worse, but maybe they would help keep the sickness at bay. Her other option would be to do nothing but bear the pain and nausea. Tough it out.

The next morning Tiffany buckled over in pain. Her lungs were constricted, and she felt achy all over. When Karlie looked in on her before leaving for school, Tiffany put on a brave face. "I'm okay, Karlie. Please don't be late for school."

"This is so unfair to her," Tiffany mumbled. It was only 6:00 A.M., but she had made up her mind to dial Dr. Ettelman's office and leave a message with his answering service. Within minutes, Dr. Ettelman returned the call.

Clearly upset at an early morning call that could have been prevented, Dr. Ettelman spoke his mind. "Tiffany, I am surprised that you would've thrown out the prescription pills. I understand that you really hate taking medication, but there will be days when you will need it. Don't kid yourself. It is better to have them and not use them than to endure a night like you did last night. You have a debilitating condition, and it will not get better."

Tiffany took her scolding like a trouper. "Yes, you're right, Dr. Ettelman," she offered meekly, ending his tirade.

Dr. Ettelman relented and softened his tone. "I will have my nurse personally FedEx you some morphine ampoules and needles. In the meantime, give my nurse your nearest drugstore information, and you can pick up some pills to tide you over till the package arrives."

"Thank, you, Doctor," Tiffany returned, then ended the call.

Dr. Ettelman's words rang in her ear. "You have a debilitating condition. . . . It will not get better. . . ."

But she had a will . . . a will to live. Tiffany looked at the clock . . . and knew she had another phone call to make.

♫ Chapter Eighteen

He was tired, and it showed. Darnell stood in his bathroom and saw the puffy eyes staring back at him. He leaned into the mirror for a closer look. "Is that a pimple? Aww, man." Darnell knew his vanity was kicking in. "Now I'm gonna feel like I'm walking around with a monstrosity on my face."

His long brown hands zeroed in on the spot on the bottom of his chin. He was about to squeeze it when he remembered the witch hazel underneath the sink. Darnell stooped his long frame and heard his knees crack. "Getting old."

Retrieving the witch hazel and a couple cotton balls he kept stashed in a Ziploc bag, Darnell dabbed the annoying area, then abruptly lost interest, knowing that it would dry up. He generally did not suffer from breakouts, not even when he was a teen. Darnell was more concerned about his puffy eyes. Last night's game ran into overtime, and he did not get home until midnight. He was the head coach at Hempstead High School, and as a result, he was often the last one to leave. Lucky for him, April and Amber were already in bed when he got home, courtesy of his mother's care. He did not know what he would do without his mother, because he sure as heck could not afford child care for two girls on his salary.

He heard the bathroom door open and looked in the mirror to see who it was. There was no reflection.

He felt a tiny pair of hands encircle his leg. He looked down and smiled at his four-year-old daughter.

"Hi, April," Darnell said, addressing the brown mop of curls.

"What're you doing?"

"I am getting ready to brush my teeth," Darnell answered and bent down to wrap his arms around his daughter. "Good morning, sunshine." April giggled and squeezed him tightly. Darnell relished feeling her little arms around his neck. It made him feel on top of the world.

He picked up his toothbrush. April grabbed on to his legs again. Darnell undid the toothpaste cap. April still did not release her hold on his legs.

"Oh," April commented. "You are gonna brush your teeth?"

"Yes," Darnell answered with extreme patience. "Watch how I do it, and then you can follow." He was used to these kinds of conversations and actually welcomed them.

"But I have to pee," April said. "I cannot watch."

"I have to pee too."

Darnell turned his head toward the other voice and smiled at another brown mop of curls. Amber was up.

Knowing the drama about to unfold, Darnell firmly addressed both of them. "You both cannot pee in here at the same time. Amber, you're a big girl, so go in the other bathroom and pee."

"But I want to pee in here with you, Daddy, and I'm not a big girl. I'm only six years old," Amber protested. Darnell saw her face scrunch as she zeroed in on her sister. He knew there was going to be war.

"Go." Darnell pointed forcefully. Then his eyes widened at what was going down before him.

April started pulling down her pants. Amber started pulling hers down when she saw what her sister was doing. April was not as vocal as Amber could be, but she was no less determined.

Darnell knew what was coming next and tried to avoid it. "Amber, go to the other bathroom," he ordered in a stern voice. "Next time you can pee in here, okay?"

Amber started crying but went to the other bathroom. April finished doing her business, and Darnell went back to brushing his teeth. He shook his head. This was what his mornings were like every day. He had not realized these kinds of conversations came with being a father, but Darnell was learning. Truthfully, he enjoyed sparring with his daughters about any and everything.

April came over for him to wash her hands, and Darnell yelled out, "Amber, get dressed." He helped April get into her clothes, which she had brought in with her and tossed on the bathroom floor.

He was so glad his mother had combed their hair and had given them a bath the night before. He did not know how he would have made it to work on time this morning otherwise.

In the midst of this chaos, the telephone rang. Darnell's first thought was to ignore it, but then he thought twice and rushed to answer the kitchen phone. He was one of those people who were afraid not to answer the phone for fear that it might be an emergency.

"Darnell King?" the voice asked.

"Yes?" *Shoot,* Darnell thought. It sounded like a telemarketer, and he did not have the time for that now. He wondered if they were even allowed to call that early in the morning.

"This is Tiffany Knightly."

As crazy as it sounded, Darnell did not instantly make the connection.

"I am calling you this early because I know you have two young daughters and I figured you would be up already."

Darnell was now a little apprehensive. This woman seemed to know a lot about him, and he did not know a thing about her. His heartbeat escalated, and he was immediately on the defensive. Darnell moved the phone from his ear to look at it with a quizzical expression. Seeing the futility of his actions, he returned it to his ear. Darnell laughed at himself. It is not as if the caller on the other end could see his face.

"I'm sorry," Darnell interjected in a slightly worried tone. "Do I know you?"

"Yes," Tiffany replied hesitantly. "We, ah, went to high school together."

Darnell paused. "Tiffany Knightly. Forgive my momentary obtuseness."

Something behind him crashed to the floor. Darnell turned his head and looked to see April in a huge mess. She had broken the jelly jar, and its contents were all over the floor and her clothes. When had she opened the refrigerator to get it? Darnell wondered. He needed another pair of eyes in the back of his head.

"Man, I honestly do not have the time for this." Flustered, Darnell glanced at his watch and groaned aloud.

Tiffany heard the commotion through the phone, his comment, and declared, "I will try to catch up with you another time."

Haphazardly, Darnell agreed and hung up the phone. His mornings were just too crazy for any coherent conversation. Boy, he wished his mother had stuck around. But knowing Leona, she had gotten up at the crack of dawn and had returned to her home. Darnell made quick work of the disaster on the floor and went to clean April. Sweating now, he put both girls in their coats to head through the door.

Just as they were about to leave, Amber declared importantly, "I have to make stinky."

Darnell dropped his bag in despair. "Sweet love of . . ." Darnell stopped before he called out the Lord's name in vain.

"Well, that wasn't really smart, now, was it?" Tiffany got off the phone with Darnell, feeling stupid. She had been inconsiderate to call the man's home so early in the morning. Tiffany resolved she would not get discouraged. Instead, she spent the day filling her prescription, reading, and resting. But still the day dragged on.

About three thirty that afternoon Tiffany made some tea and went outside to sit on the porch and people watch. She saw Myra come outside and gave her a wave. Myra took that as an invitation and walked the short distance to Tiffany's house.

"Hey, girl," Tiffany greeted with a wide smile. Today her friend was a welcome diversion.

"I came by to invite you to my church this weekend, if you're up to it," Myra said and joined her on the steps. Myra felt some sort of spiritual guidance would do Tiffany some good. Church never failed to uplift and cheer her. She hoped it would do the same for her friend.

"Okay," Tiffany agreed, too tired to put up much of a fight about how God had abandoned her, blah, blah, blah.

***

Come Saturday, Tiffany, Myra, and Neil pulled into the parking lot of the church.

When was the last time she had stepped foot inside this or any church? Tiffany asked herself. The fact that she had to think about it spoke volumes. Unsure about what she would face, Tiffany had sent Karlie to spend the day with Tanya.

Her heart thundered. *Cue burn, on the stroke of five . . . four . . . three . . . two . . . one.* Okay, she was still standing. Tiffany expelled a breath of relief. Always either on tour or undergoing cancer treatments, Tiffany barely had time for God. Correction. She needed to make time for God.

"Are you okay?" Myra asked. Neil had previously excused himself and had entered the building for parts unknown.

Tiffany saw Myra looking at her quizzically. "Yes, I am. It has been more than a minute, you know, since I have been here to church. At least I didn't explode into ashes." Tiffany made a feeble attempt at humor, but she trembled.

"Please." Myra grabbed her hand and gave it a light squeeze. "If church was for the fittest to attend, nobody would be here. You just come on in with me. You will be all right. You'll see."

Tiffany heard the music from the vestibule. "They are getting down in there. Remember when we used to sing in the choir?" she said, already moving her body to the beat.

Myra's head was bopping, and she was already singing along. "Yeah, praise and worship is one of my favorite parts. It is like what Psalms says: God inhabits our praises, and when we praise Him, the blessings come pouring down."

The usher opened the door, and the sounds from the guitars and drums intensified. Tiffany took in all the hats and fancy suits. She saw so many flashy designs and bold colors that for a second she imagined herself swimming in a box of Lucky Charms. Even Myra was decked out in her blue suit with the silver bejeweled trim. Her shoes, hat, and pocketbook were a perfect match.

Tiffany realized that, hatless and in a simple black gown, she was severely underdressed. Hmmm. The diva had been "out-divaed" today. That did not stop her from strutting down the aisle with Myra, who at the moment was—*No, please, no, yes*—heading for the second row upfront, right in the line of fire.

From the corner of her eye, Tiffany saw the hand shovers and finger pointers all looking in her direction. She pretended not to notice and focused on the choir, which was about to sing. Tiffany felt guilty. It was because of her that Myra and Neil had been late today. Well, it wasn't completely her fault, Tiffany thought. She did not know what to wear. She had to try on several dresses before Myra gave her the thumbs-up on the one she was wearing. Tiffany felt the hairs on her skin rise as the choir sang.

Before calling up the preacher, the moderator, Deacon Tiny—at least that was what she thought his name was—invited a little girl named Victoria to sing. Tiffany moved forward in her chair, amazed. Victoria could not have been more than about five or six, but she was singing Donnie McClurkin's song like a professional.

"I guess she showed me," Tiffany said good-naturedly to Myra.

Myra nodded her head. "That child is a gift from God, and her mother is this young little thing. You would never believe it."

Then it was time for the message. Tiffany wiggled her bottom on the hard pew, trying to get comfortable.

Used to the drone of older men, Tiffany perked up when she saw a younger handsome man get behind the podium. "Okay, I can tell just looking at him that this is going to be good," she whispered to Myra.

Myra gave her the eye. "Too young for you."

"Get your mind out of the gutter, lady. We are in church." She must have spoken too loudly, because Myra poked her and gestured for her to be silent.

Tiffany crossed her heart, signaling she would behave. The man had already started preaching. Tiffany found herself listening to every word. He was beginning a four-part sermon on blessings. Spiritual blessings.

"The kind that never runs dry . . . that fills the soul . . . Take a sip of that living water and you will never thirst again," he urged.

Tiffany was definitely interested in hearing more from . . . "What's his name?" she whispered, nudging Myra.

Myra drily responded, "Pastor Micah Johnston."

Tiffany liked Pastor Johnston. He was energetic and preached with sincerity. Tiffany enjoyed every minute of his words. At the end of his sermon, the entire congregation got on their feet and started rejoicing. "I am definitely coming back," she shouted to Myra. A church sister behind her must have heard her, because she patted Tiffany on the back and started jumping and shouting, "Hallelujah." After a few moments, the ushers motioned for the musicians to stop playing, and the congregation took their seats. Then the deacon read the announcements.

Before the end of the service, Tiffany got called out. The past members recognized her and remembered her when she was a young girl, carefree and singing in the choir.

"It appears we have a celebrity in our midst," Pastor Johnston said. "I'm told she used to be singing up here in these very choir stands. It seems like we can't end the day unless Ms. Tiffany Knightly comes forward."

Tiffany looked helplessly at Neil and Myra, silently urging them to rescue her from the undesired spotlight. They both raised their hands, signifying she was on her own. Tiffany stood up, feeling all eyes on her, and went down to the altar. She felt self-conscious about what she was wearing. It was not exactly church material. Her black designer dress had needed a shawl, so she'd slung one over her shoulders. The good thing was everybody was smiling, and nobody seemed to care. Nevertheless, Tiffany vowed she was going to get some church gear.

"Ah, it's good to be here. Back home," Tiffany announced, then opened her mouth and sang from her heart "Blessed Assurance." When she was finished, almost the entire church was in tears.

Pastor Johnston came over to her, anointed her, rested his hands on her head, and prayed. "Lord, as Tiffany sang that you are her blessed assurance, I pray, dear Lord, that you will make yourself known to her, that you will draw her close to you and give her that peace that surpasses all human understanding, in Jesus's name. Amen."

Tiffany had to dig her heels into the floor to keep from falling. His hands felt like a ton on her head, but his cologne, which she caught the scent of from being up close, was masculine and pleasant.

The service concluded at the end of his prayer. Almost instantly, people surrounded Tiffany just to offer their condolences or request an autograph. She dutifully listened and attached her signature to everything from a church fan to a napkin.

From his position on the podium, Neil watched Tiffany, secretly admiring her stamina. Tiffany really was a strong woman. He would make sure he said an extra prayer for her when he was on his knees. He prayed she would find some measure of peace, as Pastor had said, and also that she would find Karlie's father.

That afternoon, when she got in from church, Tiffany changed into a pair of faded jeans and a sweater. She received a text message from Karlie saying that she was having a great time at Tanya's. Tiffany returned the text, telling Karlie to call her to come get her when she was ready. Karlie texted back that she would just hail a cab.

It was time to call the next name on her list, which was Pierce. She would call Darnell back later.

A woman answered on the second ring. Tiffany assumed it was Elyse and politely asked for Pierce.

The woman did not even bother to answer, for she was too busy hollering at one of the children. "Hey, all a y'all better pipe down. I can't hear myself think."

Goodness, it sounded like a zoo instead of a home. Tiffany held the receiver away from her ear, willing herself not to hang up the phone. She heard a mild scuffle as the phone exchanged hands.

Finally, Pierce uttered a gruff hello.

"Is this Pierce Willis?" Tiffany asked.

"Yes. Who wants to know?"

"This is Tiffany Knightly from high school."

"Oh, hi, Tiffany."

She heard the sudden warmth he injected in his tone, and felt disgusted. She hoped he was not trying to make a move on her with his common-law wife and children in earshot. That would be despicable. "Do you remember me?"

"Do I ever," Pierce said. "How could I forget Tiffany Peterson? I mean, Knightly."

Tiffany was repulsed at his obviously suggestive tone. She stuck her finger in her mouth, imitating a gagging motion. If this were not such a crucial cause, she would slam the phone down right in his ear. "I was wondering if we could meet to talk," Tiffany said, fighting the inexplicable urge to cuss him out. He had always irritated her.

"Name the time and place," Pierce countered without hesitation.

Ugh. Tiffany swallowed her retort, ready to clobber him already. Pierce had been obnoxious in high school, and she saw that had not changed over time. He was extremely good looking, and he knew it. Because of his blessed attributes, Pierce believed he was God's gift to women. Tiffany sorely regretted having sex with Pierce. She had served only to feed his massive ego by doing that. Nevertheless, the fact that she slept with him made him a viable candidate in her mission to locate Karlie's father.

"What about this evening? Around five o'clock?" Tiffany asked, trying to blot out the negative thoughts in her head.

"Should I come over to your place?" Pierce asked. He lowered his voice to a mere whisper. The silence in the background indicated he had moved out of his family's earshot.

Sleaze. Slime. Fleabag, Tiffany thought, repulsed at his obvious come-on. "No," she quickly retorted. "We can meet at the Cheesecake Factory."

"It's a date," Pierce said.

Tiffany disconnected the call and looked at the receiver with contempt. "As if . . ." A few seconds later, Tiffany laughed, because she could not understand how Pierce could be so presumptuous to assume she wanted him after all these years. He was still his biggest fan, just as in high school. "Man barely has a pot to pee in, and he still think he is all that *and* a bag of chips."

Pierce Willis had been head of the wrestling team and had actually been very good. He would have been better at it if he had not allowed his ego to get in the way. Every single conversation he'd engaged in was either about a girl who liked him or his trophies from wrestling. Tiffany was amazed at how many girls flocked to him, despite his arrogance and cocky behavior. It showed their shallowness.

Pierce had asked her out even when she was dating Thomas. "Come on, girl. I will show you what you're missing," he'd told her. Bewildered, he could not get the hint that she just did not want him. Pierce convinced himself she was playing hard to get. He was the best-looking boy in the school, the homecoming king, and was voted "Most Likely to be Famous" in the yearbook. The idea that Tiffany found him repelling was inconceivable. "Stop playing hard to get, girl," he would yell, making some crude gesture. "You know you want me. You know you want this."

But when Clifford irrevocably damaged her, Pierce's persistence won out. Tiffany went out and slept with Pierce all in one night. She remembered his "This is the best. I know it is the best, girl, the best you'll ever have" speech. Detached, she'd nodded her agreement and laughed at his pugnacious attempt to please her.

Hearing her laughter had only egged Pierce on. "Yeah, you enjoyed it, girl. I know it. I can tell."

Hysterical, Tiffany thought. She cracked up now thinking about it. If women were to say the things men said in that moment . . . well . . .

She wished she knew then what she knew now as an adult. That she had been blameless and had been forced against her will to suffer through a horrible, debasing act committed by her stepfather. She definitely would not be in the situation she was facing now. She told herself that regret belonged in the past, but it was no easy feat.

Tiffany placed yet another call, trying to reach Darnell again. He answered the telephone. This time there was no doubt about her identity.

"Hi, Tiffany," Darnell greeted her warmly. "I was expecting your call."

"Oh, yeah?"

"Yeah." Darnell went on, "You are the same Tiffany who called me the other day, right?"

"Yeah," Tiffany said.

"So, Ms. Tiffany Knightly, diva superstar, what can Darnell, the small-town football coach, do for you?"

Tiffany laughed at Darnell's teasing tone. "I needed to speak with you about a very delicate matter."

"Okay." Darnell's curiosity had been piqued. He did not have a clue what Tiffany would want with him after all these years.

"Yes, it's kind of . . . sensitive . . . and personal," Tiffany said, hedging. She did not know how to get out the right words. "This is not the kind of thing a person can talk about over the telephone. Believe me."

"This sounds serious," Darnell stated, noting the gravity of her tone. "Listen, my mother is here, and the girls are down for a nap. I can shoot over and see you for a minute if you want."

Having read his bio, Tiffany felt safe allowing him to meet her at her home. "Sure. That is a wonderful idea."

"Where are you staying?"

Tiffany bit her nail. "I moved back into my old house. You remember where I live?"

"Of course. I'll be there in ten," Darnell replied and got off the phone.

Tiffany hung up the phone and ran into her bathroom. Quickly, she changed into a pink sweater and a pair of black jeans. She turned the heat on a little higher and put on a warm pair of socks. October was coming in with a blast. Next, she went into her kitchen to retrieve some finger food and put her teakettle on just in case. She felt nervous. Tiffany was intrigued to speak to him, especially after reading his profile. She wanted to know how he had survived after his wife died such a violent death.

It seemed like seconds before Tiffany heard the peal of the doorbell. She quickly answered it, and Darnell entered.

He smelled good.

Like man.

Tiffany inhaled, allowing herself the carnal pleasure. It felt like ages since she had inhaled a masculine scent. She rode the first stirrings of feminine appreciation.

♪ Chapter Nineteen

Darnell gave Tiffany the once-over. She was every bit as beautiful as he had remembered, and did not look like a woman living her last stages of life. Her shoulder-length hair actually glistened. Darnell reached out and touched it. It felt soft under his touch. It smelled good too.

Tiffany felt Darnell's hand in her hair. She was surprised at his bold gesture but did nothing to stop him, blatantly enjoying the sensations his mere touch caused. Her response baffled her. Tiffany did not expect to react to such a little gesture. She must be more starved for affection than she had realized. Compelled to say something, Tiffany uttered an eloquent "Hi."

Darnell felt something move within him and recognized it as arousal. Tiffany's scent stirred his senses. He had not expected this. After his wife's death, Darnell unknowingly closed that part of himself off. He reminded himself that initiating any kind of a relationship with her would not be a good idea. Struggling against his flesh, Darnell released his light grip on her hair and said, "Hi."

Tiffany felt a small measure of disappointment. She should be glad Darnell broke contact. She did not need any attachments.

The air about them was thick and tense. Tiffany felt like she was back in high school all over again. But she was not. She was a grown woman, and she had something she had to do. "Can I offer you something to drink?" Tiffany questioned, licking her lips. Her mouth suddenly felt parched.

Darnell walked into her living room area and sat down. "Yes, please." He watched Tiffany leave to get the drink and placed his hands on his head. What just happened? he contemplated. Darnell remembered reaching for Tiffany's hair and touching it. He had not counted on feeling the thousand electric bolts run through his body on contact. He had not anticipated becoming enticed by her scent. He exhaled.

Darnell rubbed his head, showing his distress. It had been too long since he had known the pleasure of a woman. He had devoted his time to tending to his daughters and helping them cope with their mother's premature death. "Don't even go there, man," Darnell mumbled under his breath. Being a Christian was also the major reason why Darnell had remained celibate, even though he had stopped attending church services after his wife's funeral. His wife, Lily, had introduced him to the Lord.

After her death, Darnell grew tired of the sympathetic looks and the "God knows best" comments. He also discovered that the single sisters were vultures in disguise, salivating and waiting to pounce on him at the most inopportune times. It was positively suffocating and off-putting. The Holy Spirit continuously chastised him about forsaking the assembling.

"I know, Lord, I've got no excuse," he would always agree. He was a man's man, but he was not man enough to disagree with God. It was only a matter of time before he had to heed the call.

That was why he had no business looking in Tiffany's direction. "No, I'd better leave that woman alone," he chided. Darnell could not start something with a woman who was dying. He could not bark up that tree. It had been sheer agony losing his wife, and he wasn't looking to experience that a second time. He wanted to be with someone who was guaranteed to outlive him for a change.

Tiffany returned to the living room and gestured for him to follow her into the kitchen. Like a lap dog, Darnell followed close behind her. The only consolation was that Tiffany appeared to be feeling just as discombobulated as he was. At least he hoped so.

Tiffany did not know why this was happening. She was acutely aware of the man following close on her heels. She wanted him like she had no business wanting anybody. Tiffany could not recall feeling such a powerful instant attraction before. She sang about this kind of magnetism in her songs, but she had never experienced it firsthand. She already knew Darnell in the biblical sense of the word, but she had not felt this way then. Maybe it was because she was simply a woman with no ulterior motives. It had all been about payback before.

This time, however, Tiffany wanted to sleep with him because of a potent sexual attraction. She looked down at the floor, not really looking at anything. *Uh-oh.* Self-conscious, she hugged her sweater, pretending to be cold while fervently praying Darnell had not noticed how taken she was with him. Luckily, he was too busy fitting his huge frame into one of her kitchen chairs and did not perceive her, uh, little dilemma. Thank the Lord for small favors.

"Darnell," Tiffany said, wetting her lips. She sat across from him and looked at him. Darnell gave her his undivided attention. She felt heat seep up her spine at his intense stare. She saw the passion there and knew he was also in the throes of physical attraction. Unknowingly, Tiffany's voice dropped. "I have to tell you something. Remember when we slept together?"

"Yes," Darnell answered. He remembered. Darnell adjusted himself at the memories her question evoked. *Lord, I need you to bind this feeling. Help me control it, Lord,* he silently prayed.

"Well, there is something I have to tell you," Tiffany said. She responded to the heat emanating from his eyes and instinctively crossed her legs.

"Okay," Darnell said, egging her on, but he frantically sought to bring his wayward thoughts under control.

Tiffany sat up and got her mind together. She fanned herself. It certainly felt warm in here.

Tiffany told Darnell about Karlie and the other men. Her lips loosened, and she was forthright about her stepfather's abuse as well, feeling the need to tell him what had prompted her to sleep with so many men. Finally, Tiffany confessed, "I came home to find my daughter's father."

Darnell listened intently while Tiffany spoke. Her topic of conversation had cooled his ardor significantly, but his facial expressions gave nothing away. "So, your daughter, Karlie, might actually be my child?" Darnell reiterated after mulling over all she had said.

"Yes." Her body tensed as she waited for the sure explosion to follow.

None came.

Darnell took her hands with compassion shining in his brown eyes. "I am sorry this is happening to you, and I will definitely take the paternity test. I can only imagine how you must feel. You have got a lot of guts and chutzpah, Tiffany, and that's to be applauded."

He could tell from the shock on her face that Tiffany had not expected this reaction. But he was not prepared for hers. Practically jumping across the table, Tiffany reached over to kiss Darnell softly on the lips. Acting on instinct, Darnell held her. Tiffany opened her mouth to give him full access. That was his undoing.

Darnell grabbed Tiffany without breaking the kiss and moved until his body was positioned directly in front of her. Fire seared them. He ravaged Tiffany's lips and heard her answering moan. Darnell ignored the little voice telling him to hit the brakes, and his suggestive, erotic movements left no doubt about his aspirations. She was driving him to distraction by unabashedly responding and arching her back.

Darnell picked Tiffany up with such ease one would think she weighed one pound. He then placed her across the table. *Yes,* he told himself. He was going to take her right then and there.

Desire held them captive.

Tiffany could not believe what was happening. Turned on to the max, she situated herself invitingly to give Darnell full access to her body. Filled with impatience and overwhelming desire, Tiffany began to tug her sweater over her head.

Stop, Darnell.

He knew that voice. "I will," Darnell whispered. He closed his eyes in a feeble attempt to rein in his emotions. But carnal desire weakened him, and Darnell feasted his eyes on the attractive display. He groaned at the sight of her. *Just one kiss, Lord,* Darnell thought.

Judas did a lot with one kiss too. The warning became even more insistent.

He had to get out of there. But first, Darnell determinedly blocked out the Spirit's leading. He wanted Tiffany, and there was nothing stopping them.

Both Tiffany and Darnell looked each other in the eyes, consenting. They were going to let this happen.

Darnell could hardly contain his excitement. He looked at the anxious woman lying across the kitchen table and . . .

Then the telephone rang.

Tiffany and Darnell paused. Divine intervention. God had perfect timing, or in this case, a sense of humor.

Tiffany made a lunge for the telephone. She had to answer it in case it was Karlie. "Hello?" As she listened to the person on the other end, Tiffany looked at Darnell and mouthed, "It is Pierce."

"I'll be right there," Tiffany assured him. "Wait for me, please. I do apologize, but something unexpectedly came up."

Darnell snorted. *Boy, she is so right about that.* He gathered his scattered senses and managed to cool the raging desire burning within. This was how Samson must have felt, Darnell thought, because he found Tiffany intoxicating. She was his Delilah, and he had just met her. Well, he amended, he had just met her again. For Darnell had already known her intimately, but that was ages ago, and today Darnell had been completely bowled over.

The Holy Spirit was now bringing back several scriptures to his mind that made Darnell wince at his rash behavior. *Shall we continue in sin, that grace may abound?*

At the end of her telephone conversation, Tiffany quickly filled him in that she had had a lunch date with Pierce at the Cheesecake Factory. One that she'd missed because she'd been distracted by *other* things.

Seeing Tiffany dash about to get ready to meet up with Pierce, Darnell quickly made his excuses and left. Another verse about resisting temptation was whipping at him. Darnell knew he had to obey right now.

God was not going to have it any other way. "It was just a kiss," Darnell said aloud, rationalized his behavior, once he was outside. "Nothing else happened, Lord. You stopped it just in time. One day I suppose I will thank you."

Darnell dragged his feet, but he did depart. Truthfully, Darnell did not feel triumphant. Instead, he felt an acute disappointment, especially after seeing Tiffany standing at the screen door, her body a siren calling out to him.

♫ Chapter Twenty

Jamaal walked in the house with Karlie.

"Mom? I'm home," Karlie called out. "Are you here?" She walked into the kitchen and saw a note taped on the refrigerator that stated she'd be back soon.

"Should I go?" Jamaal asked.

"No, it's okay. You can stay. My mom will be back soon. Her note said that she's running errands." Karlie walked over to the door where he stood and gestured for him to follow her into the den.

The two teenagers sat next to each other on the love seat.

Karlie snuck a look at Jamaal. Underneath the gruff exterior, he was really a sweetheart. Karlie liked him a lot and wanted to meet his parents, but when she had asked him about it once before, Jamaal had changed the subject. Karlie wanted to know why. *No time like the present,* she figured.

"Jamaal, when am I going to meet your parents?" Karlie asked.

"Huh?"

Karlie rolled her eyes because Jamaal went conveniently deaf. "Jamaal," Karlie said, "why don't you ever want to talk about your parents?"

"Because," Jamaal said simply. Karlie could see his obvious agitation as he squirmed and shrugged his shoulders dismissively. "I just do not want to talk about them right now. It's like me asking you questions about your mother dying."

Karlie bit her lip and measured her words carefully. "Jamaal, I know I just met you, but you can ask me anything you want about my mother."

"Really?" Jamaal's eyebrows rose.

"Yeah." Karlie bobbed her head with certainty. "I'll tell you anything you want to know. I'm not gonna hide my feelings from you. That's what couples do. Share their feelings."

"Well, maybe one day we can both talk about our parents and how we feel," Jamaal suggested. "Just not today."

Karlie let the matter drop.

"Let's go to the movies."

"I have homework to do," Karlie whined. She got up to get her backpack and took out her math book and worksheet. Her face fell as she eyed the math problems. Math *was* rocket science to her.

"Let me take a look," Jamaal demanded.

Karlie walked over to sit next to him on the couch before handing him the paper.

Unconcerned, Jamaal waved his hands at what he perceived as simple math. "I will finish it for you."

"Well . . ." Karlie replied, hedging. The idea of going out with Jamaal was tempting. It would be their first date. "I have to ask my mom."

"Well, ask her," Jamaal said, leaning back into the couch.

Karlie's eyes zeroed in on his frame appreciatively. He was rocking a serious body already. Imagine when he became a man. Jamaal was going to be one big ball of hotness one day. "I don't know what Mom's going to say." Her mother was cool, but there was no way she'd go for Karlie going out on a school night—and with a boy. "And I'm kind of scared leaving her alone at night. Anything can happen."

Jamaal nodded with understanding. "Well, I guess I don't mind hanging here with you. We can watch TV or something." He studied her profile from under his long lashes. He could not imagine what it was like having a celebrity for a mother. Actually, he did not even know what it was like to have a real mother. Tiffany seemed to be a good mother to Karlie. Jamaal wished he had that. He wished he knew what it felt like to have somebody who cared.

Jamaal looked at Karlie. He appreciated that she cared about him. She was always on him to go to class, and she even thought he was smart. Jamaal felt good being with her. His heart moved. "Karlie, I want to tell you something."

Karlie turned to face Jamaal, giving him her complete attention. Jamaal took her hands. They felt clammy. Karlie knew Jamaal was nervous, and she, in turn, became nervous.

"I love you," Jamaal whispered.

"You love me?" Karlie clearly had not expected that confession.

"Yes."

"Isn't it kind of sudden?" Her heart accelerated into overdrive. Karlie asked the question because she had seen enough movies to know what usually followed the "I love you" declaration. Frankly, she did not know if she was ready for it.

"No. Not to me. You are the first person I have met who truly seems to care about me, and I love you for that."

"Jamaal, are you saying this because you feel sorry for me, you know, since my mother is dying and all that?" Karlie desperately needed to know. She knew how she felt about Jamaal, but she did not want him to love her because he pitied her. That would be too awful.

Jamaal vehemently shook his head with denial. "Karlie, I know we've only known each other a few weeks, and we are very young, but I do love you. Do you think you could feel the same for me one day?"

"Yes, I do," Karlie declared, cupping his face with her hands. "I love being with you. You are thoughtful and kind and sweet."

"Sweet?" Jamaal laughed. "Please do not let anyone at school hear you say that. It would definitely ruin my reputation."

They smiled at each other. The air began to rise between them. Karlie did not recognize it. Jamaal did. He wanted to kiss Karlie really badly, but he did not want to scare her off.

"Why are you looking at me like that?" Karlie asked.

"Because—"

"Because what?"

"I . . ." Jamaal hesitated, then gulped. "I want to kiss you."

Karlie blushed nervously at his confession. She felt her palms begin to sweat. Her heart started pounding in her chest.

Using his hands, Jamaal held Karlie's head and tilted it toward him. He leaned his body into hers. Karlie retreated, but Jamaal was not dissuaded by her subtle intimation. He moved even closer to her.

"What're you doing?" Karlie whispered.

"I am going to kiss you," Jamaal whispered back.

Slowly and cautiously, Jamaal placed his lips on hers. He closed his eyes and tentatively tasted her lips, mouth closed. Karlie kept her eyes wide open. She did not know what to do. They heard the lock click and guiltily pulled apart. Her mother was home.

Jamaal was irritated.

Karlie was elated. She was glad for the interruption because she felt mortified at her apparent lack of skill. Karlie avoided Jamaal's eyes and moved away from him as her mother entered the room.

"Hi, guys," Tiffany cheerily greeted the teens, unaware of what she had just interrupted.

Karlie noticed her mother had a couple of plastic bags in her hands, and jumped up. "Mom, let me help you."

"No, I got it," Tiffany stated and gestured to Karlie to sit back down. "I just ran to the supermarket to get some fruit and snacks." She nodded in Jamaal's direction. "Hey, Jamaal."

"Hi," Jamaal said. He was still tongue-tied, but at least he spoke loud enough for her to hear him.

Tiffany left the two teenagers to themselves. She wondered if Jamaal knew any other words besides *hi* and *bye*. That was all he ever said to her. Karlie swore that he was smart and capable of engaging in conversation. She had yet to see proof of that.

As soon as she left, Jamaal looked at Karlie. He wanted to talk about what just happened, but Karlie determinedly avoided his eyes and stood up. "I think you'd better go."

"But we should talk," Jamaal protested.

"I—I do not want to talk right now," Karlie admitted. She felt ashamed at her ignorance and just wanted to curl up in her bed and sleep for days. She just knew that Jamaal would laugh at her because she did not know what she was doing. She had never kissed a boy before, and she felt like she was about to die from sheer embarrassment. Karlie quickly headed for the front

door and held it open. She could not even look Jamaal
in the eyes. Practically pushing him out the door, she
said a quick good night and closed it with a gentle click.
She saw Jamaal's puzzlement at her hasty retreat, but
she wasn't about to offer any explanations. She did not
know how she was going to go to school and face him
the next day. Karlie was horrified at the thought of him
telling his friends how green she was.

She went upstairs to her bedroom and closed the
door. Karlie picked up her pillow and placed her lips
on it. She tried to kiss it as she had often seen on TV. It
was not working. Frustrated, Karlie went downstairs to
the kitchen to get a snack out of the refrigerator. Maybe
she would ask Tanya for some tips. The next time she
saw Jamaal, she was going to get this right and impress
him. The doorbell rang. She hoped Jamaal hadn't returned to finish their conversation. Her feet dragged as
she went to answer the door.

It was Neil.

Karlie beamed and quickly opened the door to let
him in. "Hi, Mr. Jameson." Her smile was like a ray of
sunshine on a cloudy day.

"Hey, Karlie," Neil said with a smile. "I was about to
pull into my driveway when I just had an urge to check
on your mother and see how she's doing. By the way,
how's school going?"

"Okay," Karlie answered. "I'm doing okay. Math is
my biggest struggle. My friend Jamaal is helping me,
but I just can't get it."

"Who's Jamaal?" Neil queried.

Karlie blushed, then shyly answered, "He's my friend
from school."

"Oh, I see," he said. Seeing her acute embarrassment, Neil spared her any further questions.

Tiffany was resting in bed but sat up once she heard Karlie enter the room. "Hey."

"Neil is downstairs," Karlie informed her mother.

"Oh, I thought I heard the doorbell, but I wasn't sure. Is Jamaal still here?"

"No, he went home," Karlie explained. Her text message signal went off. "That's him now," she explained and wandered off to her room.

Tiffany combed her hair and rinsed her mouth out with mouthwash before going downstairs.

As soon as he saw her, Neil asked, "Want some tea?"

"Aw, thanks." Tiffany smiled at his thoughtfulness. She watched as he put the kettle on and took out the things he would need. Neil possessed a pleasant and calming aura that appealed to her on all levels.

"So how are you feeling?" Neil asked, making conversation.

Tiffany groaned and did a so-so movement with her hand. "I was in pain earlier, but I am better now. Thanks. How's Myra?"

"She's doing okay," Neil returned.

"Oh, I haven't seen her since we went to church," Tiffany commented.

"Well, I know she's been up to her neck grading history projects," Neil explained. He changed the subject. "I was just talking with Karlie about school, and she said that her friend Jamaal is helping her with math."

Tiffany rolled her eyes. "Hmm . . . Jamaal."

"Don't like him?"

"It not that. I like him well enough, but I don't really know him. Karlie says he's very smart, but, well, honestly, he looks like a thug and he doesn't speak to me," Tiffany huffed. "And I know better than to outright forbid her from seeing him."

"Well, he's probably nervous being around such a beautiful woman. Perhaps even star struck."

Tiffany blushed at Neil's compliment. "Thanks."

"I'm only telling the truth." He brought their tea to the table and dove into his main reason for stopping in. "Tiffany, I was doing some research on the Internet. I think you should get a nurse, a dietician, and start some therapy. I downloaded the research. . . ." Neil launched into sharing all the information he had found.

Tiffany listened to everything Neil had to say. She was touched at his obvious concern. "Neil, I appreciate your efforts, but all that you are telling me I already know. I just did not think I needed any of that," Tiffany explained. "I am dying, so what's the point of all that?"

"Because you have a daughter," Neil informed her matter-of-factly. "And you have got to fight this thing to the very end. That is why. Tiffany, you cannot just give up on your life because of the cancer. You can decide not to let it get the best of you. The God I serve tells me that. He never gives you more than you can bear. Tiffany, you can still fight with all your being."

"I see what you are saying. Maybe I just wanted to hear somebody say those words, you know. My own mother has not even called. She could not have cared less when I told her. It's nice to know somebody wants me around."

Neil looked at her in amazement. "God loves you too. Do not forget about Him. God is the best comforter you can have."

"I just don't know Him like you do," Tiffany countered, then shrugged. "I am going to make those calls. I do need the help, and I can afford it. I just don't know if I want somebody waiting on me hand and foot. But I do need to start some sort of therapy regimen. It could help ease the pain and discomfort I have been feeling."

"Well, if you don't want a nurse, what about asking Myra to help in the evenings when she is home?"

Tiffany harrumphed. "Myra? I don't know, Neil. Having her up the block is one thing. Having her in close proximity is another. Myra would be all up in my business. I don't know if I am too ready for her . . . piety."

"Myra is still your friend," Neil gently reminded her.

Tiffany felt guilty. "You're right. Myra is a friend. I'll consider it."

"Now that that is settled, can you do me a favor?"

"What?" Tiffany asked.

"Sing me a song."

Tiffany looked at Neil as if he was crazy or had sprouted horns. "I just sang in church, Neil. You heard me then. Besides, my songs are not religious."

"But they are about love and the ups and downs of being in love. Love is universal, so sing."

Tiffany could not argue with Neil's sound reasoning, but she still hedged. "My voice is rusty. Besides, I am nervous." She tapped her feet rapidly, a sure sign she was telling the truth about feeling apprehensive.

"Nervous?" Neil questioned in surprise. Her humility flabbergasted him. "How can you possibly be nervous when you have sung in front of thousands?"

"It never stopped me from getting the butterflies," Tiffany told him. Then she asked, "What song do you want to hear?"

"Anything. Sing me a new song. Something to stir the heart."

Tiffany thought for a moment. Tunes and words started flowing through her head. She cleared her throat and sang a few bars.

Neil clapped his hands in encouragement. His face said, "I'm waiting," but aloud he urged, "You still got it, girl. You still got it."

Tiffany's confidence returned. She sang one of her first hits, which was about being alone even though there were millions around.

Neil closed his eyes and listened to every word. The inferred meaning was powerful, and he got misty-eyed. He could definitely relate to what Tiffany was singing. It was such a shame the world was going to lose such talent.

At the end of her song, Neil dabbed his eyes with his hands before clapping loudly. "Wow, you are absolutely phenomenal," he praised profusely. "Your song touched my very core. I felt every chord and every note vibrate through my being. You are something real special, Tiffany Knightly."

"Thank you," Tiffany breathed, lapping up his much-needed praise. It was doing wonders for her psyche. The old excitement that singing usually evoked stirred within her. She started humming another tune. Tiffany closed her eyes and sang one that she had never released.

Neil was bowled over from the impact and hugged his ribs. He looked at Tiffany. She sparkled, and her presence wrapped around him and soothed his entire being. "Whoa! You have got to record that song and release it as a single. Tiffany, you simply cannot keep that song to yourself."

Tiffany basked in his compliment. "I was planning to release it after I beat this cancer, but . . ." Tiffany trailed off. "I don't have the stamina to record, but do you think I should still sing?"

"Tiffany, you need to sing. You are not dying tomorrow, so while you are still here, you need to sing. I am not suggesting you tour or anything that demanding, but think about doing a couple of local appearances, like diners and churches, you know. Think small scale."

Tiffany toyed with Neil's suggestion while she played with the curls in her hair. She admitted the idea held massive appeal. Maybe she would call Winona and ask her to arrange a couple of low-key performances around town. Winona would probably jump at the chance.

"I think I will," Tiffany declared, making up her mind. "There's no reason why I still cannot sing. Tonight proved that. I am going to do it."

"Good," Neil replied. "Focus on the here and now. God's got tomorrow all figured out, so you don't have to worry about it."

♪ Chapter Twenty-one

Ryan entered his house and went to check his son's room. "Figures. It would have been too much to ask that he be here for once." He stomped into his office, plopped into his chair, and sighed.

Exhaustion showed all over his face. Viciously, he undid his tie, frustration evident in every action. What was he to do with that boy? Brian had everything any teen his age would want, but he constantly played the fool. He was about to face possible expulsion from yet another school, and it wasn't even fazing him one bit. Brian was a gifted artist, but instead of enhancing his God-given talent, he chose to hang out with lowlifes who were about nothing and were going no place.

Ryan had been all the way in Tennessee, and he had to leave a meeting and take an overnight flight because the school principal had called. The principal had said, "I request both you and your wife's presence here at nine A.M. sharp tomorrow."

Another hefty donation. Ryan undid his shirt, carelessly tossed it on the floor, and went to get himself a drink. He needed one badly. Holding the glass in his hand, he walked up the stairs to his bedroom to check on his wife.

Patricia was asleep. He looked at her beautiful auburn hair spread across the pillow, in disarray. "I missed you, baby," he tenderly said. Ryan reached over to plant a kiss on her cheek. He really loved this woman. On his business excursions, there were so many opportunities for him to fool around, but he had never been inclined to do so. Ryan had everything he needed in Patricia. She fulfilled and completed him. Ryan did not need to look elsewhere.

That was why he did not understand what he was doing wrong when it came to his son. He and Patricia never argued in front of him, and they were always openly affectionate with each other.

Patricia stirred and opened her eyes. She smiled when she saw Ryan standing before her. Quickly she sat up to look at him. "Ryan, darling, you're home."

Ryan salaciously eyed her sheer one-piece black teddy. The ensemble was obviously his welcome home present, and he was dying to unwrap it. Ryan smiled at his wife and quickly undressed, eager to show her just how much he had missed her.

Patricia saw the hungry expression cross his face. She grinned knowingly and crooked her fingers. "I got something for you."

Ryan jumped across the bed, causing a huge squeak when he landed. Patricia's body bounced from the impact, and he shamelessly ogled all the moving parts. He greedily helped himself until he heard Patricia groan. Skipping the foreplay, Ryan apologized and promised, "I'll make it up to you later."

Brian entered the house, half expecting to see his father waiting to rip into him. But his dad was already upstairs. "Great. I know what that means." Immediately disappointed, Brian berated himself for his childish hope. He had purposely stayed out late to rile his father's temper, and it had all been a wasted effort.

Brian crept up the stairs and placed his ear against his parents' bedroom door. They were going at it like teenagers. He cut his eyes. His parents behaved like a pair of jackrabbits. "They've been married forever and still carry on like that." He stomped down the stairs and rounded the corner to his room. Now, don't get it twisted. He was happy that his parents remained committed to each other, and even his friends envied him because of it. "You're so lucky," they would say, because most of their parents were either divorced or in their second, even third, marriage. It was no use trying to explain. He often felt like he was not a part of the equation. His parents' love was for each other. Period. There wasn't enough left over for him. "It's just always about them," he'd say.

Not bothering to turn on the lamp, Brian sat on his king-size bed, not seeing all the gadgets and whatnot that were at his fingertips. He had only one question prominent on his mind. Where did *he* fit in? It was kind of like being in the Kool-Aid but not knowing the flavor. He tilted his body back to look up at the ceiling but kept his legs planted on the floor.

When his father traveled, sometimes his mother would go. No one thought to invite him to tag along. It was as if he did not exist. They both just forgot about him when they were near each other. He'd done everything he could think of to get their attention—well, mostly his father's attention. His mother made sure he ate and had clothes to wear. But would his dad spend time with him or take him out to ball games or fishing? No.

He shifted his frame until he was on top of the covers.

He had made sure he got kicked out of every single boarding school—to be home with his parents. Yet they remain dense. "They are such geniuses at their jobs, but they can't figure out something as simple as this." He squeezed his eyes. Crying was useless. It was for babies, for girls, not for him. Tell that to his tears.

The next morning Tiffany looked at the clock above the mantel. It was almost 8:00 A.M., and she was fully dressed and ready to go. Eddie had called her early to inform her that the elusive Ryan Oakes was back in town. It was mid-October, and she had finally caught up with him.

Tiffany knew this was her only chance. "I have got to catch him before he leaves for Timbuktu or the south of France." Ryan Oakes traveled more than she did. He spent months at a time away from home.

At about 9:30 she jumped into her Escalade to drive the short distance to Garden City, where his posh offices were located. Tiffany gathered her courage. "Here goes nothing." She pulled into an empty parking spot and entered the building. She went up to the receptionist and asked to see Mr. Ryan Oakes.

"Do you have an appointment?" the cute young receptionist asked.

"Ah, no, I don't," Tiffany confessed. "I am . . . an old friend, and I just need ten minutes of his time."

Pointing for her to take a seat, the young woman called Ryan's office. Tiffany walked over to the waiting area and sat. She was prepared to wait all day to see him. After five minutes, Tiffany heard, "Mr. Oakes will see you now."

Tiffany stood and followed her to the end of the hall. Through the glass doors, she saw a gorgeous and refined woman, who she knew was Dr. Patricia Oakes, and their son, Brian. She recognized them from the pictures Eddie had sent in the package. Patricia was dressed in a two-piece pastel cream suit and looked like she had stepped out of *Vogue* magazine. Tiffany saw the curious expression flitter across the woman's face and quickly introduced herself.

Patricia invited her to take a seat. "I know who you are, Tiffany Knightly. Ryan and I really enjoy your records. Come in. My husband is on a call and will be back shortly."

Ryan entered the room in an obvious hurry. "Tiffany, how are you?"

"Good morning, Ryan." Tiffany injected a pleasant tone in her voice. "I am sorry to barge in on you like this, but I have to speak with you about a very important matter."

Ryan glanced at his watch. He did not want to be rude, but he was in a hurry. "I have a meeting with Brian's principal this morning, but something came up, so I had to stop here first. In other words, I am already behind schedule."

"What I have to say will only take a couple of minutes," Tiffany assured him. Her tone indicated she was not going to take no for an answer.

Conceding, Ryan quickly sat across from her.

"We'll wait for you in the waiting area, Ryan," Patricia stated and beckoned to her son. Brian complied, albeit grudgingly.

Tiffany got right to the point and spilled her words in one breath, "Ryan, years ago we slept together, and as a result of that, you may be the father of my daughter. I would like you to take a paternity test to find out." Tiffany exhaled and slumped farther into her chair with relief. There. She'd dropped her bombshell at elevator-ride speed.

Ryan looked at her for several seconds. His eyes rapidly blinking were the only signs he'd heard her. Then he spewed, "Are you crazy? Is this about money, Tiffany? Did you squander your fortune?"

Tiffany covered her mouth with her hands to keep from laughing aloud at his questions. She should have known Ryan would think that way. "Ryan, you are clueless. Money is the least of my concerns. Trust me on that."

"She does not need your money, Dad. You heard that? She got plenty of her own," Brian spat out. He had reentered the room, unbeknownst to Tiffany and Ryan.

Ryan turned and addressed his son curtly. "This is a private conversation, Brian. Don't you think you should be worrying about getting kicked out of yet another school?"

Embarrassed, Brian bent his head to hide the flame across his face.

Tiffany felt uncomfortable watching this personal exchange between father and son. She wanted to say something but knew it was not her place.

Brian decided to ignore his father and turned to Tiffany. "I don't know who you are, but my mom said you were really big back in the day. I came back to see if I could get your autograph, anyway."

"I guess," Tiffany said and scrounged around her purse for a pen and paper. Teenagers knew how to keep a person humble. She wrote him a sweet note and signed her name. Brian blushed when he read her statement. He thanked her graciously before leaving the room.

Ryan was curious. "What did you write on the card?"

"I just simply wrote that I thought he had potential, and I signed my name."

Tiffany looked Ryan in the eyes, hoping he would get the subtle hint. It flew right over his head.

"You are about six thousand miles away from the truth. Brian has mastered the art of doing nothing." Ryan scoffed at his own comment.

"Sorry, Ryan, but I do not find that funny."

Tiffany had injected such a serious tone in her voice that Ryan felt compelled to apologize. "I did not mean that the way it sounded," he said, contrite.

Patricia came into the room to peek.

Tiffany knew that was her unofficial exit cue and made a hasty retreat. Before she left, Tiffany gave Ryan her business card, quickly scrawling her personal address and phone on the back. "Call me soon. Please."

After her departure, Ryan briefly glanced at the tiny card before he tossed it on his desk. His mind was already on other matters, and he was now in a rush to get the meeting with Principal Black over as soon as possible. Ryan did not notice when his son had again reentered the room and had pocketed the card.

"Karlie, I don't think this is a good idea."

"Tanya, quit dragging your feet." Karlie pulled her friend, and they jaywalked across the street to stand outside a moderate-size house.

"Your mom will be mad if she finds out. Bump that. My mother will have a coronary if she finds out I lied to her when I told her I was going to your house."

"Tanya, will you cease and desist from worrying already?" Karlie's chest heaved. The girls stood there for several minutes before Tanya gave Karlie a pointed look.

"Well, are you going to go knock?"

Karlie backed up, suddenly losing courage. "No. No, I am not."

Tanya stomped up. "You made me get on a bus to come over here, and now you chicken out. Make up your mind, Karlie."

"I—I guess."

"You guess what? Look, Karlie, it's either you are going to ring that doorbell or you aren't. Just decide. Because I am cold." Tanya's teeth chattered.

Karlie gathered her courage. She walked two steps, then stopped.

Tanya's fists clenched, and she huffed. "Well, I am going back to the bus stop, because my mother is making baked mac and cheese and green beans with some barbecued chicken, and my mouth is salivating."

"No, no." Karlie opened the gate and went to ring the doorbell. She pressed her ear against the door to listen for footsteps.

"Maybe the doorbell isn't working," Tanya offered from directly behind her.

Karlie jumped. "Where did you come from? Make some noise next time."

Tanya hissed through her teeth and banged the door with both her fists. "Hello? Is anybody home?"

A neighbor peered through the window to yell, "Go round the back. He hangs out in the basement all the time."

Tanya looked up toward the man and smiled. "Good looking out." Without a second thought, she moved to walk around the back.

"Dogs?" Karlie said and grabbed Tanya's shoulder. She was deathly afraid of dogs, and her wide-eyed expression showed her fear.

"Whatever." Tanya scrunched her lips, waved her hands dismissively, and kept moving until she got to the back door. She pounded the door so hard that it threatened to break free of its hinges.

"Take it easy," Karlie cautioned, "or I may have to pay for a new door."

The door flew open. "Whatever you're selling, I'm not buying," the man barked.

"How rude." Tanya feistiness couldn't be quelled. Karlie placed a cautionary hand on her friend's arm to quiet her.

"We apologize for knocking so hard, but I—I really needed to see you. Are you Thomas? Thomas Knightly?"

"Yes." Thomas squinted his eyes to take a good look at the face somewhat covered by a big wool hat.

Karlie held out her hand. "Hi. I'm Karlie. Your daughter."

✔ ♫ Chapter Twenty-two

Darnell raced into Tiffany's backyard, barely breaking out in a sweat. April and Amber were at home asleep. He did not know what he was doing here at this time of night. He had asked his mother to spend the night because he could not keep Tiffany out of his mind. He wanted to finish what they had started the other day.

Darnell had not heard from Tiffany, and given the man that he was, he decided the next move would come from him.

Darnell went over to the huge tree and looked up, eyeing the window that led into what used to be Tiffany's old bedroom. Over a decade ago, he remembered climbing this tree to get into Tiffany's room. His raging teenage hormones had made him fearless. Darnell patted his flat, toned stomach with pride. He was still in shape—he could still scale this tree in fifteen seconds flat. He wondered if Tiffany had moved back into that room. There was only one way to find out.

Darnell could simply ring the doorbell or call Tiffany's cell, but he decided to take his chances with the tree. It made him feel adventurous, although if someone saw him and decided to call the cops, he could be in some serious hot water. Adrenaline pumped through his system, and Darnell grabbed hold of the tree until he had a good grip. Bravely, he started to climb, counting on the window to be open, or his efforts would be futile.

Once he was up the tree, Darnell took a deep breath, then grabbed hold of a huge branch. Easing his body along slowly, Darnell refused to look down. His body had not changed, but his trepidation had. His armpits and upper lip sweated profusely.

Finally, Darnell extended his hand to the window. Thank God the branch had held his weight. *Er, oh yeah.* He had to remember that God was not involved in this harebrained scheme. Darnell gripped the edge of the window and gave it a good tug. "Please let it be unlocked," he whispered. *Thank God for small favors.* Well, maybe he should not be thanking God for boldly trespassing, for breaking and entering, to fornicate. In one swift move, Darnell hoisted himself inside.

He looked around expectantly. Nobody was in the room. Once his eyes adjusted to the darkness, Darnell saw the Hello Kitty decorations and knew that he had just broken into Karlie's room. "Of course," Darnell told himself. Tiffany would be in the master bedroom. Made perfect sense, now that he was standing in her daughter's room. Luckily, Karlie was not in the room.

Moving quickly, Darnell refused to dwell on where Karlie could be. He was more concerned about getting out. Karlie would probably scream at the top of her lungs at the sight of him, and he wouldn't blame her. Feeling stupid, Darnell exited the room but knew he'd come too far to turn back. He walked toward what he hoped was the master bedroom. He passed a bathroom before coming to a closed door. With extreme caution and sweaty hands, Darnell cracked the door open a little and peeked inside.

Tiffany was in bed. *Bingo.*

Just then, Darnell heard a toilet flush behind him. "Karlie." Darnell panicked and entered Tiffany's room, promptly closing the door behind him. Taking huge breaths, he felt his chest heave and tighten. He could feel the perspiration coursing down his back even though it was about forty degrees outside.

Darnell vowed he would never do something this asinine again. He was not cut out for it, and he felt like a burglar.

Darnell walked over to where Tiffany was sleeping. His feet made the wooden floor creak. Tiffany woke up almost instantly and jumped out of bed with the covers securely wrapped around her body. He saw her hands fly over her mouth in absolute shock, so he turned the light on before mayhem broke out.

"Darnell?" Tiffany looked like she had seen a ghost.

Darnell saw her hands clutch her chest as she stood immobile. He hadn't meant to give her a heart attack. "Yes, it's me," he replied, stating the obvious.

"What are you doing here, and how did you get in?" Tiffany asked, now fully awake. She pulled the covers off and tiptoed over to where he was standing.

Darnell felt foolish and cursed his rash behavior. From her befuddled expression, he could not discern if Tiffany was upset or happy to see him. His new streak of spontaneity had begun when Tiffany reentered his life. He had never done anything like this before—er, well, without permission—and you'd best believe it was his last time.

"The old tree . . ." He stopped. Now he felt stupid.

"You didn't." Tiffany giggled cheekily at his admission. "You are lucky my daughter did not wake up, or I do not know how I would explain your climbing through her bedroom window. Worse yet, you would have probably given her an idea."

Relieved, Darnell smiled, appreciating her sense of humor, and explained about Karlie being in the bathroom. Some women would have thought his actions psychotic, but Tiffany had taken it all in good stride.

He watched as she walked over to the door and se-
cured the lock before going into the bathroom. Darnell
walked over to the bed and sat down to wait for her. He
took off his jacket and placed it on the armchair. Darnell started to undo his boots but stopped, not wanting
to take anything for granted.

In the bathroom, Tiffany brushed her teeth and tried
to do damage control on her hair. She felt like a kid all
over again, having Darnell here. She brushed her teeth
and looked at herself in the mirror.

Tiffany knew she should not be entertaining Darnell,
considering the circumstances. "I must be just as crazy
as he is," she sputtered before rinsing her mouth with
mouthwash.

Tiffany knew Darnell was the kind of man she could
fall in love with, and that was no longer an option for
her. However, she could have some fun. "Just don't
fall in love with him and get all complicated," Tiffany
warned herself.

She would lay down some guidelines and make sure
Darnell understood. She was sure he would agree, because he had already lost one woman in his life. Darnell
would not be eager for anything serious with her, considering.

Yes, Tiffany was giving Darnell King the kind of deal
that most men craved—nooky with no strings attached.

Giving her breath and teeth a final check, Tiffany
went out of the bathroom and walked over to Darnell.
"Do you think this is a good idea?" she asked, although
she had already made up her mind. She was going to
make love to Darnell.

"I have not given it much thought, Tiffany," Darnell
answered honestly. "The only thing I know for sure is
that I haven't felt these feelings stir up in me in a long
time, and I just want to explore them. Beyond that I do
not have a clue."

Tiffany nodded her head in understanding. She took a finger and started circling Darnell's chest through his shirt. She could feel his deep intake of breath at her manipulative actions and allowed her hands to roam freely. Tiffany boldly looked down at the outside of his jeans. There was a noticeable bulge. Tiffany reached her hands out. "Somebody is happy to see me."

She had not made contact there—but Darnell was already moaning.

Dropping her hands, she said, "You are going to wake my daughter up with all that noise."

"I'm sorry. It's been a long time," Darnell explained.

Tiffany believed him. She continued her onslaught, and Darnell became impatient. Tiffany smiled at his obvious discomfort.

Feeling overdressed, Tiffany took off her pajama top. The silky teal top floated to the floor.

That was all the encouragement that Darnell needed. He took off his boots and unzipped his jeans before jumping out of them and throwing them carelessly on the floor. His shirt followed next. In his haste, Darnell flung it across the room. He was not sure where it landed—nor did he care.

Half dressed, Tiffany got under the covers and waited for Darnell to join her. He got in and enfolded her in his arms before placing his lips on hers for a kiss. After a few seconds, Darnell deepened the kiss.

Tiffany could feel the eager beating of his heart against her chest. Suddenly, she did not want to wait. Her body sprang to life, and passion raged within her. Tiffany sought only to relinquish the fire consuming her being and slid out of her pajama bottoms.

Darnell, however, was already having second thoughts. He stole a glance at Tiffany and saw how ready she was for something he could not give. Sighing loudly, Darnell knew he was risking the wrath of a woman in heat, but he figured that nothing outweighed the wrath of God.

Tiffany shifted underneath him.

Darnell eased away from her. He now lay beside her and looked up at the ceiling. Darnell was valiantly trying to come up with the right words to convey his apology.

Tiffany got up out of the bed, put her pajamas on, and ran downstairs.

Darnell heard her rummaging in the kitchen, but consumed with his own thoughts, he did not pay Tiffany any mind.

Moments later, she reentered the room.

Seeing what was in her hands, Darnell tried to jump out of the bed. But it was too late. Within seconds, he felt himself doused with the contents of an ice bucket.

"Hope that sufficiently cools you down." Tiffany sucked her teeth and went to get a change of linens.

Darnell departed after that, using the front door this time, of course. Tiffany kissed him on the cheek to let him know all would be well. She understood and respected his desire to remain faithful to God.

Christians and their conscience. Definite nooky blocker.

♫ Chapter Twenty-three

Neil sizzled. He watched Myra walk around their bedroom in just her bra and panties. She was talking to one of her church sisters on the telephone. It sounded like they were organizing some luncheon.

Neil enjoyed seeing certain parts of her body jiggle with every movement. Giving in to his instincts, Neil walked over to Myra and lifted the cup of her bra. He closed his eyes in delight at the sight of her curves. Neil bent over, attempting to kiss her.

Myra shooed him away, as if he were an insistent fly. Neil felt hurt and mouthed the question "Why not?" to her. Myra, still listening to the other woman ramble on, pointed to her watch and mouth the word "Time."

Instantly, Neil became angry. Everything with her was about time. Like a defiant child, he marched down to the kitchen and stomped over to the calendar. By the looks of it, the right time would not be until the following week. "Surely, she doesn't expect me to wait that long." With a sudden spurt of masculine indignation, Neil tore the calendar off the refrigerator door and crushed it into a ball before throwing it in the garbage. He left the house and slammed the door behind him with a loud crash. He seriously needed to cool off, or he was going to tell Myra about herself. Neil walked to the corner store and purposely bought a fresh pack of cigarettes.

Neil felt a personal satisfaction as he lit one, but before he drew its contents into his mouth, he thought he spotted Karlie walking toward him. Swiftly, he spit the cigarette out of his mouth and onto the sidewalk. Neil used his shoe to make sure it was fully out. As the girl came into view, Neil realized that it wasn't her. "Thank you, Lord," Neil said, looking up toward the heavens. It had been eons since Neil had touched a cigarette, and God knew he did not want to, anyway. It was a stupid, childish way of getting back at Myra. However, God had used the right tactic to help him live up to his promise not to seek comfort in a butt. He had help from the Lord. God was his refuge and strength. He threw the pack of cigarettes into a trash bin at the end of the street.

Neil decided to pay Tiffany a visit.

Tiffany watched Neil as he plopped his body in the chair. His whole demeanor and body language said something was seriously disturbing him and rattling his mind.

"What's on your mind?"

"It's Myra," Neil explained. "The thing is—"

Seeing his distress, Tiffany rushed to reassure him. "You know you can tell me anything."

"Well, she has endometriosis, and it's making it difficult for her to have a child, you know. But Myra is becoming obsessed about having a baby, and it's beginning to interfere in everything." There. He'd said it, laid it all out there.

"You aren't getting any, huh?" There. She'd said it, laid it all out there.

"You got that right."

Tiffany smirked at his quick response. She retrieved a box of cheese crackers and shared some with Neil. The two crunched until Tiffany asked, "You want me to talk to her?"

"I—I do not know." Neil hesitated, unsure if that would be a good idea.

"I would be discreet about it. Talk to her without being obvious. It's up to you."

Neil considered her suggestion. At this point and time anything was worth a try. Then he blurted out, "Yeah, go for it. Maybe if another woman spoke to her, it would make a difference, because she is driving me crazy. I mean, I am a child of God, but this is trying for a saint."

Tiffany laughed in commiseration. "I feel your pain, man." She told Neil about her confrontation with Thomas and her make-out session with Darnell.

"You could still . . ." Neil trailed off, trying to be tactful.

Tiffany laughed. "Evidently. I am dying, but I am not dead yet." She chuckled when she saw his face redden with embarrassment. He was cute when frazzled.

"So the hormones are still kicking." Neil gave Tiffany the once-over.

Tiffany noticed and accurately interpreted Neil's speculative look. "Yeah," she admitted. She squirmed a little, hoping he was not getting any ideas in his head, because in her opinion men could probably understand the concept of friendship only for so long. She knew Neil was firmly dedicated to God, but he was also a man with blood running through his veins—a man seriously deprived at home from the sounds of it.

"By the way, I forgot to give you an update on my meeting with Pierce," Tiffany said, trying to keep things light between them. That was her unspoken declaration that she had no intentions of going down that path with Neil. Ever.

"How did that go?" Neil questioned. For a second there, his fantasy carried him on a useless journey of what might be, but he just as quickly dismissed the notion of anything between himself and Tiffany. Neil rebuked the devil for putting such dangerous thoughts in his head. Neither one of them needed that complication. Neil cherished their friendship too much to risk ruining it in any way.

He could not afford to mess up his ministry either. Then he would have to answer to God for himself and for Tiffany. No, he would not even go there.

"It was interesting," Tiffany began. "I left Darnell in a frenzy, raced over to the Cheesecake Factory, and Pierce greeted me with a hug. The problem was that the hug lasted just a little longer than necessary, and I pulled out of his hold. I was drowning in his cologne. I mean, it smelled as if he took a bath in it or something, because my nose started itching." She scratched her nose as a reflex action. "Well, we ordered our meal, and Pierce spent every single second flirting with me when he has a hundred kids at home. I mean, I was disgusted, but I did what I had to do, you know."

Tiffany went into the kitchen and returned with water for both of them. Neil thanked her and motioned for her to carry on, riveted by her conversation.

"I finally got around to telling him about Karlie and the need for a paternity test, and do you know what the idiot did?"

"What?"

"He had the gall to ask me about money. He wanted to receive compensation for taking the paternity test. I know Pierce is strapped for cash, but to come right out and . . . It goes without saying that I was angry. Karlie would just be a commodity to him. I already knew he was going through financial struggles, but Pierce was tactless."

"Scumbag," Neil commented.

"Yeah. . . Well, the conversation went downhill from there. I told him distinctly that I was not about to pay him to do that. I would not put a price on my daughter, because she is not for sale. He's even called and left his banking information on my voice mail. I mean, who does that?"

"Maybe you should just pay him," Neil interrupted.

"What?" Tiffany was outraged and looked at Neil with an expression that told him so.

"Before you blast me, isn't finding out who Karlie's father is the main objective here? I knew Pierce from high school, and he seemed okay to me. He probably only asked because, like you said, he needs the money."

Tiffany thought about it. She could call Winona and ask her to find her a paternity specialist. Then, once Pierce donated his specimen, Winona could pay him, and she'd be done with him forever. Tiffany gulped. She hoped.

"At this moment, money is not the main object. You have a limited amount of time to find her dad," Neil continued.

His rationale was slowly beginning to make sense to Tiffany.

"I understand why you would be outraged, though," Neil noted.

"I guess it just leaves a bad taste in my mouth."

"Yeah, that was tacky."

"Thank you, Neil." Tiffany said. Then she mumbled, "Might as well get this over with." She placed a call to Winona, had her wire the money into Pierce's account, and asked her find a paternity specialist. When she ended the call, Tiffany ranted, "I hoped Thomas would've changed his mind and spared me from pompous jerks like Pierce. But it doesn't look as if Thomas will bend."

"Probably not," Neil concurred. "But, unfortunately, you don't have the luxury of time. So take Pierce up on his offer."

Tiffany didn't wait long to keep her promise to talk to Myra on Neil's behalf. She decided to pay her friend a visit. Tiffany rang the doorbell. Within moments, Myra opened the door.

"Hi," Tiffany greeted. "I just dropped in to see what's going on."

"Nothing much. Just getting dinner started." Myra graciously invited her in and commented, "You look well."

"Yeah, well, I called Dr. Ettelman and renewed my prescription, so I am pretty zoned out now and liking it."

"You had stopped taking your meds?" Myra looked concerned.

"For a minute—then reality set in. He sent me some morphine ampoules and needles. Lucky for me, I have a nurse to help with that, but this glow is about something entirely different," Tiffany coyly explained.

Myra came over and sat down at that spicy tidbit.

Tiffany smiled to herself. She knew her friend well. Myra's curiosity was piqued by anything that sounded like gossip. "I was thinking about how I almost got me a little something, something." Tiffany cracked up at the resulting expression on Myra's face.

"In your condition, is that wise?" Myra was aghast. She could not imagine thinking about sex if she were dying.

"My body is still very much alive." Tiffany chuckled, highly amused. She knew Myra would react like this and actually found it endearing.

"But when did you start dating?" Myra tried a more delicate approach. She really wanted to start some serious praying, but Myra knew this was not the time. She did not want to appear too judgmental, either.

"I don't have to get your permission. I am grown."

Myra wanted all the salacious details.

"Quell the enthusiasm. Obviously, you are still hooked on your stories. Remember Darnell?"

"Darnell," Myra repeated.

Tiffany could see Myra's mouth drool with that juicy piece of info. A sly smile crossed her face.

"I knew you two liked each other in high school. How romantic that you should get together right now!" Myra supposed she should be preaching about staying away from the possibility of fornication, but she was a real romantic at heart, and she had always liked Darnell.

Tiffany cracked up at the delightful expression on Myra's face.

Myra had always sought the proverbial happy ending to everything. Tiffany recalled how Myra would refuse to read a novel if she knew it did not end with the traditional happily ever after. She was determined to see the world through rose-colored glasses for the rest of her life. However, Tiffany knew firsthand that the world was not always pretty. Correction, the world itself was magnificent. It was its people that were all messed up and confused.

"So enough about me," Tiffany said, changing the subject. "What's going on with you?"

"Nothing much."

Myra became quiet and a little withdrawn at the question. Her answer told Tiffany there was actually a lot going on. She did not know what to say to make Myra talk without betraying Neil's confidence.

"You sure? Why you say it like that?" Tiffany asked.

"Well, I . . ." Myra stopped, feeling unsure. She did not know if she could talk to Tiffany about what she was feeling. Tiffany had a child, and Myra did not think she would be able to relate.

"Well?" Tiffany asked gently.

Myra took a deep breath and cleared her throat. She wanted to talk about it badly with someone. Myra looked into Tiffany's face and saw the genuine concern reflected in her eyes.

"Neil and I have been trying hard to have a child, but . . ." Myra could feel tears stinging her eyes already. "But I have endometriosis. Do you know what that is?"

Tiffany shook her head, signaling that she did not have a clue.

Myra briefly explained her condition. She knew so much about it that she sounded like a physician. "Endometriosis is when the tissues that normally line the uterus grow in other parts of the body. It causes unbelievable pain, heavy bleeding, and in my case, infertility. On rare occasions, when I have a bowel movement, it is incredibly painful. I guess I lucked out, because so far I haven't felt any pain during intercourse," Myra explained. She shrugged, then stated, cheekily, "I guess that is a good thing."

Tiffany listened intently. Her heart expanded at her friend's plight. She did not even smile at Myra's attempt at humor. "Is there any cure for endo . . . endo—"

"Endometriosis," Myra said. Then she answered. "No, none that I know of. The doctors say that having a baby might help. But—"

"You cannot get pregnant," Tiffany said, finishing her sentence. She felt genuine empathy for Myra's situation.

"Well, I can," Myra said, "but the chances are slim."

"I feel it for you, girl." Tiffany did not know how to word her emotions. "How's Neil taking it?"

"He has been a trouper," Myra answered. "He is wonderful and caring and says all the right words. I honestly could not ask for any more."

"I am glad to hear that. But that sounds like it could put a lot of pressure on your relationship."

"No," Myra replied, denying that that was true. "It hasn't. I mean, there are times when Neil gets frustrated because we have to wait for the right time to . . . you know."

Tiffany raised her eyebrow, intent on letting Myra believe that she had not heard this all before. She was glad for the opening so she could broach the point that she needed to get across.

"Myra, operating under those conditions could be hard on a man."

"I know," Myra agreed. "But what other option is there if we want to have a child?"

Tiffany struggled to find an answer to that question. She could truly understand Myra's position. But, on the other hand, Neil had a legitimate concern as well. Tiffany did not think Myra understood that. Sometimes her friend could be very one dimensional.

"What about in vitro?"

"I prefer to let things happen naturally," Myra quipped.

"Then why not?" Tiffany proposed. "Why don't you just dispel with all the charts and timetables and just give Neil an old-fashioned spanking."

Myra blushed at Tiffany's sexual reference and gave a hesitant laugh. "I do not know."

"It could work. Maybe if you both relaxed and just enjoyed each other, it would happen. Get Neil in a frenzy, and rejuvenate those lazy sperms."

Myra laughed at Tiffany's blunt speech. The church sisters never spoke about sex in such terms, but maybe they should. Myra admitted that though she was red-faced, she was slightly intrigued. A sexual adventure with no holds barred sounded appealing. Myra still had her doubts, though.

"What if it doesn't work?"

"Then you would have had too much fun to even care."

Myra gave Tiffany a hug and thanked her for the advice.

"Do not thank me. Just do it," Tiffany advised with a raunchy quip. "Give the man some backbreaking exercise and hold your legs up high."

"I do not think that works." Myra cackled with laughter.

"You can try."

♫ Chapter Twenty-four

Jamaal and Karlie had been playing some serious cat and mouse, and he was about to change that. He ran after Karlie before she got to her next class, determined to confront her. She had been painstakingly avoiding him, and he wanted to know why.

"Karlie, why haven't you returned my calls?" Jamaal asked without preamble. His class was on the other end of the campus, and he did not have time to mince words.

"I have just been busy," Karlie said, hedging.

"Too busy to talk to me?"

Karlie heard the hurt in Jamaal's voice and knew she had to respond. She had to tell him the truth no matter how embarrassing it was for her. "No, it's not that. It's just—"

The late bell rang, interrupting their conversation.

"We'll talk after school," Karlie suggested, glad for the respite.

"All right," Jamaal agreed before going to class.

Karlie was waiting for him by the gym after school. Tanya was there as well—for backup, he supposed. As soon as the girls spotted him, Jamaal saw Tanya wave before she walked off. He was glad because he and Karlie needed to have a private conversation.

"Hey," Karlie greeted him.

"Hi."

"I guess I owe you an explanation," Karlie began. The two fell in step as they started walking home. They chose to walk instead of taking the bus because it gave them time to talk and truly get to know each other.

"Please, just tell me what's going on."

Karlie hesitated but then blurted it out just to get it over with. "After our kiss, I was so embarrassed that I guess I was avoiding you."

Jamaal stopped and looked at her with bewilderment. "Embarrassed about what?"

"Kissing," Karlie said in a low voice. "I got scared because—"

"It was your first time?"

Karlie nodded her head. Her chin was on her chest, and she knew her face was beet red.

"Karlie, I do not care about that." Since she would not look him in the eyes, he used his index finger to lift up her chin. "The first time for anything is always special, and I feel good that you would even let somebody like me kiss you."

"Somebody like you?" Karlie creased her brow with indignation. "You are great, Jamaal. Can't you see that?"

"You are the only person who thinks so, besides my grandma," Jamaal said, "And I love you for it." He pulled her close to him and kissed her gently on the lips. After several moments, he released her, and they started walking while holding hands. "There. Now you've moved on from the first kiss."

"I love you too," Karlie said. "Now I feel stupid for avoiding you."

Jamaal stopped to look Karlie in her eyes. "Karlie, you don't have to hide anything from me—ever. I got your back no matter what."

"Thanks, Jamaal. I am here for you too if you ever decide you need to tell me something." Though she didn't come right out and say it, Karlie was referring to Jamaal's parents. She had yet to meet them, and Jamaal had remained mum on that topic. Hopefully, he would trust her enough to share all of his life with her.

That very evening, right outside Karlie's house, another boy stood there for several minutes. He turned his nose up at the regular-looking structure, but he was pretty sure his eyes were seeing things right.

Brian double-checked the business card again to make sure he had found the right place. He looked around the neighborhood with barely concealed disdain. He could not imagine Tiffany living *here*. She was a former diva who should be living somewhere fit enough for *MTV Cribs*.

Shrugging his shoulders, Brian opened the gate, walked to the front door, and rang the doorbell. Brian rubbed his hands together. "It's cold out here." Now he wished that he had listened to his mother and worn his gloves. He zipped up his jacket and rang the doorbell again.

Moments later, Tiffany opened the door. She gave him a huge grin and opened the door even wider. Brian felt relieved that she obviously remembered him and was glad to see him.

"What brings you over here?" Tiffany asked, surprised to see the young boy on her doorstep, but Tiffany wanted him to feel welcomed. She did not know what it was about Brian, but when she looked through the peephole and saw him standing there, her heart went out to him.

"I saw your card on my dad's table, and I was in the neighborhood, so . . ." Brian stopped, feeling stupid about showing up at her house uninvited. He regretted his rash move.

He turned to walk away, humiliated.

"You want to play twenty-one? My daughter and I were just in the midst of playing, and we were playing for nickels. Want in?"

Brian smiled and made a U-turn. Meekly, he followed Tiffany into the kitchen and stopped when he saw Karlie. Brian was entranced. His expression was positively comical.

Tiffany saw Brian eyeing her daughter and paused. Her mind whirled with possibilities. *No, this could not happen.* She had not considered or foreseen *this* possibility. Brian could not drool over his potential half sister.

She was going to nip that in the bud before it got ugly. Evidently, Ryan hadn't confided in his son about anything to do with Karlie—which wasn't surprising—but that also explained the goofy expression all over Brian's face.

Tiffany saw her daughter return a shy smile at Brian and knew she had to do something. Thinking fast, she rapidly performed the introductions and made a point to ask Karlie to invite Jamaal over to even out the team. She hoped mentioning Jamaal's name would cool Karlie's interest in Brian.

Lucky for her, Karlie obediently went to make the call. Brian watched Karlie walk over to the telephone, liking what he saw. Tiffany could practically smell his testosterone level escalating. She did not know how to curb his ardor without revealing the truth. Then an idea occurred to her, and she grabbed it like a lifeline.

"Brian, you and Karlie are about the same age, I think."

"Oh, I am seventeen. How old is Karlie?"

"Fifteen," Tiffany gleefully pointed out.

She saw Brian's face drop and hid her smile. To him, two years were like an eternity. Karlie would not be able to do anything he could. She could not drive yet. She could not get into R-rated movies. Tiffany delighted in the fact that this romance was probably ending before it began. Maybe Brian would readjust his thinking and view Karlie as sort of a little sister, and that just might not be a far stretch from the truth.

"Brian, would you like some snacks? I have pretzels, cheese curls, all kinds of goodies," Tiffany offered.

"Oh, yes, thank you."

Tiffany drew him out in conversation until Jamaal arrived. The four of them played a mean game of Monopoly until Tiffany excused herself to order some pizza for all of them.

Neither Jamaal nor Brian seemed in a rush to get home. Tiffany wondered about that. Come to think of it, she never heard Karlie once say she was going to Jamaal's house. Not that she would like that.

Tiffany made a mental note to ask her daughter about that. She already had a good idea why Brian was here. He did not think anybody cared if he came home. Tiffany thought about that some more. All she had done was give him a little attention, and here he was, on her doorstep a few days later. He had great poise and manners and was acting like a regular teen. She could not imagine Brian doing anything to precipitate an expulsion from school.

The telephone rang, and Tiffany answered with a soft "Hello." She smiled when she heard the voice at the other end. "Hey, Darnell."

Tiffany left the teenagers to entertain themselves and went upstairs to take the call. She went into her bedroom and sat on the bed. Darnell called her every night, and they stayed up until the wee hours, talking about all sorts of things. He had given her a renewed outlook on her life.

But she was going to die, and there was no getting around that fact.

Tiffany knew the best thing to do would be to cut Darnell loose before this thing between them became more than she could handle. Darnell made her yearn for something she had no business wanting in her condition.

Hope.

Her mother was in her room and on the phone again, and Karlie wondered who was calling on the regular. She did not like it one bit. Unless it was Neil. She envisioned her mother with him.

Karlie knew that Neil was married, but that did not deter her fanciful thoughts. If he was happy with his wife, Karlie did not think he would be over at their house all the time. Besides, people got divorced like it was nothing. Many of her friends in L.A. were the products of divorce. Look at her. She barely knew her father. Thomas Knightly had not even bothered to visit her, even though she was only a stone's throw away now.

Neil could divorce that woman and marry her mother. Her mother laughed and seemed happy whenever he was around. That meant a lot to Karlie. Maybe if her mother were with him, she would live. Karlie's face remained pensive.

Brian and Jamaal each caught the other one looking at Karlie. Jamaal immediately went over to her to give her a hug. He was claiming his turf and wanted Brian to know it. Brian realized what the younger boy was doing and shrugged. Karlie was too young for him, anyway.

Brian pulled out his cell phone to look at the time. It was getting late, and neither one of his parents had called to find out about his whereabouts. He knew they would be shocked to know where he was hanging. They probably assumed he was up to no good.

Brian jumped up, went out the front door, and stepped outside to get a smoke and to think. Jamaal came out a couple of seconds later to head home. Brian supposed he should be getting ready to leave as well. If he were honest with himself, he would prefer to stay here. He did not want to go home. This was the first time in months he had played and just had some clean fun.

Brian heard the front door squeak and saw Tiffany at the door. He spat the cigarette out of his mouth and snuffed it out with his feet.

"Those will kill you. That is not a lie," Tiffany warned.

"I know," Brian said. "I cannot even stand the smell of them."

"Then why are you smoking them?" Tiffany asked. She moved aside to let Brian back into the house.

"I only started in the first place just to . . ." Brian stopped before he said too much.

Tiffany took pity on him and let the matter rest. She could fill in the blanks. Brian was at that crucial stage between boyhood and manhood, and she knew that maintaining his pride was a must.

Tiffany offered him a cola, and Brian gladly accepted her offer. She knew Brian was probably used to consuming a different kind of beverage, but he was still a minor.

"So, what brought you here?" Tiffany finally asked the question prominent on her mind.

"I came by because I heard you tell my father you needed to meet with him, and I wanted you to know that you are probably wasting your time. My father does not have time for anything but his job and my mother."

Tiffany reeled at the bitter tone in his voice. The problem with Brian and his parents was deeper and more complex than she had realized. Tiffany wondered what she could say or do to help.

"I am sorry to hear that," Tiffany stated. "But your father is going to have to make the time to talk to me. It's important."

"Well, good luck," Brian told her. Then, feeling as if he had said too much, Brian uttered a hasty "I'd better go." He thought about calling his friends but felt too tired to do anything else. Deciding to head home, he hopped on his motorbike and revved the engine.

"Well, feel free to drop by whenever," Tiffany called out.

Brian gave an unenthusiastic response, trying to pretend that it did not matter. He was trying to be cool and appear unaffected. He pulled away from Tiffany's house and headed down the street. Now that he was alone, Brian smiled.

Tiffany must genuinely want him around to extend a second invitation. It felt good getting such a sincere welcome. Brian felt at home with her and Karlie. Such comfort and love had surrounded and engulfed him, and Brian had just basked in it. He'd relished every minute of it. He knew that he would visit again. Wild horses could not keep him away.

♫ Chapter Twenty-five

Neil stood outside and watched the sunrise. It peeked through the clouds with sparkling brilliance, a lovely shade of gold that no kind of paint or artist could capture. The first verse of Psalm ninety-one popped into his head. It was so true; the heavens did declare God's glory.

He could never get over just how lucky he was to be able to see this sight whenever he wanted to. So many other brothers his age missed this because they were locked in a four-walled cage. They would give their soul to be standing in his shoes.

It was so peaceful at this hour, when the neighborhood was still asleep. There was no one hanging on the streets, trying to sell drugs. There were no fights going on. The scenery could fool a person into thinking this place was a dream. However, Neil knew that by midday it would become a living nightmare.

Neil wrapped himself even more in his robe. It was a cold and windy Thursday afternoon. The wind was tossing the trees branches. November was coming in with a bang, which meant the possibility of a deadly winter.

He quickly retreated into the house.

Myra should be up soon to get dressed for work.

Tiffany must have done well with her promise, because things with Myra were grand. She seemed to have relaxed about her "mission" for a little while. Neil was glad for the reprieve. They had been having some great sex, and things were feeling right between them again. Neil prayed that this "vacation" from baby boot camp lasted.

Her internal alarm clock went off, and Myra stretched languidly. She knew it was time to get up. Sleepily, she headed for the bathroom to shower and get ready for her day.

Myra sat on the toilet to relieve herself. Looking down at her underwear, she saw a tiny spot of blood. Myra knew what that meant. By the middle of the day, she was going to be in a significant amount of pain. She was surprised that she was not vomiting as usual, and Myra prayed it stayed that way.

Myra dutifully went to work with the enthusiasm of a fish out of water. It took every ounce of willpower she had to ignore the throbbing pain in her lower abdomen and in her legs. Myra knew from experience that this month would be bad. She was going to have to take the next day off, for sure.

Then one of the other teachers dropped a bombshell at work. Ms. Wise was pregnant.

Myra smiled upon hearing the news. "Oh, I am so happy for you. You must be so excited!" she told Ms. Wise. She laughed and offered her congratulations with the rest of her coworkers, but inside she was dying all over again.

On the drive home, Myra gripped the wheel and re-played Ms. Wise's announcement in her head. "Even Ms. Wise is pregnant, and she is forty-three. Forty-three and she got pregnant. Why is God doing this to me?" Myra pulled over to the side of the road to look up at the sky. "God, why are you punishing me like this?

Why won't you open my womb? You gave all these other women children, and they don't even deserve them."

She plopped her head on the steering wheel and whispered, "I want a child of my own to love and cherish." She wanted a new life, which she would treasure and shower with love. Myra could not figure out why God denied her that right.

She knew without a doubt that she would make a good mother and would be better at it than some of the people she knew. Myra put her car in gear to continue her drive home.

Myra touched her abdomen and felt the tears streak down her cheeks. She stopped at a light and noticed that the driver in another car was looking at her. Myra quickly wiped her face, feeling discomfited.

She made a dramatic U-turn and drove up to her favorite bakery. Things had been going so well that she had even managed to drop a few pounds. It had been weeks since she had baked any cookies or pies.

Myra climbed out of her car, slammed the bakery door, and went to the counter. "I'd like two dozen of your chocolate chocolate-chip cookies and a box of your éclairs." Once she received her order, she stomped out of the store and sat in her car. Myra ate the entire box of éclairs. The chocolate chip cookies she would carry home.

Sensibly, Myra knew there was no use beating herself up about her infertility. She had to accept what she could not change. She just did not know how to do that. Myra firmly believed in God and was certain that He could perform miracles. She accepted all the stories she read, and knew God had come through before. He had done it for Hannah, and for months Myra had prayed, fasted, and studied the scriptures. However, it had been to no avail. It was as if God had closed His ears. Her pastor kept saying it was all about God and His timing, but her clock was ticking. To herself, Myra confessed she had lost a little faith that God would come through.

Myra stopped at the supermarket to pick up some feminine products she would need. Though she had the cookies in the car, she went to the dessert aisle and selected a couple boxes of Louisiana Crunch Cake and some doughnuts. The way she felt, she knew she was going to need them.

Tiffany carefully steered her Escalade out of her driveway and turned onto Main Street. She was on her way to Ryan's home. She had been surprised by his telephone call, and grateful for it. She had not expected it, since it had been almost two months since she had barged into his office, asking him to take a paternity test.

Ryan saw Tiffany drive up and opened the door to meet her. He was eager to sit and chat with her. Brian had spoken so highly of Tiffany that Ryan had eventually called to arrange a meeting.

Ryan wanted to know how she had managed to earn his son's evident respect. It was because of her that he and his son had engaged in an actual conversation consisting of more than monosyllabic words. Ryan figured that meeting with Tiffany would keep him on Brian's good side. The boy had gotten up this morning without a hassle and was now in school. For that simple feat, Ryan would give Tiffany his right hand.

He would volunteer his specimen, even though he prayed he was not the father. He could barely handle the one child he had, and was not sure he would be able to cope with another. He had filled his wife in on the nature of Tiffany's visit, and thankfully, Patricia had been forgiving and supportive.

Ryan greeted Tiffany and took her jacket. The two went into his study to carry on their conversation. Ryan did not skirt the issue but plunged head-on.

"I invited you over because I know we did not have a chance to discuss your situation the last time we met. I just wanted to let you know in person that I will take the paternity test. However, I'd be lying if I said that I hope I am your daughter's father, because frankly, I can hardly handle the one child I have now."

Tiffany nodded her head in understanding. "I appreciate your frankness, Ryan. I will make all the necessary arrangements and get back to you."

"Okay, then." Ryan gave Tiffany his private cell phone number.

"How's Patricia?" Tiffany asked. She could not imagine this was easy on his wife.

"Remarkably well, considering the circumstances," Ryan answered. "Patricia knows I love her and nothing can shake that. She told me she sort of suspected I had been with someone else all those years ago. She just never imagined that my, ah, momentary lapse in judgment could have such lasting repercussions."

"That is good to hear," Tiffany said, unsure of just how to reply, as she was a part of his "momentary lapse." "It seems as if you and your wife have a great relationship."

Ryan smiled. "We do. Patti completes me. She means the world to me. Funny enough, being with you that night proved that to me. I knew without a doubt there would be no other woman to fill her shoes."

Tiffany smiled pleasantly and got up to leave before she asked Ryan how he felt about his son. She wanted to know if Brian also meant the world to him, but she knew it was not her place to ask any questions, particularly because of the favor she was asking of Ryan.

Tiffany did not know why she felt such a pull toward Brian. Maybe it was because he had so much potential. Or maybe it was because she knew firsthand what it felt like to wonder if your parent loved you. Maybe it was a combination of both. Whatever the reason, Tiffany determined that anytime Brian graced her doorstep, she was going to let him into her home, no questions asked.

Tiffany heard her cell phone go off just as she entered her car. She quickly put her Bluetooth in her ear and took the call. "Hello?"

"Hi, Tiffany. How are you?"

"Okay. I miss you. I think we need some girl time."

"I totally agree." Winona was then all business. "I have arranged a few limited performances for you at Nakisaki starting next Saturday night."

The restaurant served Jamaican and Chinese cuisine and hosted a nightclub in the basement. Tiffany had been there a few times with her friends and remembered how much she had liked the general ambience of the restaurant.

"Sure. Thanks. I will do it."

"Let's definitely get together," Winona said before ringing off.

Tiffany made a U-turn and headed toward Nordstrom at Roosevelt Field to purchase several gowns for her performances. Tiffany called Winona back and asked her to line up a piano and a voice coach. She wanted to get her voice back on track for her performances. Tiffany had to admit that she was excited about returning to the stage. It had been ages since she had sung live, and she was looking forward to it. She realized she missed all the drama, tension, and work that went on backstage during her acts. Myra's church had requested that she sing again, and Tiffany relished the opportunity. That would serve as even more practice for her.

She looked at her watch. It was a little past four o'clock. Tiffany wondered if Karlie was home yet. She texted her but didn't get a response. She had invited Darnell and his daughters over, and she would need Karlie's help. However, Tiffany wasn't too concerned. Sometimes a parent just had to cut the umbilical cord and trust their children.

"You cannot ignore her, or me, forever, you know," Willie advised.

Thomas continued his painting, determined to ignore his mother. "I can certainly try."

Willie let out a huge sigh. She waited several seconds before leaving the room. Thomas put down his paintbrush and thought about Karlie. Karlie had been dropping by his place and he had been spending time with her ever since she showed up at his door, but he had kept her away from Willie. Thomas could not chance his mother saying the wrong thing.

"What am I going to do?" he muttered. Thomas loved Karlie, but knowing she might not be his had him twist tied. Though he had been missing in action for every birthday and every Christmas, Thomas had faithfully sent his daughter a gift. But a part of him strongly wanted to forgo the tradition this year. However, the better part of him did not want to disappoint Karlie, even though he was furious at Tiffany for lying to him all these years.

Spending time with Karlie did not appease his anger.

Why had Tiffany deceived him the way she did? Underneath all his anger was the hurt. Hurt that Tiffany had kept the truth from him. The sad thing is that the truth would not have deterred him from marrying her. Thomas despised the fact that Tiffany had taken advantage of his genuine love for her. It ate him up inside.

Thomas packed up his supplies and prepared to go home. He put on his sweater and jacket before going outside to start up his F-150. The powerful engine roared, causing Willie to come to the screen door.

"You weren't going to say good-bye?"

"I'm sorry. I just have a lot on my mind," Thomas lied. He wanted to avoid any further discussion about Tiffany. He backed his truck out of the driveway and spent the ten-minute drive to his own home filled with thoughts of Karlie.

He knew from their conversations that Karlie had no idea about the real reason Tiffany was back in town. Thomas vacillated between wanting and not wanting to tell her the truth. Thomas walked up the three steps to enter his home.

"Hi, Dad." Karlie sat on the couch. Judging by the empty Chinese food containers, she'd been there awhile.

"You finally used your key!" Thomas exclaimed. He'd given Karlie a key to his home and told her to come and go as she pleased, but she always rang his doorbell, anyway. He'd even found her waiting on his porch once.

"Yeah." Karlie blushed. "It was cold outside. I waited about twenty minutes before I decided to come inside. I have to get home soon."

"I told you I much prefer to drop you home. The bus takes one hour, when I can have you home in fifteen minutes."

"I just don't know how Mom would feel about me coming here."

"Tiffany would prefer honesty." Thomas almost choked on his words. He felt bitterness rise within him and squelched it down.

Karlie looked guilty. "I know. But my whole reason for reaching out is that I'm scared. Mom was all I had my whole life, and I'm going to lose her one day. Being here with you makes me feel closer to her somehow. Like I will always have a connection, you know."

Suddenly overwhelmed, Karlie started to cry.

Thomas hugged the teen and kissed the top of her head. "Karlie, from the depth of my heart, I truly apologize that I wasn't a better father to you. I should have been there. I should have played a more active role in your life. My reasons at the time seemed viable, but now that I see you here face-to-face, I realize that my fears dictated my life."

"It's okay, Dad. All my life, I've heard nothing but good about you. I have no reason that I know of to hate you. I know you said you left me alone for a short time when I was a baby, but I was obviously okay. I admit that when I was younger, I did wish you were there. I cried about it sometimes, but I had Mom. I was okay. I'm just glad I have you now."

Thomas looked at Karlie with amazement. He shook his head, unable to fathom her words. "Karlie, you are mature beyond your years. I am grateful to have you in my life, and no matter what, I love you." Thomas refrained from calling her his daughter, but he spoke the truth.

"Next time I come, may I bring Jamaal?"

"Oh, is that the guy you were telling me about?"

"Yeah, he's my . . . boyfriend."

"Boyfriend." Thomas touched his chin as thoughts of what he was like at that age surfaced in his mind. "I hope you're being careful?"

Karlie blushed. *How like a dad.* "You have nothing to worry about in that department."

Thomas visibly relaxed, and though the words stuck in his throat, he felt compelled to ask her something. "Well, do you have any, ah, questions for me? You know, like a man's point of view?"

"No. Mom told me everything I need to know." Karlie peered up at him from under her lashes, feeling tongue-tied. "But I will try not to be too embarrassed to ask you a question if I need to."

"Whew. That is good enough for me. And to answer your earlier question, bring Jamaal with you the next time you come."

"You're not going to threaten him or anything like that, are you? 'Cause he is still scared of Mom. I keep trying to convince her of his intelligence, but Jamaal keeps proving me wrong every time she comes within two feet of him."

Thomas cracked up. "What does he look like?"

"A little like Ludacris."

He could picture Tiffany's face. "Well, I know better than to judge a book by its cover. Believe me, people are not always what they seem."

♫ Chapter Twenty-six

Darnell arrived at Tiffany's house promptly at seven o'clock. April and Amber were with him. It had taken him an hour to get them dressed and to put their hair in some semblance of order. He was going to drop them off at his mother's house when he left Tiffany's. She had offered to get them off to school and to keep them that weekend.

"Open the door, Daddy," Amber demanded.

"I can't, honey. I have to wait."

"Daddy, just open it." April pushed past his legs to turn the knob. Darnell lightly swatted her hand away, but then Amber put her hand on the knob.

"Guys, just wait."

"We're not guys, Daddy." Amber chuckled.

"Yeah, we're girls," April pointed out. "We do not have peanuts."

Thankfully, the door opened, sparing him further conversation about "peanuts" and "bresses," and "veggies." Darnell felt his temperature rise. This was the first time the girls were going to meet Tiffany and Karlie, and he was nervous.

On the drive over, Darnell had pondered at length if he was doing the right thing. He debated how his young daughters might react and considered the awful possibility that they would hate Tiffany. In the end, Darnell brought them and decided that he would play things by ear.

Karlie answered the door. "Hi, Mr. King."

Darnell noticed her pleasant smile but noted the guarded expression in her eyes. He wasn't the only one feeling trepidation. "Hi, Karlie. How are you?"

"Awww, twins." Karlie bent to give his daughters a warm hug. She rubbed her face between them so each of her cheeks touched their faces. The girls squealed.

"Actually, they're two years apart," Darnell explained, though Karlie was too enthralled with the girls to pay him any attention.

"I'm April."

"And I'm Amber."

"I like her, Daddy." April turned toward her dad to share her news.

"What's your name?" Amber quizzed.

"Karlie."

"I like that name."

By that time, Darnell had gotten out of his brown tweed jacket. He bent to help Amber get out of her faux leopard-print jacket. Karlie assisted April with hers. She then led the girls from the foyer through the living room, and they bounded up the stairs to see her room.

Darnell couldn't help but dwell on the fact that his daughters had received a much warmer greeting than he had. Darnell tried to shrug it off but knew that Karlie's reserved attitude made a warning bell go off in his mind. He decided to tread carefully with Tiffany's daughter because she might not like the idea of a man coming around after all these years. Darnell made a mental note to ask Tiffany about that as soon as the opportunity arose.

The doorbell rang. Tiffany called out, "Get the door!"

Since he was the closest to it, Darnell answered it. "Hey, Neil."

"Darnell, how have you been?"

Karlie raced down the stairs. When she spotted Neil, she gave him an exuberant greeting and a quick hug.

Tiffany came out of the kitchen. "Neil. I didn't expect to see you."

"Karlie invited me since Myra is at a women's meeting. She's coming by when it's done."

"Cool. The more the merrier." She would find out what he thought about Darnell later.

Tiffany added an extra leaf to the table and two extra place settings. Darnell and Neil rushed to help her get the table ready, but Tiffany shooed them away. She called Karlie to assist, while the men caught up on their lives since high school. April and Amber were playing with Karlie's Wii. She rarely played with it anymore, and the girls were enjoying it.

"Why did you do that?" Tiffany asked her daughter.

Karlie played dumb. "What?"

"You know," Tiffany said. "I wanted you to get a chance to meet Darnell and really get to know him and his girls. I wasn't expecting extra company."

Karlie shrugged with the unconcern of a teenager. "I invited Jamaal over too."

"When were you planning on telling me?" Tiffany injected a serious tone in her voice so her daughter knew she was not happy about the situation.

"I'm sorry, Mom. I didn't think you would have a problem with it." Karlie sounded appropriately contrite, so Tiffany decided to let it go.

"So what do you think of Darnell?"

"He is all right. I guess." Karlie shrugged. Her dry tone revealed that she didn't relish this conversation at all.

Tiffany did not like the deadpan response her daughter gave her. She looked over at Darnell. He looked good, and there was nothing just "all right" about him, either. "Is it because he is a teacher at your school?"

"What? I said he's okay. Give it a rest, please, Mom." Karlie heard the doorbell and went to let Jamaal in.

Tiffany let her daughter off the hook. Communicating with teenagers was a nightmare at times. Their acerbic, monosyllabic answers made their true feelings hard to ascertain. Generally, Tiffany and Karlie always managed to have a good rapport. That was why Tiffany felt puzzled at her daughter's one-liners and tepid responses. She decided to let it go for now, telling herself, "I'm going to drag the truth out of her later."

Myra and Neil held hands as they walked the short distance to their home. They had had a great time at Tiffany's house.

"Karlie is a dream. I've seen her walking about the neighborhood, but I really got a chance to know her tonight," Myra commented, deciding that Tiffany had obviously spent a lot of time with her daughter and had done some good parenting. Karlie was well mannered and extremely respectful.

"Yes, Karlie is a sweetheart," Neil agreed. "Aren't Darnell's daughters just precious?"

"Yes, they are." Myra smiled. "They are so precocious and rambunctious. Darnell obviously has his hands full. I think it's because they will be with his mother this weekend that he agreed to come with us to church this Saturday."

Neil chuckled. "I'm glad he decided to come. Good thinking on your part to invite him, Myra. Hey, did you see when he covered up Amber's mouth when she mentioned Tiffany had nice breasts? Well, her word was 'bresses', but it took everything in my power, to hold my laughter in."

Myra cracked up. "Yes! That was hilarious. Tiffany turned purple from embarrassment."

"Kids say the craziest things. That was definitely a funniest video moment." By now, they stood outside their gate.

Myra squeezed Neil's hand to get his attention. "Neil, I had a great time, but I felt a little funny, though."

"Why?"

"I guess it's because we were the only ones there without any children."

Neil sighed internally. He did not know how many times he could say the same thing. It was becoming slightly monotonous. "Myra, I am quite sure nobody paid attention to that. Most of our friends actually envy us. We are free to travel and do whatever we want."

"I know," Myra said. "I guess I am just being paranoid."

"Yes, you are," Neil assured her. "Myra, I am okay with us not having a child of our own. I am just happy to be with you, and you are enough for me. If God does not choose to bless us with a child, I can live with it. Myra, please just try to be happy."

"I love you, Neil," Myra said wholeheartedly. "I am lucky to have a warm, loving man like you. I guess that is why I wish I were able to conceive. You would make a great father."

Neil patted Myra on the shoulders and said nothing. He yearned for the day when Myra would not base her worth on her ability to bear a child. He wished she could see that there was more to her than that. He looked at her and tried to communicate his true feelings in words.

"Myra, I love you whether you have a child or not. I love you for you, warts and all."

***

"I want to point out that all the letters Paul wrote were to actual churches. He addressed regular folks with struggles just like you and me. It's in the book of Romans that we find what is commonly known as the Sinner's Prayer. And that prayer is the same today. If you confess your sins and profess that Jesus is the son of God, then God will wipe your slate clean. I know He will. He did it for me."

"Hallelujah," Myra yelled, pumping her hands in the air.

"Tell it, Pastor," another voice shouted from behind.

Tiffany said a low "Amen." She was still self-conscious about shouting out praises to God.

"So, the question is, what is stopping you today? What is making you stay in your seat instead of coming forward?" Pastor Johnston reached into his pocket and pulled out his handkerchief to wipe the sweat from his brow. He motioned with his hands to the congregation.

"Darnell is going up." Myra nudged Tiffany. "He is going up to the altar."

Tiffany looked on as Darnell sunk to his knees. He had both hands extended in the air, and tears streamed down his face. Pastor Johnston went over to pray with him.

"Go up with him," Myra urged.

"No," Tiffany whispered. "It's gonna look like I followed him up there."

"Who cares?"

"I do."

Tiffany looked behind her and spotted Karlie sitting next to Tanya. Karlie had asked her mom if Tanya could join them. Their eyes met, and they smiled. "I love you," Tiffany mouthed.

"I love you too," Karlie mouthed back.

Tiffany tilted her head toward the altar. Karlie got to her feet and walked down the aisle toward her mother. The choir leader began singing, "Let Jesus fix it for you. . . ."

They joined hands and went up to the altar for prayer.

"Are you going to ask Jesus to heal you?" Karlie asked.

Tiffany didn't answer but just smiled..

"I'm going to," Karlie whispered. "God can do it, Mom. He can heal you. You just have to believe."

"Okay," Tiffany said just to end the conversation.

Pastor Johnston was heading their way. When he placed his hands on her shoulder to pray, Tiffany felt an instant calmness permeate her body.

At that moment, Tiffany recognized and accepted His divine presence. God was here. She could feel Him all around. His Spirit filled the atmosphere. Inside she prayed, *God, thank you for my life. Help me accept whatever you will for me and give me peace.*

At the end of the prayer, Neil enfolded Tiffany in a warm embrace. He placed a soft kiss on top of her head and leaned back to smile in her face.

Karlie noticed and smiled.

Myra noticed and frowned.

♬ Chapter Twenty-seven

Ryan and Patricia fell out of the shower and onto the floor in a huge mass of bubbles and soap. They howled with laughter like kids.

Ryan rubbed his body against her, basking in the rippling sensations. "Patti, I will never get tired you." She rocked his world even after all these years.

He had caught a shuttle from Boston to make it here tonight. Brian had insisted that he be there to see Tiffany's performance at Nakisaki. Ryan did not want to disappoint his son, who had specifically requested he come, so he had bent over backward to make it home on time. The problem is that Patricia had been waiting for him too, which explained why they were now a soapy mess on the bathroom floor.

They heard a loud rap on the door. "Are you two still in the shower?" Brian yelled through the door.

Ryan and Patricia looked at each other guiltily. He placed his hand over her mouth to stifle her laugh. "Shhh," he warned.

"We are coming, Brian," Ryan said. Patricia squirmed beneath him, shattering his concentration. "Keep still, Patti. You are distracting me."

"Fantastic. Can't you two ever control yourselves?" Brian sounded disgusted. "We are going to be late, for crying out loud. It's a Saturday night, and we have to get there before the crowd. . . ."

"He sounds pretty upset," Ryan whispered to Patricia.

"Give us ten minutes, Brian," Patricia called out. "We'll be right out."

"You guys are disgusting," Brian said before walking off.

Brian went into the foyer to mope and wait for his parents to finish their business. He looked at the clock. "Great. I'll be lucky if they're ready to go in a half hour. I should just leave." His only reason for not leaving was that he had promised Tiffany he'd bring his parents. She had given him complimentary tickets, and if his parents came, then Brian would get into the club without a hassle. He did not know why he allowed his parents to get to him after all these years. He should be used to it by now. Brian just did not know why he continued to hope against hope for some attention from them.

Even tonight Brian had been thrilled when his father walked through the door. It meant a lot to him that his dad had made the big effort to make it tonight. His father had also been on time. Then his father had busted his bubble, as the first chance he got, he jumped between his mother's legs. Brian had tried to distract his father with some conversation, but it was to no avail. When it came to Patricia, his dad had a one-track mind. He could keep his attention diverted only for a couple of minutes before his father rushed off in search of Patricia.

That was why Brian had urged his mother to dress before his father got in, but he was willing to bet that she had been stalling on purpose. Brian knew that if she was not fully dressed when his father got in, they were going to be late.

Another glance at the clock confirmed his predictions were accurate. Not knowing what else to do, Brian sulked.

Forty minutes later, and still waiting in the living room, Brian was fuming.

Over at Nakisaki, Tiffany glanced up at the clock. She had ten minutes until showtime, and she was a pack of nerves. She looked out in the audience and saw Neil and Myra. They must have been looking out for her, because they waved as soon as she poked her head out.

Tiffany went into the small dressing room to get herself together. She was afraid that her voice would crack tonight, even though her voice coach had repeatedly assured her that her voice was "dynamite."

She pulled on her green floor-length sequined dress. "Did I gain weight?" she wondered aloud, because she suddenly felt claustrophobic. "Please don't let me throw up on the stage." Tiffany quickly chided herself for even voicing her fear.

Tonight was going to be perfect.

Tiffany wondered if Darnell had gotten there yet. His mother was supposed to be babysitting. She looked out again and saw him. Tiffany smiled and waved like a schoolchild. Darnell gave her the thumbs-up sign and blew her a kiss.

Tiffany beamed. She really liked Darnell and enjoyed his company but refused to entertain the notion that she felt more than like for Darnell. She did not want to take that final step and admitted that she was falling in love with him. Tiffany knew that would not be fair to either one of them to expose her growing feelings. Darnell did not need that from her now. She did not need it, either.

Tiffany's cell phone rang, and she rushed to answer it. "Hi, Karlie."

"Hi, Mom. Just calling to tell you I love you and I hope you break a leg tonight. I'm having a great time with Tanya and her parents. We're going bowling."

Tiffany smiled. "Thanks, honey. I love you too, and I'm so glad you called. Well, I'd better get going. You and Tanya have fun tonight, and mind your manners. I'll come get you in the morning."

Winona called next. "Sorry I couldn't make it, but I know you will do your thing."

"Thanks, Winona. I got your flowers, or should I say, your entire garden," Tiffany said, eyeing the huge centerpiece. "It barely fits in this small dressing room."

"Only the best for you, babe," Winona said. "Now, don't worry. Everything will go without a hitch, and you are going to be great."

"Thanks, Winona. You are doing wonders for my psyche. I don't even know why I am so nervous."

"I would be nervous if you weren't nervous," Winona assured her. "Now, let me get off this phone so you can get in your zone."

Before Tiffany knew it, it was time for her to go on. She greeted the crowd and sang her heart out. She saw when Brian and his parents came in and gave them a barely perceptible nod. During the performance, she even gave Brian a shout-out, which seemed to brighten him up a bit. Tiffany sang ten songs before closing out to a standing ovation.

She felt good knowing that tonight had been a success.

The deejay took over and started pumping out some solid tunes. Tiffany quickly changed before she and Darnell hit the dance floor. She saw Ryan and Patricia getting their groove on. They were grinding each other so close that it looked as if they were doing it on the dance floor.

Tiffany did not understand how they could be behaving like that with their son present. Tiffany knew she could not dance like that with Karlie watching.

Patricia looked her way, and Tiffany motioned to Brian. She must have gotten the hint, because Tiffany saw Brian and his mother dancing a few minutes later.

Now that Ryan was back in town, Tiffany made a mental note to get a set date from him for the paternity test. She could not continue to put it off.

Tiffany grabbed Ryan as soon as she and Darnell got back to the table. On the dance floor, she said, "Ryan, I know you are busy, but I need a date from you for when you are going to take the test. As you know, time is of the essence."

"Have you told your daughter yet?" Tiffany took a misstep, and Ryan had to do some quick maneuvering to keep her from losing her balance. "I guess I have my answer."

"I don't plan on telling her until I have everything in order as far as getting these tests done."

"I know it is not my place, but she is old enough for full disclosure."

Now Tiffany was adamant. "No. I can't take the chance. I want to give Karlie more time to settle in. Maybe after the holidays we'll get down to business."

"Well, for the record, I think you're making a grave mistake."

"For the record, it's my mistake to make."

♫ Chapter Twenty-eight

That Monday Brian ran up the steps and rang the doorbell. This time he was sure of his welcome. Each time he'd stopped by, Tiffany had been gracious and inviting. He had made sure to call ahead to ensure Tiffany was up to seeing him.

"Hi, Brian. How's school?" Tiffany asked when she opened the door.

"School is school," Brian replied.

"I guess," Tiffany said with a laugh and moved aside to let Brian inside. She shivered from the cold. Trees swayed, and the leaves flew all over the place. "I don't know how you ride your bike in this kind of weather."

Brian chuckled. "I got skills."

Tiffany pulled on the screen door, and the wind caused it to close with a loud bang. She shuddered from another chill. The cotton pajamas and warm, fuzzy socks she wore did nothing to ease the cold seeping through her bones.

Brian made himself at home while Tiffany went to get herself a blanket. She turned the heat up when she saw that underneath his jacket Brian had only a T-shirt on.

"Where's your sweater?"

"I'm okay," Brian replied. "It's not that cold."

"It's freezing out there," Tiffany disagreed. "You should be dressed warmer than that. And are you planning on riding your bike all through winter?"

Brian looked at Tiffany and saw genuine concern reflected in her eyes. He gave her a penitent response. "Okay, I promise to wear something warmer next time. And I will talk to my mother to see if she'll let me drive her car, since she always drives the Escalade to work."

"That sounds much better," Tiffany said, feeling mollified. She looked at Brian to see if he was simply being patronizing but realized the young man was being genuine. She felt pleased at that.

"So, what brings you here?" Tiffany asked him.

"I did not feel like going home," Brian told her, "and I did not want to hang out with my friends, so I took a chance and called you." He did not add the fact that his mother had called him to tell him that she was going to be home late and his father was out of town again.

That pretty much left Brian to fend for himself. He hoped that Tiffany had some food because he was starving for a home-cooked meal and tired of takeout.

"Well, I am always happy to see you," Tiffany assured him. "Karlie should be home soon. She is at her friend Tanya's house, working on an art project of some sort. She has to turn it in before Thanksgiving."

"Oh." Brian did not know how to reply. His stomach growled loudly.

"Are you hungry?" Tiffany questioned once she heard the loud rumbling sounds from his stomach.

"A little," Brian shyly confessed.

"Well, you are in luck. I have a housekeeper now. Her name is Annie, and she comes in every morning for a few hours to cook and clean for me. I think she made steak, mash potatoes, and veggies. Would you like some?"

Brian practically drooled at the mouth. His stomach responded for him with a huge rumble. "That sounds good, if you have enough."

Tiffany smiled. Seeing the hunger written all over his face, she said, "I will get you something to eat right away." She picked up the television remote and handed it to him. "Turn on the television. See what's on."

Tiffany went in the kitchen, out of Brian's sight, and released a little laugh. She thought about his parents. They did not realize that they had been given a precious gem.

Tiffany made Brian a huge helping and put his food to warm in the microwave oven. "Are you okay out there, Brian?" she called out.

"Yeah, I'm just channel surfing."

Tiffany heard the front door open and then listened to Karlie's and Tanya's excited voices as they greeted Brian. She retrieved two more plates and dished the girls out some of the hearty repast. She knew from experience they were also going to be hungry.

"Brian, your food's ready," she called out before putting another of the plates in the microwave to warm.

Tiffany did not know if it was in style, but the girls rarely ate lunch. This meant that when they came in, they were ravenous.

Tiffany heard the girls and Brian talking. "That explains why I got no answer." Tiffany shook her head and smiled. She removed the hot plate from the microwave and put the last one in to warm.

"Maybe you should put your feet up," Brian suggested when Tiffany walked back in the den..

"I think I might just do that," Tiffany stated and turned to go up the stairs. "You all can watch TV a little longer, but, Karlie and Tanya, do not forget about your art project."

"I will help them, Tiffany," Brian volunteered.

"Thanks." Tiffany was grateful.

As soon as she left the room, Karlie went inside the kitchen to get their food. She was more than a little concerned about her mother. She felt a presence behind her and almost jumped when she saw that Brian had followed her into the kitchen to get his plate.

"So, tell me about your friend," Brian whispered.

"Who? Tanya?"

Brian nodded his head and then peered over his shoulders to make sure that Tanya could not hear him.

"She is sixteen," Karlie revealed. "She'll be seventeen next May, and she is graduating because she skipped a grade."

Brian bobbed his head up and down, liking what he'd heard. "So, does she have a boyfriend?"

"No," Karlie said. "But I do not know if she would give you the time of day."

"Why not?"

"Because *we* are good girls."

"And?" Brian demanded an explanation.

"And guys like you definitely do not date girls like us," Karlie noted. She took three glasses out of the cabinet to serve them some drinks with their food.

"Guys like me?" Brian questioned. He wanted to know what Karlie meant by that comment. What had Tiffany said about him to her daughter?

"Yeah, cool, popular guys like you. You all just want one thing." Karlie pressed the ice button on the fridge to fill their glasses.

Brian relaxed once he heard Karlie's rationale. "I am not like that. Put in a good word for me with Tanya, please. C'mon, you are practically my little sister."

Karlie looked at Brian and laughed. "Just because you come here to visit, it does not make me your little sister, okay?"

"Yeah, well, I heard my dad could possibly be . . ." Brian trailed off. He stopped as he considered the fact that Karlie might not know anything. His parents had told him that it was possible that Karlie was his sister and that his father was going to take a paternity test to find out. They'd discussed it with him, and Brian was all for the idea. He would love to have a little sister. But looking at Karlie's bewildered expression, Brian guessed she did not have a clue about the situation.

"Your dad could possibly be . . . what?" Karlie demanded.

"Forget it," Brian said and went to sit with Tanya.

Karlie followed him out of the kitchen at a much slower pace. Something about what Brian had almost said gave her the chills, and she didn't know why. For the first time Karlie wondered just how her mother even knew Brian. She had just introduced him, and that was it. Karlie had never thought to ask her mother about Brian at all. Maybe she should. Karlie looked at Brian, who was charming the socks off Tanya. Karlie did not doubt the pants would soon follow.

Neil ran up the steps to Tiffany's house as if the devil were on his heels. Myra was acting crazy again, and he did not know how to deal with her erratic mood swings. He hoped Tiffany would talk some sense into his wife.

Neil rang the doorbell, and Tiffany answered. "Hi, Neil. Come on in. I was just about to take a shower. Follow me."

Neil followed but thought to ask, "What about Karlie?"

"She's fast asleep," Tiffany replied. She carefully closed the door behind them before walking to the bed and turning to face him. In slow motion, Neil really looked at the woman before him.

Tiffany wore a small, sheer blue robe, and from the looks of it, she had nothing on underneath. She shifted, and her robe slipped open.

Neil's breath caught as his suspicions were confirmed. Tiffany was completely naked underneath that robe. "Oh," he exhaled and went to sit on the edge of her bed.

Suddenly, the air in the room became tense.

Neil could see her chest heaving up and down as she glanced at him with speculative eyes. He moved toward her like a cat stalking its prey.

Seductively, Tiffany opened her robe and allowed it to fall to her feet. She moved over to him, and Neil buried his head in her abdomen. Tiffany took her hands to hold his head against her midriff.

Neil smiled, knowing exactly what she wanted. He breathed in deeply, inhaling her scent, and began kissing her navel. He heard Tiffany moan, encouraging him to do as he pleased.

He groaned loudly.

Whoa.

Neil jumped up to a sitting position in a sweat, now fully awake. He looked around his bedroom, half expecting to see Tiffany standing there. But she was not. It had only been a dream. But it had been real enough to awaken him.

Neil looked at the woman asleep next to him. He leaned over to peek at her. Yep, it was Myra. He released a huge sigh of relief and wiped the sweat off his face. Neil could not remember the last time he had dreamed about another woman. Guilt hit him with the force of a ton of bricks. What in blue blazes did this mean? It was too late for any rational self-interrogation, so Neil dismissed the question. Besides, he had an even bigger issue to deal with right now. His "friend."

Neil moved a little closer to Myra, hoping to nudge her awake. He spooned her and tapped her shoulder lightly. He was definitely in the right mood.

Myra only groaned. She was too exhausted and mumbled a quick "Not tonight, babe."

"I need you," Neil whispered urgently.

Myra yawned. She barely opened her eyes but turned over until she was lying on her back. Unceremoniously, Myra said, "Go ahead then. Just hurry up so I can sleep."

Neil took what she grudgingly offered, though he felt grimy. In that moment, his need far outweighed his guilt.

Unable to sleep, Darnell opened his desk drawers, not looking for anything in particular. His eyes fell on his Bible. It was a large burgundy leather-bound minister's Bible. His wife had bought it for him. Slowly, Darnell picked up the Bible and placed it in front of him. Gently gliding his hands across the smooth leather, he remembered the countless times he had sought the Word for comfort and for answers.

Darnell realized it had been ages since he had actually opened his Bible. Flipping through the pages, he saw the many Bible verses he had highlighted at one point or another. A bookmark jutted out of the edges, and Darnell opened to that spot. He saw Psalm 43:1. It stated, "Teach me to do thy will; for thou art my God." The Word whipped at his heart immediately, and Darnell stopped reading. He could not go any further for tears filled his eyes.

"Lord, help me live according to your will. Help me accept your will for my life." Darnell prayed for he knew he had not come across that verse by accident.

Even though he now regularly attended church with Tiffany and had been at the altar several times for prayer, Darnell had not recommitted his life to God. He knew God was calling him back into the fold.

♫ Chapter Twenty-nine

Tiffany and Karlie entered their home after church that Saturday after Thanksgiving on a real high. Pastor Johnston had preached such a powerful sermon that Tiffany had walked up to the altar for prayer.

He had also asked her to sing, and when she did, there was not one dry eye in the place. Tiffany felt a completeness using her gift for God. She also knew that God wanted *her,* not just the use of her gift.

Karlie headed up the stairs, but Tiffany stopped her. "Karlie, I need to talk to you. Let's have a cup of hot cocoa."

"Sure." Karlie turned around, and Tiffany ushered her into the kitchen.

Dreading the impending task, Tiffany put the kettle on and made conversation. "I can't believe all that snow. I think it must be about six inches already. If this keeps up, I think you may be looking at a snow day."

"This will be my first snow day," Karlie proclaimed. "Sit down, Mom. Let me do it."

Tiffany remained quiet until Karlie brought the bubbling cups of hot cocoa to the table. "Thanks, honey." Holding her cup gently, she took a couple of sips and allowed the hot liquid to warm her insides.

Karlie stirred her hot cocoa to cool it down before taking a tentative sip. She was not trying to scald her tongue, because then she would not be able to eat well for days.

"Karlie, I have something important I have to tell you."

Hearing the serious tone in her mother's voice, Karlie paused with alarm. "What is it? Is it the cancer?"

Tiffany held her hands up. "No, honey. It's nothing like that. I just want you to promise that you will hear me out." Her stomach rolled over, but Tiffany could not delay the moment any longer. It was time Karlie learned the truth.

"Okay, Mom." Karlie's heart rate accelerated. Had her mom found out about her secret visits with her dad? Was it Jamaal? If it was not the cancer, then what was it?

Tiffany ignored the butterflies inside the pit of her stomach and began. "Karlie, I have not been completely honest with you. I moved back home because I had something I had to do before I . . . go. My reason for coming back to Hempstead, back to where I grew up, was that I needed to find your father."

"Dad? But, Mom, I know where he is. As a matter of fact, I have been—"

"Karlie, please let me finish." Tiffany held up her hands. Now that she'd started, she had to get the story out. Tiffany had let things drag on too long already, and she needed to tell Karlie the truth. "I was a little older than you when something really bad happened to me—something that I made sure never happened to you." Tiffany took Karlie's hands in hers. "My stepfather raped me."

"What?" Karlie pulled her hands away in shock, her eyes as wide as saucers. "You were raped? I can't believe it. How did that happen? Well, not how, but why did he rape you? I just don't understand!"

"I don't know why," Tiffany replied. "But it happened prom night. Clifford Peterson raped me right before my mother got home. When I told her, she didn't be-lieve me. She thought I was lying and had made it up."

Karlie's mouth hung ajar. It took several seconds, but she broke down. "Mommy, I'm so sorry that hap-pened to you."

Tiffany nodded her head but knew she was only half-way through. The worst was yet to come. "Karlie, when my mother didn't believe me and then accused me of seducing her husband, I went crazy. I started acting out. Karlie, I had sex with four boys after that."

"TMI, Mom." Karlie scrunched her nose. She did not relish the image of her mother having sex with so many people.

"No," Tiffany stated. "I have to tell you. I can't chance you hearing about it or finding out somehow. I have to tell you myself. Trust me, this is hard for me, but I won't be here forever, and I—I just need to do this."

Karlie undid the jacket to her two-piece Pierre Car-din, suddenly feeling warm. She wore a cream ruffled blouse underneath her checkered suit.

Tiffany followed suit and removed her scarf from her black turtleneck dress before rolling up the sleeves. Then she continued. "I had never done anything like that before. I was one of the good girls, you know. But I just didn't know how to handle or cope with what Clifford did to me, and my mother refused to press charges. She called me a whore so much that I guess I just started acting like one. I know now how stupid and risky that was. I could have been killed or caught a disease, but instead, I got . . . pregnant."

"With me?"

"Yes," Tiffany replied. She waited until she saw the question reflected in Karlie's eyes. "I became preg-nant with you. I was young and scared, so I convinced Thomas to marry me, and we ran off together. The rest you pretty much know."

"Mom, what are you saying? Are you saying what I think you're saying?" Karlie asked, filled with disillusionment and disbelief. "'Cause I'm beginning to feel like I'm on a *Maury* episode or something. When did you find out that Thomas was my father?"

"I didn't."

"Didn't what?"

"I never found out who your father was," Tiffany quietly confessed. "I told Thomas he was the father, and that's when we got married."

"So, Thomas Knightly is not my father?"

"No . . . I'm not sure. He could be. Actually, I hope he is your father, which is why I met with him and asked him to take a paternity test. But he was angry, and he refused."

"So Dad . . . I mean Thomas . . . knows I am not his child?" Karlie now felt betrayed by two people instead of one. "Mom, I went to see him. I have been spending time with him, and he never said a word. Instead, he pretended that he loved me and that he was my father." Karlie sprang to her feet as anger rose in her. "I don't believe this. Who am I? Am I your daughter, or am I adopted?"

"No," Tiffany asserted. "Karlie, you are my daughter. That's who you are. You can be sure of that. I never regretted you for an instant. I was frightened, but I never once considered aborting you. You are my best accomplishment."

Karlie barely listened, too caught up in her own tirade. "Every year he sends me gifts, and even now he welcomed me into his house, and he didn't say anything."

"His house? I had no idea you were in contact with Thomas."

"Yes. I reached out to him."

"That's . . . that's wonderful." Tiffany went to hug her daughter close.

Karlie shrugged out of her mother's embrace. "No! Don't you dare touch me! You are not who I thought you were. You just changed my whole life all over again. First, you tell me you're dying, and then we have to move, though I didn't want to come here. And now you tell me my whole life is a lie."

Karlie cried as her heart disintegrated and shattered into tiny pieces. "I can live with growing up with an absent father because at least I knew who he was. But I can't deal with this. Are you seriously telling me that you have no idea who my father is?" Karlie's voice rose an entire octave. She looked at her mother with repugnance written all over her face. "No clue at all?"

"Well," Tiffany said, hesitating, "I told you it has to be one of those four men."

"Don't you mean five?" Karlie pointedly asked.

"No . . . there is no way that . . . I just know in my gut that Clifford Peterson is not your father," Tiffany assured her.

The two engaged in a stare down before Karlie continued her tirade. "Wow. A one-in-four chance. How comforting," she viciously spat. "Will my real father please stand up? Did you even know them, or did you just pick up random guys? Like, wow. I can't believe I'm having this conversation right now."

Tiffany's tongue felt parched, and her mind drew a blank. Karlie, her beloved daughter, was now looking at her as if she were an alien. She reached out her hands toward Karlie, intending to comfort her.

Ruthlessly, Karlie shoved her mother's hands away, rejecting her.

"Well, Thomas and I were high school sweethearts. Darnell and Pierce also went to my school. Ryan, though, I met at a bar."

"Seriously? You slept with my high school coach. Great. Just great. Is there anybody in Hempstead you haven't slept with?"

"I have all their information in a file if you . . . need . . . to read it."

"You had them investigated? Like, I feel as if I am in a novel right now, 'cause this is not happening. This is surreal. You're not who I thought you were. You are a liar and a first-class hypocrite."

Tiffany felt the old feelings that Merle had evoked within her swell to life again. They resurfaced vigorously. She began to cry as guilt and self-hatred engulfed her.

In one violent motion, Karlie jumped from around the table and ran toward the door.

"Karlie," Tiffany yelled. "Where are you going?" She lunged and grabbed on to Karlie with all her might.

"Get off me!" Karlie screamed before going to the front door. She opened the door so hard that the crash reverberated throughout the entire house. In a fit of rage, she went outside, heedless of the snow and the cold.

"Do not do this, Karlie. I beg you." Tiffany followed her outside and pleaded. "Please do not reject me like this. Let's talk about it."

"I have absolutely nothing to say to you, and I think you've said enough," Karlie shouted back at her mother. The snow fell hard again in heavy flakes. It was settling quickly, but Karlie ignored it and waited until her mother stood before her. Then she contemptuously declared, "I want nothing to do with you. You are nothing but a . . . a . . . slut."

Tiffany's mouth hung open, and she stepped back with hurt and alarm. "I can't believe you would call me something like that." In one quick move, she lifted her hand and slapped her daughter hard across the face. "Don't you ever in your life think of speaking to me that way again. Do you hear me?" Tiffany clenched her teeth in anger.

Karlie was past the point of caring, as her emotions spiraled out of control. "I spoke to you that way because I no longer have any respect for you. You are not who I thought you were. I don't know my grandmother, but she was right. You are a whore."

Tiffany wailed as Karlie's words crushed her very core.

Karlie watched her mother slowly crumple onto the snow on the ground but did nothing to stop her. She sped out of the yard and ran off, not caring if her mother lived or died.

"Karlie, Karlie, come back," Tiffany called out until her voice croaked.

She knew Karlie had heard her but blatantly chose to ignore her. Emotionally drained, Tiffany sat in the snow and cried. She did not know how long she sat there before Neil came by and saw her.

"Tiffany!" Alarmed, Neil effortlessly lifted her into his arms and took her inside. She was so cold that Neil worried about hypothermia. He quickly removed her cold, wet clothes and put pajamas on her. Tenderly, he placed her under the covers in her bedroom to warm her up.

"Tiffany, what happened? Where's Karlie?" he asked repeatedly, but Tiffany was too zoned out to answer him.

Moving quickly, he made Tiffany some soup and forced its contents down her throat, but she still felt deathly cold to the touch. He fretted, unsure of what to do. Looking at the fireplace in the living room, Neil decided to throw some logs in and get a cozy fire started. He bolted up the stairs and hoisted Tiffany, along with her blanket, to take her back downstairs.

"That should warm you up," he said as he laid her on the couch.

Tiffany shivered, and to Neil that was a good sign. He rubbed his hands along her body to give her some much-needed body heat. At the same time, Neil prayed and prayed for God's help.

It took almost an hour before Tiffany opened up enough to let Neil know what had transpired. "I've lost her, Neil. She ran off and left me, and I don't know if she's okay."

Neil was worried about Karlie too, but he was also angry with her for deserting Tiffany when she knew her mother's delicate condition.

Darnell called on the telephone, and Neil quickly filled him in. Darnell briskly said, "I'm on my way."

As soon as Darnell arrived, Neil said, "I'm going to go look for Karlie to see if I can talk some sense into her, and if that doesn't work, I am going to throttle her."

♪ Chapter Thirty

Karlie walked several blocks before calling Jamaal on her cell phone. "Jamaal, I—I'm so upset."

"Karlie, what's wrong?"

"I—I can't even . . ." Karlie was at a loss for words.

"Where are you?" Jamaal said, responding to the urgency in her tone.

"I don't know. My mom just upset me, and I left the house."

"Karlie, you're scaring me. Where are you?"

"I am near the pizza shop not too far from my house," Karlie offered. She crossed the street to enter the pizza parlor and ordered a soda before sitting at a booth.

"Okay, I know where that is. Hang tight. I'm on my way."

Jamaal got there in just under ten minutes. He raced into the pizza shop and frantically searched for Karlie. He didn't know what was up, but it had to be serious, because Karlie had had a meltdown over the telephone.

"Karlie," Jamaal called out as soon as he spotted her.

Karlie turned toward him with bloodred, puffy eyes.

"Is it your mother? Is she . . . has she . . ." Jamaal stopped, unable to get the question out.

"Died?" Karlie said, finishing for him. She shook her head wildly. "No, she is not dead. But I might as well be."

Jamaal heaved a sigh of relief, sat down right next to her in the booth, and gently asked, "Karlie, what's wrong?" In all the time he had known her, this was the first time he'd seen her so completely undone.

Karlie wiped her tears with a napkin before spilling her guts. She told Jamaal everything that had transpired, holding nothing back. When she finished, Karlie flung herself into Jamaal's arms and cried uncontrollably.

Jamaal held on to Karlie for several minutes before letting her go. "Karlie, I feel it for you, but you were wrong to leave your mother like that."

"What? What?" Karlie wrinkled her eyebrows, slightly confused, before becoming angry and jumped up out of her chair. "Well, excuse me for looking to my boyfriend to give me sympathy. But do I get that? No. Instead, you take her side."

Karlie stormed out the door of the pizza shop and was halfway up the block before Jamaal caught up with her.

Jamaal grabbed her arms, exerting enough pressure until Karlie stood still. "Karlie, you have got to calm down, because right now you are not listening to anybody." He made a quick decision. "C'mon," Jamaal commanded. He held Karlie's hands and practically dragged her the five blocks to his house.

Karlie went along with Jamaal mostly because she didn't have a backup plan. She couldn't go to Thomas's house now that she knew the truth. Tanya was out with Brian or something, so that had left only Jamaal. Karlie noticed beer bottles had been thrown all over the lawn and were peering out from underneath all that snow. She saw some apartments with cardboard for windows and could not help but let out a sigh of alarm. There was graffiti all over the walls, and it smelled like urine.

Jamaal tightened his lips at the sound of her intake of breath but did not say a word. He had been trying to avoid bringing Karlie to his place for this very reason. Then he stiffened his spine. This was where he lived, and it was time he stopped being ashamed. Karlie had to learn to toughen up and realize she lived in a real world with real people. She had to know places existed that were not covered with sunflowers and daffodils.

Jamaal pulled her up a flight of stairs and walked down the hall. Karlie shivered from the cold emanating from the hallways and snuggled closer to Jamaal. She wrinkled her nose from an odd stench.

Outside his apartment, Jamaal took out his key and opened the two locks that would guarantee their entry, and they quickly went inside.

Karlie rubbed her hands together, trying to get warm and curiously looked around. It was nice and clean inside Jamaal's place. Karlie's face reflected her surprise.

"What were you expecting my house to look like? A dump?" Jamaal asked somewhat defensively. "Do not judge a book by its cover."

He took off his jacket and held out his hands for Karlie's. Then he hung them inside the hall closet.

"My grandmother's at work," Jamaal said.

Karlie nodded. Jamaal was in a crazy mood, and she didn't want him going off on her again. "Where's the bathroom?"

He pointed in the general direction, and Karlie found her way.

While she was relieving herself, Jamaal used that opportunity to call Tiffany. He told her that Karlie was with him and that he would bring her home shortly. Jamaal heard Tiffany's cry of relief and anger, and it touched his heart. Karlie had no idea how lucky she was, and Jamaal decided that it was time that she knew that.

As soon as Karlie reentered the room, Jamaal beckoned for her to sit next to him. "You are lucky. You know that?"

"I do not feel that lucky right now."

"Well, you should because you have a mother that is worried sick about you. That is more than a lot of people have."

"Yeah, right," Karlie said, sulking.

"It's more than what I have," Jamaal informed her quietly.

Karlie became thoughtful at that comment. "What do you mean?"

"I mean, some of us wish we had a mother to love us the way you have."

"I—"

"Do not open your mouth to say another word," Jamaal demanded, holding his hands up to stem her comments. "It's time you listened to what I have to say."

Karlie looked at Jamaal expectantly.

"I do not even know where to begin." Jamaal paused. "Karlie, what I am about to tell you, I have never told another living soul."

"You can trust me, Jamaal," Karlie told him.

"Well, I am going to tell you what I have been told by my grandmother." Jamaal wiped his hands on his pants and licked his lips. Then he took a deep breath before continuing. "My mother was fifteen years old when she became pregnant with me. She tried to hide it from my grandmother, but eventually, Nana found out. My mother, Stephanie, decided to try to get an abortion when she was about five months pregnant. Fortunately for me, that was illegal in this state. So my mother had no choice but to keep me." Jamaal took a sip of soda before continuing with his story.

"She carried me to full term and went into labor. Nana was at work. So Stephanie went into labor and gave birth to me right here inside this apartment. Then she ran around the corner and dumped me in the garbage can. It was early March, so you know it was cold outside. Then she disappeared."

Karlie let out a sharp breath of surprise. She wanted to say something, but Jamaal waved his hands dismissively.

"Lucky for me, again, somebody heard me crying and scooped me out of the trash. The cops and the news were all over here, and my grandmother heard about it. She came home and saw all the blood and accurately put two and two together. Nana called the cops and told them what had happened."

"Your grandmother spilled the beans on her own daughter?" Karlie barged in to ask.

"Yes," Jamaal said matter-of-factly. "Just because we live here, it does not mean we aren't honest."

Understanding his gentle reprimand, Karlie nodded her head and did not say another word.

"So, Nana got custody of me, and I have lived with her since then. I was into all kinds of things until I met you. Now I know for sure what I want to do."

"What's that?" Karlie asked.

"I want to be a journalist," Jamaal said. "It's because of the news system that my grandmother found me, so . . ." He trailed off, embarrassed.

"But what about your dad?" Karlie wanted to know.

"Never knew him. Nana told me that my mother never confessed who the real daddy was," Jamaal answered.

"Wow."

"Yeah, so, you should consider yourself lucky that your mother kept you. She obviously loves you and dotes on you. My mother threw me in the garbage."

Karlie started to cry again. Her eyes were so puffy that they hurt. She did not even know where the tears came from, because she had already cried tons in the last couple of hours.

Jamaal moved over and gave Karlie a hug. They hugged each other closely, not wanting to let go.

"All I am saying is that you should give your mother a second chance. You did that for your dad," Jamaal urged with a whisper.

"Yeah, but that's different."

"How? How is it different?"

"I am only just now getting to know Thomas. Mom has been there with me all my life. I depend on her, and she betrayed me. I just never imagined she would lie to me so easily. I do feel bad about calling her those nasty names. I've never spoken to her that way before."

"Your mother was young," Jamaal said, defending Tiffany. "She made mistakes, but I am sure that she loves you, and I know that you love her too."

Jamaal leaned over and gave Karlie a gentle kiss. Karlie returned the kiss passionately. Jamaal took that as a sign of encouragement and moved his hands under her shirt. Tentatively, his hands crept higher.

Karlie jumped back. She did not intend to have sex until she was good and ready and old enough to handle it. She definitely did not want anything happening without using protection.

"What?" Jamaal asked in a daze.

"Jamaal, I am not doing this," Karlie stated firmly. She got up and went to retrieve her jacket out of the closet.

Jamaal went over to Karlie. "I am sorry, Karlie. I just got carried away with the moment, you know. You do not have to worry about doing anything that you are not ready to do."

"Okay." Karlie smiled.

Jamaal kept his eyes planted on Karlie's face. He rapidly blinked his eyes for they itched to look down at the tempting display, clearly outlined against her sweater. Taking a chance, Jamaal looked down. He could not resist the urge.

Karlie saw him and criss-crossed her hands to protectively cover her chest area. "Jamaal, please I want to go home, and I do not feel comfortable."

Jamaal chastised himself for his actions, and he quickly apologized. "Sorry, Karlie, I just think you are so beautiful. You are the best thing to happen to me, and I am not about to mess things up with you."

"Thank you," Karlie said with a blush.

Jamaal reached over to give her another kiss. To prove himself to her, he kept his hands to himself.

Darnell cuddled underneath the blanket with Tiffany and waited for Karlie and Jamaal. Jamaal had called again to say that they were on their way. He placed a call to Neil and let him know that Karlie had been found and was on her way home.

Tiffany alternated between cursing herself and crying her eyes out. Darnell soothed her. "Karlie will come around. You'll see."

"She hates me. She's not going to forgive me."

At his wit's end, Darnell took Tiffany's hands in his and prayed. He mumbled assurances and quoted scriptures that came to mind.

They heard the screen door open and sat up.

Karlie entered the house, waved at Jamaal, and said, "I'm in. Text me when you get home."

Darnell left Tiffany on the couch and said a terse "Wait here" to Karlie, then went out to thank Jamaal for seeing Karlie home. He extended an invitation to come in at Tiffany's behest.

Jamaal declined, politely saying, "Karlie and her mom need to talk. I'm just glad to help." Darnell even tried to give him cab fare, but Jamaal assured him he was quite comfortable walking home.

Back inside, Darnell watched as Karlie slowly hung her jacket on the hook. He pulled her aside and used his sternest teacher tone with her. "Karlie, what you did tonight was totally uncalled for. You caused your mother unnecessary worry and pain without once considering her illness. Look at her. She's so cold that she has not stopped shivering for almost two hours. Neil found her literally sitting in the snow, crying, because of you. Right now your mother needs a reason to live and hang on. You are that reason, Karlie. Think about that carefully before you speak to your mother."

Karlie wanted to resent Darnell for what he'd said to her. But she could not. He was right. She should have stopped to consider her mother's serious condition. If anything happened to her mother, she would not be able to live with herself.

Darnell calmed down. "Karlie, I know I had some tough words for you just now, but I just want you to think about your mother and put yourself in her shoes. Her entire life has been about you and what you want."

Karlie went into the room, afraid and ashamed to face her mother when she thought about how she'd call her a slut. "Mom?"

"Karlie." Tiffany simultaneously smiled and cried with relief. She opened her arms to receive her daughter.

Karlie lunged into her mother's arms and hugged her tightly. "Mom, I am so sorry for what I said. I didn't mean it, honest."

Jamaal and Darnell went out the door, and Darnell gave Jamaal a ride home.

Tiffany and Karlie barely noticed when the men left. They were too busy trying to console each other.

"I know you didn't mean it, Karlie," Tiffany said. She sneezed three times and pulled the blanket closer. Karlie started to fuss over her mother, but Tiffany stopped her. "No, I am fine. I am just glad that you are back. Karlie, can you ever find it in your heart to forgive me? Because of my stupid actions, I have made your life a complicated mess."

"No, Mom. You do not have to apologize. You are the best mother a daughter could ask for, and I love you." Karlie spoke honestly and sincerely. "I am sorry, Mom. I do respect you, and if I had a choice, I would still choose you as my mother."

Tiffany's eyes filled at Karlie's declaration, and she said a mental prayer of thanks to Jamaal, because she knew, without any doubt, that he was the reason why Karlie came home. She would have to thank him later. He was truly a remarkable young man.

♫ Chapter Thirty-one

It was almost dawn when Darnell entered his house and vigorously knocked the snow off his boots. The temperature had dropped several degrees. He walked quietly up the stairs to check on his daughters. Both of them were asleep in their room

Darnell found his mother waiting for him in the kitchen. He reached over to give her a gentle kiss of appreciation on her cheek. "Sorry, Mother. I did not expect to be this long."

Leona looked at her son. "Darnell, what're you doing?"

"What do you mean?" he asked.

"I mean with Tiffany Knightly," Leona said. "She is dying, Darnell, of lung cancer. You know any kind of a relationship with her would be pointless."

Darnell sighed. "Mother, I know that she is dying. I just . . . I like her."

"But you have two young girls to consider, Darnell. I mean, you should have heard them talking nonstop about Tiffany. I can see how much they love her. They even asked me if you two were going to get married so they could have a new mom."

Darnell paused at that new piece of information. When his daughters had told him how much they liked Tiffany, he had been relieved. But now he could kick himself for this lack of foresight.

"What do I do? I guess I never thought that far ahead." He sat down at the table and put his head down.

"I know what you need to do. You need to consider your daughters first, Darnell. It's not about you anymore and what you want. When you have a child, it's about them." Leona got up to leave.

"The weather is nasty out there," Darnell said, "I think you should bunk over here for the night, or what's left of it."

Nodding her head, Leona left her son with his thoughts and went to sleep in his guest room. She hoped for his children's sake that Darnell knew what he was doing.

"Daddy, are you going to marry Ms. Tiffany?" Amber asked her father.

Though three weeks had passed since his mother had given him a heads-up, the question still caught him off guard. It was the first day of his winter break, and Darnell relished these days off that came along with his career choice. It was well worth the salary cut to spend quality time with his daughters. Next year he planned to take them both to Disney World.

Right now, though, with that question hanging in the air, Darnell wished he had some place else to be. He did not have the answer to that question, so he decided to ask one of his own. "Why would you ask me that, honey?"

"Because." Amber looked up at her father, and Darnell knew that was her final answer.

He stooped down to her level and then called April in the room. He might as well talk to them both at the same time, even though he knew they would ask this same question a million times again and not get tired.

"Girls, I like Ms. Tiffany, but it does not mean that we are going to get married," Darnell explained.

"Why not?" April asked with a look of innocence.

"Because Tiffany and I are just friends. Okay?"

"Okay," they said in unison. They sped off to their room, momentarily appeased.

Darnell, however, was not. He wondered if it was fair of him to engage in anything with Tiffany when he had daughters. They needed a mother. Common sense dictated that he end whatever this was between himself and Tiffany. Yet he heard himself call out to tell his mother that he was leaving. He still put on his coat and went to meet Tiffany.

He was powerless to resist the pull that Tiffany had on him. He missed her like crazy, and as soon as he left her, Darnell found himself missing her again. What he was feeling sounded like love to his ears, but Darnell refused to acknowledge that emotion. He figured that as long as he did not delve too deeply into his heart and as long as he did not say anything aloud, it would not be real.

However, somewhere deep inside him, Darnell knew he was kidding himself. He could not stop the love from flowing or growing in leaps and bounds. He could not rein in his feelings any more than he could stop the rain.

"Hurry up, Darnell."

Tiffany had shipped Karlie off with Tanya to guarantee them the privacy they would need for what would be their first and last winter break together. She opened the curtains to look outside again. Still no sign of him. "Where is he?" She looked at the clock on the mantel. Suddenly, she shivered, feeling unnaturally colder than usual. Tiffany abandoned her post at the window and checked the thermostat. She raised the lever to warm the house and lit the fireplace.

Twenty minutes later, she still felt chilled down to her bare bones. Her teeth shattered, and her body quivered. "This is ridiculous. I should be warmer than toast by now." Tiffany stomped up the stairs to her bedroom to get an extra pair of socks.

On the way back down the stairs, a brief dizzy spell came over her. "Whew." She sat at the bottom of the stairs to get herself together. "Please God. Not now. I'm not ready."

The doorbell rang. Tiffany got up off the step and walked to the front door. It took every ounce of willpower she possessed just to accomplish that small task.

"Hi. How are you doing?" Darnell greeted her and drew her in for a deep kiss.

"Okay, now," Tiffany returned. She purposely refrained from mentioning how she felt because she did not want to worry him. She moved her body as close to Darnell as she could to draw his body heat.

"Hmm. Hmm." Darnell gripped her bottom and pulled Tiffany even closer. As the kiss continued, their passion ignited. Darnell broke contact to grab Tiffany in his arms and carry her up the stairs.

On the drive over, Darnell had cautioned himself to slow things down between the two of them. He planned to have a long talk with Tiffany to voice his concerns. But now all thoughts of verbal conversation flew out of his head. Now he realized it was sheer madness on his part to imagine for one second that he could turn his ardor on and off as if it were a light switch.

Darnell knew only that he wanted this woman with an intensity that stupefied and humbled him. He had never believed until this moment that instantaneous passion of this dimension was possible.

Darnell decided to give in to the urge gripping his mind and body. He practically threw Tiffany on the bed and was completely naked by the time her shirt came over her head. He stood proud and tall before her, leaving nothing to the imagination.

"Whoa." Tiffany saw the fever reflected in Darnell's eyes and felt her insides heating up at his hot glare, but nature spoke first. "I have to use the bathroom," Tiffany shyly admitted.

"Take your time, but hurry up."

Tiffany chuckled at the contradiction. "Give me two seconds."

She went into the bathroom and looked into the mirror. Suddenly Tiffany felt another presence. It was odd, but it was as if she was not alone.

God's eyes were watching her. Tiffany keenly felt His presence and instantly felt ashamed. "Lord, if that is you," Tiffany softly commented, "if that is you, I don't know if you can get me out of this. Honestly, I don't even know if I want to be rescued, but if it is you, then do something."

Just like that, her body cooled down.

Tiffany did not know much about praying, but she was going to need the Holy Ghost when she faced Darnell to tell him she had changed her mind. She quietly opened the bathroom door and poked her head out. Darnell was lying on the bed. Slowly she crept forward until she stood over him.

He was asleep and was snoring loudly.

Tiffany curled her lips and covered her mouth to keep from laughing. Snatching a warm blanket, Tiffany went into the smaller guest room.

God had a sense of humor. Not only did He stop things, but He kicked her out of her own room in the process.

About three o'clock in the morning, Tiffany woke up and entered her bedroom to find Darnell lying there with a pensive look on his face.

"What's the matter?" she asked.

"Just thinking about how I fell asleep on what could have been one of the luckiest nights of my life."

"You know it would have been, but let's agree to face the obvious. God is at work."

"He must be," Darnell concurred.

After their previous two foiled attempts, Tiffany and Darnell decided not to have sex, but that didn't stop their hands or curb their imaginations. The most significant event took place when they went to church together that Saturday. After Pastor Johnston's pointed message, both Darnell and Tiffany went to the altar to commit their lives to the Lord.

For Darnell, it was a return home.

For Tiffany, it was hope. Hope for a life devoid of pain, tears, and sadness. When Pastor Johnston asked her to pray, she cried out, "Lord, I thank you for all the good and bad things I have endured in my life. For they led me to you. Take my life, Lord, and make me become a blessing for you. Lord, thank you for the gift of salvation and for the promise of eternal life. Thank you for showing me your love."

Standing at the altar with Darnell, Tiffany knew that she had made the best decision of her life. She looked behind her to see Karlie sitting in the pews. Tiffany prayed that her daughter would also accept the gift of salvation one day.

When they returned to their seats, Tiffany surreptitiously wrote Darnell a quick note. He quickly perused the contents before nodding his head in agreement.

Karlie saw the note pass between her mom and Darnell, and her curiosity blossomed. She really wanted to know what her mom had said to Darnell. She eyed the note, hoping to catch a glimpse, but Darnell tore the paper into tiny pieces and stuffed it into his pants pocket.

Tiffany felt her chest lift at Darnell's consent. She had been as nervous as a schoolchild but felt it was imperative to communicate what was uppermost on her mind. God had said no more touchy-feely stuff.

Tiffany and Darnell prayed together. They read and studied together, growing more and more in God's grace. They lived in His favor. It was a huge sacrifice, but Tiffany knew it was worth it.

♪ Chapter Thirty-two

"Four."

"Yes."

"Let me get this straight in my head. You slept with four men in the space of one year?"

"Yes."

"So Thomas may not be Karlie's father."

"No."

"Wow."

"Big wow."

Myra subconsciously played with her wedding ring. She experienced a momentary loss of words. Well, actually, she had been silent through Tiffany's entire story. Myra was not about to put her foot in her mouth. She'd learned well from their last conversation to keep her mouth closed, since it was less likely she'd come off sounding condemnatory. When Tiffany came to her door this morning, she had no idea what she was in for.

"So did you finally set a date for the paternity test? I mean tests? 'Cause I mean, I wouldn't have waited this long if it were me. Ah, please don't just say yes again."

"Yes," Tiffany responded before she caught herself. "I'm sorry. Yes, I did set a date.

January nineteen, since that was when I could get everyone in together. I spoke with Karlie about it, and she wants to be there when I get the results."

"That's understandable. It's only right that she hear firsthand who her father is," Myra agreed. She sure was glad she was not standing in Tiffany's shoes right now. "How are you feeling?" She asked the first thing that came to her mind while she tried to process the latest in the Tiffany Knightly saga.

"I have some really good days when I entertain the thought that God healed me. But then they are followed by some really bad days. So, you know, I try to take things day by day."

"God knows what is best for us, even when we don't know. At least that is what I hold firm. Tiffany, I am taking a personal leave from work."

"You're taking a leave of absence? Why?" Tiffany scooted her chair closer to Myra.

"More tea?"

"No, if I drink another cup of chamomile tea, I'm likely to start singing "Come By Here" or something."

Myra giggled. "You're hilarious. I'm going to get myself another cup." While she busied herself with the necessary ministrations, she answered Tiffany's original query. "Honestly, my reasoning is twofold. I need some time away from work, and I just want to be here for you, as well."

"Myra your offer sounds appealing, and I do want the help, but I get the feeling that this has nothing to do with me."

Myra self-consciously wrapped her sweater tighter about her waist. "Your perceptiveness is so uncanny. Yes, Tiffany, I genuinely want to help you in any way I can. That's from the heart. But—and please don't think less of me as a woman of God—but I have been questioning God lately, sort of."

Tiffany leaned back into her chair. She felt uneasy hearing someone as devout as Myra questioning her faith. "What do you mean, Myra? As a new convert, that is scary for me to hear you say, because if you're questioning God, then where does that leave me?"

Myra closed her eyes, feeling slightly embarrassed, but her eyes watered from her inner pain. "I can't keep it boxed in anymore, Tiffany. I just don't get why it hasn't happened. Why hasn't God given me a child? It is eating away at me, and all I do is bake and eat, bake and eat. Look at me. I am almost three times the size I was in high school. I pray, I fast, and I pray, and I am not getting any answers. Then there are women like you who got pregnant without even trying, and you may not have even wanted a child."

Tiffany instinctively gave Myra a hug. "Oh, Myra."

"Please don't take offense at what I'm saying. I just feel this big, empty void in me, and nothing else matters. I want a baby so bad, it consumes me. There is not a single day that goes by that I don't think about getting pregnant. And I know it sounds selfish, but I can't stand to see Ms. Wise."

"Whoa. Myra, you just lost me. Who's Ms. Wise?"

"My coworker. She's pregnant, and I have to see the joy on her face and listen to her talk about things I can't relate to, and it is tearing me up inside. I am doing everything . . . counting days . . . everything. It's like it's never going to happen."

Myra cried, and her potent anguish brought tears to Tiffany's eyes. Tiffany drew her into the living room area, and they sat together on the love seat. "Myra, you keep saying what you are doing, but what about faith in God? I know I sound childish, but that is what I hear Pastor Johnston talk about, and it helped me. I put my life and my faith in God, and I know that whatever happens to me, God will be there with me. I have to believe that, Myra. Don't you believe that?"

"Yes, I do. It's just . . . I don't know. I'm confused, I guess, because I keep wondering if God is not going to do what I am asking Him to do."

"But we are God's creations, and we can't dictate what God should do with us."

"Somebody has been paying attention to Pastor Johnston's messages," Myra said with much self-deprecation. "I know I am not being much of an example to you right now, and I am sorry for that." Myra bent her head and cried.

Tiffany lifted Myra's head. "Myra, I don't think less of you. I think of you as human. Maybe God allows us to go through certain situations to bring us closer to Him. If I hadn't been diagnosed with cancer, I probably would be too busy trying to stay on top of the pop charts to even think about God. But now I am a daughter of Christ, and I finally feel truly loved."

"You're right, Tiffany," Myra acknowledged. "God is testing me, and I keep failing the test."

"No, Myra, you're testing God. You can't test the one who knows it all. I've learned that, and I have to accept that."

Myra wiped her face and looked Tiffany solemnly in the eyes. "Tiffany, look at you, a newborn babe preaching to me."

Tiffany gave a self-conscious chuckle. "Well, I wouldn't say that I'm preaching, but I will say it has to be God."

"Hallelujah." Myra exhaled. "Thank you. It felt good just to unburden."

"I feel the same way, Myra. Hey, did you talk over your taking a leave of absence with Neil?"

Myra squirmed. "No. Not yet."

"Well, are you going to?"

"Yes."

"Will you tell him today?"

"Yes."

"Can you say something other than yes?"

"Yes. I love you, girl."

"I love you too, friend."

Chapter Thirty-three

Monday, January 19. Martin Luther King Jr. Day. How had it gotten here so fast? Tiffany wondered. Darnell was at her house at seven o'clock in the morning.

Winona had referred her to a specialist known for discretion and quick results. She had previously arranged for Pierce to provide his specimen, so Tiffany, Darnell, and Karlie huddled in her Escalade. Darnell drove them to the clinic that would finally answer the big question of Karlie's paternity. At the last minute, Ryan had been called away on business, but he promised to reschedule.

Two days after they took the test, Tiffany received the phone call.

The results were in.

The four of them raced over to the center as if there was a three-alarm fire. It was 99 percent conclusive that neither Darnell nor Pierce was Karlie's father.

"No, no, please. It cannot be." Tiffany clutched her chest. Darnell grabbed Tiffany to keep her from falling.

Pierce shouted, "Test it again. I know I'm her father. Just look at the resemblance. She looks like me." He continued his diatribe in the vehicle until Darnell dropped him outside his gate.

"You'll get your check in the mail," Tiffany coldly informed him. Not even Karlie's presence had kept his greed at bay.

"Thank the Lord for that small favor," Darnell said as soon as the car door slammed. He took off at great speed.

"I'm relieved that Pierce is not. I'm just glad to get that leech off my back for good." Tiffany directed her words to Darnell, but her eyes were pinned on Karlie, who had remained conspicuously silent.

Karlie turned her head. She had nothing to say, but her pain was evident by the tears that she wiped away.

When Darnell pulled up to the house, Karlie got out of the car. "I'm going to Tanya's," she said and took off.

Tiffany knew better than to stop her daughter then. Truly, she also needed some time alone to deal with the disclosure. "I was so sure—was hoping actually—that you were her father."

"I know it would have made things easier," Darnell agreed.

"I've got to go," Tiffany said and opened the door. She dashed up the steps, opened her front door, ran up the stairs, and locked herself in the bathroom. "I thought Karlie was his, Lord. At least I had hoped she was." She cried so hard that she started vomiting. Tiffany heaved over the toilet bowl countless times before she stretched out across the bathroom floor. Feeling the bile rise again, Tiffany started to get up when she saw blood. Tiffany knew that was not a good sign. Panic hit her full force, and she started hyperventilating.

Hyperventilation led to more tears.

"Tiffany. Are you okay in there?" From his tone, she knew Darnell's mouth was pressed against the door.

Darnell had not gone home, she realized. In a haze, it all came back to her that she had left her front door ajar. Tiffany dragged her body to the bathroom door. From her position on the floor, she answered him. "Yes, Darnell, I am okay. I just need some time. Okay?

Go home to April and Amber. I promise to call you later."

Darnell tried to coax her into unlocking the door, but Tiffany just needed him to go.

"I've got to talk to God," she whispered.

Those magic words led to his departure and a promise to call.

"Lord, this is way too much for me to handle. I don't know how to deal with this life-terminating disease and baby daddy drama at the same time. Plus, how do I handle falling in love with Darnell? God, please, just help me. I need you."

Tiffany finally found the strength to get to her feet and cracked open the door, expecting Darnell to pounce on her. Fortunately, he really had gone home. Disappointment washed over her being, and she walked into her bedroom. She dug out some kind of sleep apparel, changed, and went under the covers.

Tiffany curled her body in a fetal position to enclose all the pain and hurt she was facing. If it were not for Karlie and God, she would end everything right there. She would imbibe all the pills she had left just so she would not have to deal with another day. However, Tiffany knew she could not. She was going to be there for her daughter to the bittersweet end. She owed Karlie that much.

"Why didn't you tell me? Why did you let me go through life believing a lie?" Karlie accused.

Seeing the tears stream down Karlie's face, Thomas knew the moment had come. He had just walked down the stairs to make himself some cereal when he saw Karlie sitting there.

"So, Tiffany finally told you the truth?"

"Yes, Mom told me, and when she did, I was so angry at you that I vowed never to call or speak to you again. But I realized that I needed answers and that instead of running, I need to face things head-on. My mother ran, and look where it got her. I refuse to run."

Thomas admired her courage. "You know you're nothing like your mother was at your age. You got spunk. She did a really good job with you."

Karlie knew an evasion when she heard one. "Can you please just answer my question? Why didn't you tell me the truth when I first came to see you all those months ago? Why did you keep on pretending to be my father, though you aren't?"

"Well," Thomas said, hedging, "I don't know for sure I am *not* your father."

"But why didn't you tell me?" Karlie asked, persisting.

She just wouldn't let up. Thomas huffed. "Maybe I didn't tell you because—"

"Because what?"

"Because I wanted you to be. That's why. Karlie, I've loved you from the first time I saw you."

Karlie's shoulders drooped, and she shook her head dejectedly. "Considering how you left when I was a baby and barely had any contact, you really expect me to believe that?"

Thomas took her by the hand. He could see her reluctance, but at least she didn't pull away. *Good.* That meant he could still rectify things. "I can see you don't believe me. Put on your coat, and come with me."

"Aren't you going to get dressed?" Karlie asked when she saw him push his feet into his house slippers and put a coat on over his plaid pajamas.

"Don't need to. Just come on."

The two left his house and got into his car. Thomas did not wait for the engine to warm up before he pulled off.

"Where are we going?"

"You'll see. Just be patient."

Karlie sulked the entire ten minutes, until he expertly pulled the car into the driveway. "Where are we?"

"My mother's house."

Karlie looked skeptical, but she got out of the car without a word. She did slam the door to make her displeasure clear. Just as they got to the front door, Karlie stopped and put a hand on his shoulder. "Uh, I'm a little scared. I mean, I've never met your mother before."

Thomas slapped his head. "Karlie, I am sorry. I am such an idiot. I didn't even explain. My mother is not here. She's at church or volunteering or something. She has nothing to do with why I brought you here. Come on."

Karlie breathed a sigh of relief. She didn't know what to call Thomas, her maybe dad, and to meet her grandmother or non-grandmother would have been too much.

Thomas walked Karlie through the house and into his art room.

Karlie ran her hands all over his supplies and eyed his paintings.

"Be careful," Thomas called out sharply. Seeing her jump back, he softened his tone. "I'm working on a major commission and am just paranoid about something happening before I get done."

"I understand. Thanks for bringing me here."

Thomas went into his storage area and hunted through his paintings. He searched until he found what he was looking for. Triumph evident in every step, Thomas walked back into the room. "This is for you."

Karlie appeared quizzical, but she unwrapped the huge frame until she recognized the face. "It's me."

"Yes, you were nine months old. I painted it from memory."

"Are you serious? You really painted this from scratch?"

"Yes," Thomas confirmed and with his finger poked his temple. "From here. I loved you from the first time I saw you. You were my little angel with all those curls. I mean, I just couldn't get enough of you."

"Wow." Karlie was speechless. It was impossible not to feel his love, as it was evident in every brushstroke.

"Thanks. I don't ever intend to part with it. I usually keep it hanging in the front foyer at my house, but I took it down to . . . you know . . . I don't even remember why now." Thomas scratched his head before taking the painting and placing it by the door. "I won't forget it this time." He grinned. Then he retrieved a gift-wrapped package and handed it to her.

Holding her questions at bay, Karlie opened the present and lifted out a chenille blanket. "Ooohh. It's so soft." She rubbed it against her cheek.

Thomas jumped like a kid. "Open it. Open it."

Karlie opened the blanket and stood up to get a good look at it. Her mouth dropped open. "The painting. You put my picture on here."

"Yes." Thomas beamed. "I had it made for you. Karlie, I hope you like it and that you will keep it. It would really mean a lot to me."

"I will. Thanks so much. Daddy, are you going to take the paternity test?"

Her calling him Daddy was not lost on Thomas. Karlie had judiciously avoided calling him anything before. "Um, Karlie, that's between your mother and me."

"Listen, I know you're angry with Mom, but think about me. I need to know who I belong to. Mom is dying . . . dying. I don't know what's going to happen to me once she's gone, and . . ." Karlie broke into tears.

Thomas felt like a heel. "Karlie, please. I just don't want to know. And, okay, yes, maybe I am punishing your mother too. But I need time."

"I understand." Karlie shrugged and looked down at her feet. In a small voice, she asked, "Can you take me home please?"

"Karlie, I—"

"Please just take me home."

Thomas complied, but when he dropped her off, he did say, "I'm sorry to disappoint you, Karlie."

"Neither Darnell nor Pierce passed the test. I mean, the paternity results were negative."

Thomas nodded. This meant he had a fifty-fifty chance. "I'll think about it. Just give me some time to get my mind settled."

"Time is one thing I don't have," Karlie replied sadly.

Neil walked over to Tiffany's house, acknowledging that he had been purposely avoiding her. He'd had another dream about her that had totally perplexed him. He wished that he could just keep it out of his head. His throat was sore from the prayers of pardon to God. But his concern for her welfare overshadowed everything else.

"Hi," he greeted her once she answered the door.

"Hey, yourself." Tiffany stepped aside and silently watched him enter.

"Came by to check on you," Neil explained.

"It's been a while," she commented wryly. "I missed you, Neil. Seeing you at church is not the same as when you call or come by."

Neil at once berated himself for his inconsiderate and selfish feelings. "I figured with Myra coming by and you dating Darnell that I am now low on the totem pole. I did leave a card in your mailbox."

"Don't tell me you are going to get funny on me like that." Tiffany slapped him playfully. "I need you. You know that, and I appreciated your card."

Neil saw the sincere emotions reflected in her eyes and smiled. "It's good to hear that."

"Yeah, well, you'll always be special to me in so many ways you cannot even begin to understand."

Neil wished her statement did not cause his insides to swell with happiness. "So how're you feeling?"

"Things are not looking so good lately."

"What do you mean?" Neil at once became alarmed. He knew from experience that Tiffany tended to understate everything.

"I started coughing up blood again, and lately I have been so weak and cold. Nothing I do helps the chill," Tiffany confessed. "Then the results came back, and neither Darnell nor Pierce is Karlie's father."

Neil enveloped Tiffany in a huge embrace before releasing her. "So what about Ryan and Thomas?"

"Well, I have to reschedule with Ryan, and I haven't contacted Thomas since that day at the restaurant. I know Karlie has been spending time with him, but that hasn't moved him to take the test."

"Tiffany, you have to," Neil implored. "That way you will know for sure who the father is and eliminate the guessing game."

"You are right," Tiffany confirmed. "But Thomas hates me."

"He does not," Neil disagreed. "He is just angry."

"I don't know." Tiffany was not too sure.

"So how's Karlie taking the news?" Neil asked, changing the subject.

"She seemed to be okay."

"And how's everything with Darnell?" He asked the question uppermost in his mind.

Tiffany blushed. "They could not be better. Things are going so good that I'm scared to tell him about how sick I've been feeling."

"You should," Neil advised her. "He is your partner, and what affects you affects him."

"It's not like that with us, Neil," Tiffany argued. "We both agreed not to get emotional."

"You mean to tell me your heart is not involved?" Neil asked the question, though he knew her answer.

Tiffany could not look him in the eyes but gave a small telling shrug.

"I thought so. So you'd better open up to him and tell him what's going on."

Neil left her house shortly after that and went home. As soon as he opened the door, he saw Myra waiting for him. They had barely spoken to each other ever since she started her leave of absence. Neil felt she should have spoken to him first about it, and the ensuing shouting match was one of the worst of their entire marriage.

Myra wore the frown of a judge, and she had a huge box of doughnuts open. He knew what that meant. Nevertheless, he put on a brave front.

"Waiting for me?" Neil asked, making light conversation.

"Where are you coming from?"

"Tiffany's," Neil answered and then asked, "Is there a problem with that?"

"What's going with you two? I mean, you are always over there and always up in her face. You know more about her business than I do."

Neil looked at his wife as if she had suddenly sprouted horns. "She is dying, and she needs a friend. You know that because you are supposedly her best friend, and you've been going there, so you know how she is feeling. What else do you need to know?"

"Did you ever sleep with her?"

"What!" Neil exclaimed, and his eyes popped open at her question. Myra had hit him from left field with that question. For a split second, he wondered if he had called Tiffany's name in his sleep during that dream, but then dismissed it. Myra would have mentioned that.

"Did you ever sleep with Tiffany?" Myra spelled it out again. She picked up another doughnut and took a huge bite. "I want to know. It seems as if she has slept with everybody else around here, so why not you too?"

"Myra, are you all right?" Neil looked keenly at his wife. Her dark mood was hard to handle, and Neil was unsure of how to communicate with her. It was ironic how he was able to help others with their relationships but seemed to be clueless when it came to his own.

"Of course I am all right. Just quit stalling, and answer my question." Myra got up and went to the refrigerator. She popped open one of the bottles of wine that they usually kept chilled and poured some in a paper cup.

Neil watched, completely stumped, as she guzzled the liquid contents as if they were water. He wished he knew what had brought this on. Myra was behaving like she was on the verge of a breakdown.

His confusion led to anger. "I can't believe that you would even open your mouth to utter such garbage. Use all those degrees you have to think coherently. If you do not know me better than that by now, then I must be wasting my time."

Neil put his coat on, threw the door open, and slammed it behind him.

Myra sat down at the table and cried. What was wrong with her? She knew that Neil was a rare breed of man that was capable of being committed to one woman. Myra berated herself that she had even allowed that thought to take root and fester in her mind.

Myra knew it had a lot to do with the fact that her period was due in two days and her hormones were out of whack. She always seemed to go a little psycho because she was going to be in pain again. She was going to face the agony of having another potential child ripped from inside her. Myra honestly did not know if she could handle it. She needed a miracle.

♫ Chapter Thirty-four

Ryan entered his home and slumped into the couch, tremendously exhausted. He was going to have to slow down. He was getting too old for the constant running around his business dictated. He had been gone for a whole month, and he missed his wife.

He called out, but no one was home.

Ryan placed a call to Tiffany. "Hi. I am back in town until Thursday. So I'll take the test if you can work your magic to get me in."

"Thanks, Ryan. Karlie and I both appreciate your doing this. I just want to get some closure."

"Okay. Just give me a time and place, and I will be there."

"Okay. Thanks for keeping your promise to call, and I will make all the arrangements and get back to you."

After getting off the phone, Ryan allowed his mind to wander to thoughts that were more desirable. He thought about Patricia and how he missed her terribly when he was away.

Ryan moved, and something crinkled beneath him. Realizing it was a crumpled piece of paper, Ryan picked it up.

It was Brian's report card. Ryan leaned forward once he saw the grades listed there. He had not known his son was even going to school. But evidently, Brian had been doing the right thing and had the Bs and Cs to prove it. There was not one derogatory comment from any of his teachers, and they all spoke about his dramatic improvement.

Suddenly, Ryan remembered that Brian had called him and left a voice mail asking him to call him back. Ryan had played the message right before the plane took off and had completely forgotten to return his son's call. He did not know how that had managed to slip his mind.

Ryan placed a call to Brian's cell but got his voice mail. "Brian, this is Dad. Please call me."

For the first time in a long time, Ryan felt awful and shamefaced. He had not spoken to or seen Brian in days, and that was unacceptable. Ryan had not even been there to see Brian's expression when he received his new car, which Patricia had bought him. Thinking about it, Ryan doubted he could identify Brian's favorite food or movie, or anything else, for that matter.

"I've got to do better."

Brian was obviously trying to reform his ways, and Ryan was never around to congratulate him on it. He felt an urgency to correct that.

His cell phone rang. "Hello?"

"I'd like to speak to Mr. Ryan Oakes please. This is Detective Younger."

"This is he."

"Mr. Oakes, I'm going to need you to come down to the precinct. Your son, Brian Oakes, and a friend were arrested tonight."

Ryan's heart almost stopped beating at that news. "Arrested? What are the charges?"

"Mr. Oakes, we will tell you more once you are here. You might want to give your attorney a call."

As soon as the call ended, Ryan called Counselor Graham and then Patricia. She was in surgery, so he scribbled a quick note and left it for her. He then drove over to the police station. His heart pounded and ached at the same time. He visualized Brian behind bars, and the image shook him to his core.

Chilled, Tiffany pulled on a sweater over her turtleneck and went back to the window to wait on the private car service Winona had previously arranged for her. Tiffany did not feel well enough to drive, so she already planned to tip the driver, who was crazy enough to venture out in weather like this.

She prayed while she waited. "Lord, I pray for Brian. Help him. Heal his heart." It was simple and to the point. Though it lacked the flowery embellishments of others' never-ending prayers, Tiffany believed God heard.

About twenty minutes later, Tiffany entered the police station. Ryan saw her at once and got up to give her his seat. But he couldn't hide his surprise. "Brian called you?"

"Yes. So what's going on?" Tiffany didn't feel she had to explain the relationship she had with his son. That was something Ryan would have been aware of had he been actively involved in his son's life.

"I don't know," he whispered. "The only thing they told me is to sit here and wait and someone would see me." Ryan grappled with the fact that Brian had called Tiffany—and not him.

"Where's your attorney?" Tiffany asked.

"He's still on his way."

"So did you at least get to see Brian?"

"No."

Tiffany saw the worry and love etched all over Ryan's face. She only wished Brian could witness that. Someone moved, and Ryan was finally able to sit next to her. He grabbed Tiffany's hand for some comfort. She literally felt his hand shake in her grasp and gave it a tight squeeze to reassure him.

After exactly thirty-three minutes, Counselor Graham walked through the door. He met with Ryan briefly before going to talk to the arresting officer. After a brief exchange of words, Graham went back to the holding cell to speak with Brian.

A couple of minutes later, Graham walked into their view. He spoke to the arresting officer before heading over to them.

"Brian is scared but all right. The police are about to question him, and I am going to be there to guide him through the process."

"Has he said anything about what he did?" Ryan asked Graham. He did not wait for a response before firing off another question. "Can I go in to sit with him?"

"Brian told me that he went by his friend Alfred's house to hang out since he was home alone. Alfred asked him to drive him somewhere, and Brian agreed. He said that he was not speeding or anything, but the police pulled him over. The officer searched the car and found that Alfred had marijuana in his pocket. The officer arrested them both immediately. I believe they impounded his car. I will get the address for you." Graham excused himself for a minute to get a cup of water.

Once he returned, he said, "Brian was not doing any drugs, Mr. Oakes. He did not know his friend had any on him, either. The good thing is that Alfred is backing up Brian's story and confessed that the drugs were his. Hopefully, they should release Brian after all the paperwork is done."

Ryan repeated his other question. "So am I allowed in there for this? After all, Brian is still a minor."

"Well, you are allowed, but Brian does not want you in there," Graham admitted.

"Say what?" Ryan went red in the face and looked as if he was about to blow his top.

Tiffany had remained silent during their exchange but now stepped forward to place her hand on Ryan's arm. "Ryan, respect your son's wishes."

"Ask him again," Ryan commanded. "Tell him his father wants to be in there."

Graham declined to comment and went back into the room to speak with Brian. But Brian could not be cajoled or persuaded. Graham stuck his head out and mouthed the word "No" before going back into the room.

Hearing the door close with a bang, Ryan lost his fire and slumped back into his chair. Tiffany empathized with him, but she knew that Brian had good reason to feel the way that he did.

"Why doesn't he want me in there with him?" Ryan said with a small sob. "I am his father. I should be there."

Tiffany felt Ryan's desolation and knew she had to make him at least understand. "Maybe Brian does not want you there because he thinks you are going to jump on him. Maybe he does not like the fact that the only time you seem to pay him any attention is when he gets into trouble. Maybe he resents the fact that you are never around."

Tiffany paused, half expecting Ryan to take a swing at her for her candor. She had no right interfering in his affairs. Ryan's relationship with his son, or lack of it, was not her business. Tiffany wondered if she should have bitten her tongue but dismissed any regret. He had asked a question, and she had told him no lie. He was a grown man and the head of major corporations. Ryan could surely handle a few tough truths.

Ryan took out his handkerchief and wiped at the tears that filled his eyes. "You are right. Brian wants nothing to do with me because I am a bad father."

Tiffany had not expected Ryan to react with such emotion and sensitivity. He didn't seem like the type to break down in tears. She felt her heart soften, especially since he had not taken affront at her statement.

Tiffany held Ryan in a loose embrace and soothed him. "Ryan, you are not a bad father. You need to spend time to get to know your son. Ryan, that is something you can change, starting today. Brian loves you, and he only wants to know that you are going to love him unconditionally. He only wants to know that you believe in him."

"What if he rejects me? Or tells me it's too late?" Ryan said, worried.

Holding his hand, heedless of who was there to see, Tiffany prayed again.

At the end of her prayer, Tiffany was glad to see his tears ebb. She was not used to seeing men cry like this and did not know how to handle it with finesse. "Ryan, I do not think it's too late. It is never too late for love. Just know that Brian does not need your censure. He needs you to shower him with a lot of love and attention. He'll never be too old for that."

He must have been contented with her answer, because he seemed occupied with his own thoughts after that. Tiffany remained quiet to give him time to digest everything that she had said to him. She hoped that Ryan would make something positive come out of this incident, because Brian needed him desperately.

Tiffany could not help but think about her own comment. *It is never too late for love.* As she'd heard herself say it, Tiffany realized that it was true. She should not prevent herself from experiencing love because she was dying.

Not God's love.

Not Darnell's love.

Tiffany knew that she needed to embrace life with everything that she possessed. She needed to live her life to the fullest, just like anybody else.

Tiffany waited with Ryan for two hours, until Brian was finally released. Patricia called, but Ryan told her it was best for her to wait at home. Tiffany's heartstrings literally constricted when she saw Brian walk out with his head hung low. She only hoped that Ryan heeded her advice and went easy with his son.

Tears came to her eyes when she saw Ryan rush over to embrace his son. Brian looked up at his father with surprise before awkwardly returning the hug.

Brian's arrest had been a much-needed wake-up call for both of them, and she could only hope both men heeded the warning.

Tiffany got home that night and dashed under the covers, knowing she was going to pay for her stint out in the cold tomorrow. Going to the station and staying there so long was not a wise move on her part, for now tiredness seeped through her spine. Yet she had felt so strong when she was there. Now her aching joints were a big reminder that she was not well at all. She reached over her bed to check the answering machine.

Karlie had called to say she was staying the night at Tanya's.

Darnell had called too, to tell her that he was coming over early in the morning to take her out to breakfast.

It was almost eleven o'clock, but Tiffany returned his call. "Hey. I just wanted to hear your voice."

"Hi," Darnell said. "How did things go with Brian?"

Tiffany filled him in. She ended with, "I told Ryan we could just put off the testing until another time, and knowing him, we're probably looking at next month some time, which I hope is not the case."

"How do you feel about that?"

"Honestly, I am fine. I need a mental break, Darnell. I am just so tired." Tiffany yawned.

"Okay, I'm going to let you get some rest. So I'll just read Psalm ninety-one, and then we'll pray." She heard a drawer open and close and Bible leaves being shuffled before Darnell began reading. "He that dwelleth in the secret place of the most High shall abide under the shadow of the Almighty. . . ." Tiffany enjoyed listening to his voice. It soothed her, and she finally drifted into sleep.

Patricia entered Brian's room. Ryan had showed her his report card, and she was so proud of him. She was relieved to see him finally making the most of his God-given potential. Brian was so talented and gifted, and she was glad that he was beginning to do something positive with his abilities. Patricia knew that Tiffany and Karlie had a lot to do with that. Brian seemed to be flourishing under their friendship.

Privately, Patricia conceded that in a way she had given up on her son. She had stopped expecting him to do the right thing. Tired of the phone calls and the complaints from Brian's teachers, she had consoled herself with the fact that even though she could not do anything for her own child, she was saving the lives of others. Patricia also did not have a clue how to reach

Brian. Her hat went off to Tiffany. Tiffany seemed to share a bond with her daughter and with Brian that amazed Patricia.

Patricia watched the way in which Tiffany communicated with the teens and marveled. She was beginning to see that all the parenting books that she bought and read could be wrong. Patricia was learning that every child was different, and she had to make a bigger effort to get to know and accept her son the way that he was. That required some rethinking on her part, because science and reason had governed and dictated her entire life. Raising a child put all those theories in the garbage can. It was completely out of her realm.

Nevertheless, Patricia needed to have a heart-to-heart talk with her son. She was very upset about his arrest. Luckily, Brian's friend had come through for him, or else he would be facing time. God had definitely smiled on him.

"Brian." Patricia gently shook him awake.

Brian swatted her hand away and burrowed deeper into his pillow. Patricia shook him again. This time Brian slowly opened his eyes.

"Brian, I need to talk to you."

"Mom?"

"Yes. Brush your teeth, and meet me in the kitchen in five minutes."

Brian hurried to do her bidding and went into the kitchen. He glanced at the clock. He could not remember the last time he had been up at eight o'clock on a Saturday morning.

"Sit down, Brian," Patricia instructed.

Brian did not argue with her and took a seat around the small dinette. It was an antique made out of solid mahogany wood. The refurbished chairs were exquisite. Most of the time, Brian did not eat in here. He often camped out in the family room. That way if he spilled anything, his mother would not lose her cool.

"Brian let me start off by saying how proud your father and I are of you. Your grades are a great improvement. That is why I cannot understand why you would still be hanging out with those lowlifes that you call your friends." Patricia looked at him, demanding an answer.

Ryan came in on the tail end of her comment and sat down to listen. He wanted an answer as well.

Brian gulped. This was the first time in a long time that Brian could remember both of his parents sitting before him. He thought about the censure in their voices and wondered if they were ready for the truth.

He decided that it was time that he told them what was on his mind. His brief stint in jail was his wake-up call that he couldn't keep his feelings hidden. He was ready to come clean. "You both do not have a clue how I feel, do you?" Brian said with repressed anger. He jumped from the chair and walked around the table several times, grappling with how to express himself.

"Then please explain." Ryan sounded tortured.

"We are listening, and we want to understand," Patricia added gently.

"Is this what it took?" Brian bellowed, coming to an abrupt halt. "It took me getting locked up for you two to pay me any attention."

"That is not true," Patricia fervidly denied. "We both love you, Brian."

"It *is* true," Brian vehemently shot back, with tears falling from his eyes as his emotions came bubbling to the surface with full force. "All my life I have lived in the shadows. You both love each other so much that you have no room left for me." Seeing his father's mouth open, Brian held up his hands to thwart an interruption. "All my friends think I am so lucky that my parents are still together. But I do not feel the same way, because I have always had to compete for your love." Brian began crying again. "You two are always off together somewhere and never once think to include me."

"We did not think you would want to hang out with a couple of old fogies. We didn't think kids your age thought it was cool," Ryan defended with a gasp.

"You never asked," Brian accused. "You just assumed. The only time you two ever pause from your busy schedule is when I get into trouble. You ask why I still hang out with my friends. Well, I will tell you. It is because when Alfred called, he told me how much he missed hanging out with me. I thought that I owed it to him to go, because I could not remember the last time my parents ever said those words to me. I am so sick of being in this lonely house all by myself. Tiffany was the one who made me realize that I was only hurting myself with all the crazy stunts I pulled just to get your attention. That is why I started going to school, and I even quit smoking. But you both were too busy to even realize that."

Patricia started to cry from the impact of his truthful words. She saw now just how selfish she and Ryan had been. Brian was right. She had not noticed that he had quit that bad habit.

"You made your mother cry," Ryan said to Brian. "Is that what you wanted?"

Brian got up. "No. I just want . . ." He stopped, unsure of how to continue.

"What do you want, Brian? Please tell me, because I do not have a clue," Ryan stated.

"I want to feel as if my parents love me. Especially you, Dad." Brian finally found the courage to utter the words that he had been dying to say for years.

"I love you, son," Ryan said with tenderness. "I have loved you from the day I saw you. That is why I love your mother so much, because she gave you to me."

Brian choked up at his father's admission. The burden around his heart lifted, and he felt joy surge within his body at his father's sincerity. He saw love shining from his father's eyes. Eyes that were centered on him, not his mother. Overcome, Brian jumped up to give his father a tight hug. "I am sorry, Dad."

Ryan squeezed his son hard. This was the first time in ages that his son had called him Dad. Brian usually did his very best to avoid calling him anything at all.

Patricia looked at the father and son embrace and dried her tears. "Things are going to be better with the three of us from now on." She had been too busy working to notice how truly wonderful her son was, and that was going to change. "Brian, you will never doubt our love for you ever again."

♪ Chapter Thirty-five

After an interminable amount of time, Karlie and Jamaal broke their kiss. Since their first kiss, kissing had become their favorite pastime.

Everywhere and anytime they could, Karlie and Jamaal spent time engaging in some serious tongue action. They were at Tanya's house, and not even the thought of Tanya's parents busting in on them cooled their raging hormones.

For her part, Karlie knew it had a lot to do with the turmoil going on in her life. She needed something that felt stable in her life, and this was it.

As for Jamaal, Karlie suspected that it was just his libido. She did not mind as long as he kept his hands pressed against her back. The last time he had tentatively copped a feel of her behind, but Karlie was not having that.

Pastor Johnston's sermons about God's love stayed with her. Her mother constantly played CDs with gospel songs and scriptures.

Kissing would be her only guilty pleasure.

Karlie was grateful for Jamaal at this point and time in her life. He was a solid presence that she had come to rely on to keep her sanity. Karlie felt comfortable telling him everything that was going on. She'd cried on his shoulder when she learned that neither Darnell nor Pierce was her father. She had not wanted her mother to see how much the news devastated her. Karlie supposed it had a lot to do with trying to discover where she came from. She needed to know that.

She needed to feel like she belonged to someone.

She needed a father to claim her.

You have me.

Ignorantly, Karlie interpreted that to mean Jamaal. She would have fainted had she known it was the Father reaching out to her.

Karlie's thoughts flowed back to Jamaal. She had not known when they first met that he would come to mean so much to her. He was her best friend and her rock. Jamaal appeared so tough in school that Karlie felt special to see this gentle and caring side of him.

He became impatient and moved closer to kiss her again.

Karlie backed away and put her hands against his chest. "Jamaal, we have to stop."

"Why?"

"Because I do not want things going any further."

"But I won't let it. You know that by now. I'm not going to make you do something you don't want to do," Jamaal pleaded.

"I know, but I am more worried about me," Karlie explained. "I am worried I might throw caution to the wind and do something stupid."

Jamaal moved even closer at that intriguing confession. "Really?"

"Yeah," Karlie admitted to him. Her face was beet-red.

"Well, I would not allow you to," Jamaal told her.

Karlie smirked with disbelief. She did not think there was a hot-blooded teenage boy out there who would say no to something like that.

"It's true, Karlie. I know what you are going through, and I would not take advantage of your vulnerability by having sex with you. When we have sex, it's going to be because we both want to, not because of any drama going on in our lives. Look what happened with both our mothers. Also, I know you've been reading your Bible."

"Did you say '*when* we have sex'?" Karlie was still stuck on that bold remark.

"Yes, when. As a matter of fact, it won't be sex, because we are going to make love," Jamaal promised. He had done it before with other girls, but they did not mean anything to him. Karlie did. To prepare, he'd borrowed romance novels out of the library to get some creative and romantic suggestions that would make their first union both memorable and enjoyable. Jamaal particularly wanted to give Karlie a night she would never forget.

"When . . . ," Karlie repeated, a little apprehensive at that thought.

"When," Jamaal confirmed. They had a good number of years ahead of them, but Jamaal was going to marry Karlie. He was confident their love would be that strong. It was the real thing, and he did not need to go looking anywhere else.

Tiffany was sick of the snow and the way it was making her feel. It was almost the end of March. Where was spring?

She stood by the window and watched the snow fall in huge clumps. The only thing nice was its beauty when it first fell. After that came the massive cleanup and the car accidents. At this moment, Tiffany missed the sun and warmth of Los Angeles.

Soon her thoughts returned to Darnell. She was in a serious conflicting position. On one hand, she wanted to be around him and just soak up all he had to offer.

But, on the other, she wanted to let him go, because she was only going to cause him heartache later on.

She knew Darnell was the best person to talk to about this, but she always stopped herself from disclosing that she was in love with him. That would only serve to complicate things even more between them. Worse yet, Darnell might agree and end things between them. Tiffany could not bear that possibility. Then what would she do?

Cancer was raging an even more powerful war against her body, and it was winning. Tiffany felt twice her age. She had to expend a lot of effort to even complete the exercise workouts. She might as well just stop with the whole thing.

She ate, but the food tasted paltry. It had lost its savor. Tiffany swallowed her food because she knew she needed the nutrients.

Nothing seemed right with her. She was just a shell of her former self.

You are more than a conqueror.

"I don't feel like one now, Lord."

Tiffany had been compelled to cancel several shows Winona had lined up for her. She had even had to renege on her television appearance with Lifetime and MTV for some type of "Where are they now?" program. She just was not well enough to do all that. In addition, trying to hide just how sick she was from Karlie was taking a strain on her system.

Unexpectedly, Tiffany sneezed and saw blood. She ran to get a napkin to stem the crimson flow. It was gushing from her nose and into her hands. Blood stained the cream sweater that she was wearing.

Upset, Tiffany raced up the stairs and into the bathroom to wash her hands. She swore that she was going to move in here soon given how much time she spent in here. She pulled her sweater over her head and ran to her bathroom sink to soak it in some Woolite. Then she climbed in bed.

Karlie called to say she would be home soon. Tiffany groaned a reply. She tossed and turned in her bed until daybreak.

Then, finally, she went to sleep.

Karlie called to her mom when she got in, and went to her mother's bedroom to check on her. Her mother was asleep. "Aw," she cooed in a low tone. Karlie touched her mother's forehead before giving her a tender kiss on the cheek. Tiptoeing out of the room, Karlie went to bed, unconcerned.

Darnell came over at precisely eight o'clock the next morning. "Hey, Karlie. Is your mom ready?"

Karlie looked at him in confusion. Her mother hadn't awakened yet, so she had no idea about her plans. "I don't know," Karlie replied. "I'd better go check on her."

Halfway up the stairs, the doorbell rang. Karlie was about to execute a U-turn to see who was at the door, but Darnell waved her up the stairs. Hearing Myra's "Hey. How is my patient?" Karlie bounded up the stairs and entered her mother's room.

She tapped her mother's shoulder and even tried to get her to sit up, but to no avail. Fear crept up her spine, and Karlie panicked and hollered, "Darnell, come quick! It's Mom. She's not waking up. I can't get her to wake up!"

"Jesus, have mercy," Myra called out as she raced up the stairs behind Darnell. Saying a quick prayer, Myra punched in the numbers for Neil's job to tell him what was going on.

***

Everybody gathered in the lounge at Winthrop University Hospital. They were all in various degrees of shock and disbelief about Tiffany's sudden decline.

Darnell had called the ambulance at about eight thirty, when neither he nor Myra were able to help her regain consciousness. Tiffany was in a deep sleep.

It was now three o'clock in the afternoon, and still she slept.

Karlie was completely devastated. She had not been allowed in the room, because Tiffany was in critical condition. "I want to see my mom," she cried into Myra's shoulder.

Darnell drank his fourth cup of coffee and wondered, What happened? He had just spoken to her the night before. They were supposed to have breakfast together. How had they ended up here at the hospital? Darnell did not relish that he had to make the necessary phone calls and spread the news. This was like what he went through with his wife all over again.

His mother was right. As he sat in the hospital lounge, Darnell knew that he did not have the constitution to go through this. He could not watch Tiffany get sicker and eventually die.

Somehow or another, he had suppressed the idea that Tiffany's death was imminent. Today was a harsh jump back into reality. Withholding a sob, Darnell got up to go to the restroom. He relieved himself and briskly washed his hands. Darnell looked at the face staring back at him in the mirror and saw how Tiffany's illness had taken a toll on him. His hands shook, and his insides hurt.

He had to pick up April and Amber soon. Darnell battled with guilt because he knew that he was secretly glad for a legitimate excuse to leave. He actually welcomed it because he did not want to be here. He could not stand the torture and the agony.

Darnell dried his hands and went back to the lounge to make his excuses to everyone. He determinedly ignored his conscience. He knew that if Tiffany awakened, she'd expect to see him. But he had to get out of there, or he was going to suffocate on his memories. He was not sure if he would be back.

Neil drove like there were devils chasing him. He screeched into the parking lot of Winthrop University Hospital and barged into the waiting room with a huge bang. His eyes scanned everybody in the room. Myra, Ryan, Patricia, Tanya and her parents, Brian, and Jamaal were all there. He saw Pastor Johnston and his wife as well and felt comforted that the man of God was there to lend his support.

Finally, his eyes locked with Karlie's.

Myra loosened her grip, and Karlie rushed over and fell into his arms. She started crying earnestly. Neil held her and tried to quell the tears forming in his eyes. "She is going to wake up, Karlie. Tiffany would not leave like this. She would not leave without saying good-bye."

"I don't know," Karlie cried. "I want my mother." Her tears made everyone else cry. "What am I going to do if she leaves me, Neil? I have nobody. I do not even know where I am going to live," Karlie cried with deep anguish.

"There, there." Neil patted her on the head. He did not have any direct answers to give her. "Everything always has a way of working out. Do not worry about that right now. You have to believe your mother is going to wake up."

Myra listened intently as Neil talked to Karlie. He knew the right words to say to calm the girl. She had to hand it to him; Neil had a gift for talking to people. Watching the two of them together, an idea began to form in her head.

♫ Chapter Thirty-six

Tiffany jumped awake. She raised her arms, only to find them connected to all sorts of machines and devices. By the beeping sound, Tiffany knew they were monitoring her heart rate and blood pressure.

She looked at the clock. It was eighteen minutes after five. She was up too early. How would she kill time before Darnell came for their breakfast date? She could work on the song she'd begun composing.

Then everything clicked. This wasn't her home. She was in a hospital ward.

Panicked, she jumped off the bed. She had to get out of there before Karlie came home.

With all the contraptions and wires, it was inevitable that Tiffany would fall. And she did with a loud thump.

Neil woke with a start. He had drifted off but now moved like lightning to assist Tiffany back into bed. "Hey, look who finally decided to wake up. You had me—I mean all of us—worried." Neil fetched her a glass of water to drink.

Tiffany took a huge gulp before asking, "What happened?"

"You have been asleep since last night. You did not wake up all day. I had to fight to get the doctors to let me in here. I finally convinced Karlie to get some sleep in one of the empty rooms. I'll go get her in a minute."

"What time is it?" Tiffany almost fainted when he told her it was 5:20 in the evening. "I have been asleep that long? Neil, it's scary, but it feels like I have been sleeping for just a couple hours."

"It was much longer than that," Neil responded.

"I've just been so tired and sick the past few days. I didn't think that—"

"That you could end up here? Tiffany, you have end-stage cancer. You know what that means. You cannot afford to ignore your body when it is time to rest. Tiffany, you have to accept that your body is going to . . ." Neil stopped, unable to go on. "Let me go get Karlie. I'll be right back."

At the door, Neil turned. "Tiffany, you have to get rest. I don't know what I would do without you." He left before she could respond.

Tiffany gulped down her tears. "I can't let Karlie see me like this." She smoothed her hair and straightened her gown. Tiffany shifted her body weight and moaned when she realized that a Foley bag had been inserted. She hated that thing with a passion because it took away the sensation of letting her know when she had to pee. It also hurt like heck when they removed it. Tiffany could be glad only for the fact that she was unconscious for the catheter insertion.

A doctor entered the room and identified himself as Dr. Layton. "Hi, Mrs. Knightly. I have conferred with Dr. Ettelman and will be overseeing your care."

Tiffany nodded her head.

"Your tumor continues to grow, and I do concur that surgery is not advisable, because it is in a precarious position. I see where you had previously attempted to shrink it using radiation therapy, but that proved unsuccessful. I will do the best I can to assist with your medicinal needs and to make your stay here as comfortable as possible."

Tiffany nodded her head at his tough news. "Thank you, Dr. Layton."

"We will keep you overnight, and you can choose to enter a specialized facility or to go home."

"I'm going home," Tiffany declared firmly.

Dr. Layton left after that.

The door cracked open.

Karlie sped over to her mother and grabbed her tight. Tiffany could see how red and puffy Karlie's eyes looked.

"I am so sorry I am putting you through all this," Tiffany whispered in her hair.

Karlie straightened and looked her mother in the eye. "Mom, you can't help that. I am just glad that you are still here. I was so . . ." She paused before finishing her sentence. "Scared."

Over Karlie's head, Tiffany mouthed, "Where's Darnell?"

Neil shrugged.

Tiffany spoke to Karlie for a little bit before she convinced her to leave the room to tell the others that she was okay. She wanted some more alone time with Neil.

As soon as Karlie left, Neil came over to sit on the bed. He leaned over and gave Tiffany a tender kiss on the lips.

"Welcome back," he greeted her again.

"It's good to be back," Tiffany replied before urgently saying, "Neil, I have got to find Karlie's father."

"I know." he agreed. "I will take care of it."

"It's too much to ask."

"No, it isn't," Neil assured her. "There's nothing I would not do for you. Just rest and let me be a friend."

"Okay." Tiffany felt her eyelids get heavy with sleep. Before sleep claimed her again, Tiffany grabbed Neil's hand with a strength that belied her illness. She moved in toward him and placed her lips against his to give him a small kiss laced with pure love, nothing sexual in nature.

Once she fell asleep, Neil took out his cell phone. It was time to make a certain call. It was time to call Merle, Tiffany's monster of a mother.

Tapping his feet impatiently, he heard the call go straight to voice mail. Neil left a brief detailed message. "Hi, Ms. Merle. This is Neil Jameson. Not that you give two cents, but I'm calling to let you know that Tiffany was admitted to Winthrop Hospital today. She's here if you care to see her—although judging by your past record . . . Well . . ." Neil hung up the phone without saying good-bye. He knew it was futile, but he hoped Merle returned the call or showed up. The witch would probably delete the message without a second thought.

Merle played her answering machine for the fifth time. "Who does Neil think he is? I don't want to hear anything from his scrawny behind. I have known him from when he was knee high, and now he leaves me this disrespectful message as if I am nothing."

Merle played with a huge bracelet on her left hand. "Tiffany has enough people always fawning around her. I am not going anywhere." She refused to change her stance after all these years because her daughter was dying.

Merle squeezed both her legs tightly with her hands. Her arthritis was acting up because of all this bad weather, but thankfully, it would finally feel like spring in a few days. She opened her door to check the mail-box, for her check usually came in around this time.

Merle did not feel an ounce of guilt for accepting the money. "She owes me after what she did."

You know Clifford raped her.

"Please." Merle refused to hearken to her conscience. There was no way she was wrong about Clifford. She had a sixth sense about those things, and Clifford had been many things, but he wasn't no pedophile and he wouldn't have done something so heinous—so vicious.

No, Tiffany instigated it. There was no other plausible explanation for why Clifford would have sex with her. Merle had never denied him any sexual favors, but Tiffany seduced him with her fast-trotting behind, and Clifford had been too drunk to turn that down.

Now, *that* Merle could understand. It was a classic case of the apple not falling far from the tree. Tiffany's daddy had seduced her and then run off with another woman without a backward glance. Clifford had been her father until he succumbed to emphysema, and Tiffany was so ungrateful to accuse Clifford, who had doted on her, of raping her.

Still, Merle felt a pull to draw close to her only child. Tiffany was her blood.

"No." Stubbornly, she resisted. If she tried to repair her relationship now, it would be an admission of her doubt. And she wasn't doubtful. She was sure about her, even though Tiffany seemed to have everyone fooled. A mother knew her child, and Tiffany's innocent act did not wash with her. Despite the fact that she sang like an angel, her daughter was still common trash.

"No. Sorry, Neil. Let Tiffany find her way out." Merle pressed the delete button and erased Neil's message from the machine and from her heart and mind.

"Hi. I'm looking for Tiffany Knightly's room."

"Sure. She's in room three-sixteen."

He saw Karlie with Neil from high school. Guilt attacked him with a renewed vengeance. He should have been there, and he could've kicked himself for not agreeing to the paternity test earlier.

Karlie spotted him and walked over to him. "Hi. Are you here to see my mom?"

"And you," Thomas replied. "I just wanted to check on you." Karlie hugged him, and his heart melted. "Oh, Karlie, I don't know why it took me so long to take the test, and now I fear I am too late."

Karlie looked up at him. "No, it's not too late."

"I just want you to know that no matter what the results are, I love you."

"I have loved you all my life. Mom didn't teach me anything else."

Overcome, Thomas decided to depart. "I'll come by and see your mother once she is out of the hospital." He nodded at Neil before heading home, feeling lighter than he had in years.

Days after she went into the hospital, the nurse escorted Tiffany in a wheelchair out of the hospital and into Neil's Benz. She put on a cheery face for Karlie, not wanting her to see how her heart was aching that Darnell had not visited or called. Tiffany understood why, but that had not eased the pain in her heart.

Karlie had noticed his absence and wanted to choke Darnell with her bare hands. When she returned to school, she was going to confront him and give him a piece of her mind. Teacher or not, nobody treated her mother that way.

Neil and Karlie settled Tiffany in the rear seat. Once they arrived at the house, they fussed over her until she was safely inside. There she greeted by a small group of friends. Tiffany saw the balloons and the WELCOME HOME banner and fought back tears.

"Myra even baked some of your favorite pies," Karlie told her.

"Oh, this is just too much." Tiffany held on to her heart. "Thank you, all."

Their love and concern made Darnell's absence easier to bear—almost. However, Tiffany would trust and lean on God.

Pastor Johnston walked over to her. "I am going to share a brief word with you, Tiffany. Remember, you are not alone. God is with you. All you have to do is cast all your cares upon Him. God can bear it all. Whatever you are facing, God can take it."

She held on to those words in the ensuing days, until she got on her feet and felt like herself again. Her appetite returned, and Myra had her on a newer and stricter holistic regime. She hired a night nurse so Myra could be home when Neil got in from work.

She was alive. That was what mattered. She'd been given more time, and she was going to grasp it with both hands.

Myra sat nervously at her kitchen table, waiting for Neil to come home. She wanted to discuss an urgent matter with him.

"Hi, babe," she called when he walked through the door.

Neil raised his eyebrow at his wife's cheery greeting. "Hi," she said as he walked in the kitchen. He was scared to say anything more for fear it would change her mood.

"I wanted to run something by you," Myra said.

Uh-oh. Neil sat down cautiously into the nearest chair, unsure what Myra had up her sleeve.

Myra read his dubious expression and laughed. "Relax. I just wanted to ask how you would feel if we were to take Karlie in."

Neil pulled his chair out and looked at Myra with amazement. That had to be the most selfless thing he had ever heard her say.

"I mean, if Tiffany agreed, it would be the perfect solution for everybody. Tiffany would have us to take care of Karlie, and I would finally have a child to call my own."

He had thought too fast. Myra was still always about Myra. He put his hand to his chin in thought. Even though her motives were selfish, Myra's suggestion was a good one. It was something that he had considered, but Neil had not broached the subject, unsure of how Myra would react.

"It is a good idea," Neil finally said.

Myra whooped and gave him a hug. "It's settled, then. I think you should be the one to tell Tiffany. If I do, it I might sound too desperate."

"Whoa." Neil attempted to slow Myra down. "Myra, Ryan and Thomas still have to take the paternity test, and then one of them has to make a decision. We have to wait."

Myra's face fell. Then she perked up. "I am going to trust God to work things out for me. I have been praying for a miracle, and I figured that Karlie is it. Karlie is my miracle child."

"Myra," Neil cautioned, "you know the saying about counting your chickens before they hatch."

"Yeah. Yeah," Myra declared, unconcerned. "But this chick has already hatched, and she is practically full grown." She chuckled at her own joke before going to busy herself upstairs.

"I'll go see Tiffany tonight and talk to her about it. But first let's pray about it and seek God's face."

When Neil arrived at her home, Tiffany was already in bed. He patiently waited as the night nurse took all the necessary vitals and filled in the chart. As soon as they were alone, he broached the subject of Karlie. Myra had already texted him to ask about Tiffany's response to their suggestion.

"Tiffany, I wanted to talk to you about something," Neil began.

Tiffany gave him a wide, trusting smile and patted a spot on the bed. Neil complied and sat on her left side near the edge of the bed. Gently, he took her hand in his.

"Myra and I had a talk, and we both would be delighted—honored, actually—to . . ." Neil paused, not sure how to put it into words.

"Just say it," Tiffany urged.

"Well, Myra and I were thinking that we would love to have Karlie. I mean that is if you need us to, we would welcome the idea of caring for her as our own." Neil knew his words sounded jumbled, but was there a correct way to tell a mother you wanted her child? He didn't think so.

"Neil, are you saying that both you and Myra would be willing to take care of my daughter when I am gone?"

"Yes," Neil said, "I like the way you phrased it better. It's not that we want you to die, but we just want you to know that the offer stands if you need it."

"Oh, Neil," Tiffany said. "I am so touched by your willingness to bless me. I cannot explain what it would mean to me." Tiffany burst into tears. It was as if a fifty-pound weight had been lifted off her shoulders. "I would love it, actually. You and Myra would be the most amazing parents for Karlie."

Neil smiled and patted Tiffany's hand. Tears filled his eyes. "No, Tiffany, it would be you blessing us by entrusting us with your most prized possession."

Tiffany gulped and whispered again, "Thank you, Neil, and thank Myra for me. Well, I'll thank her tomorrow."

"Well, I know that this is all contingent upon Ryan's and Thomas's test results and decisions. But if they have any qualms at all about caring for Karlie, then you know you have us." Neil felt a peace come over his being. He began praising God, and Tiffany joined in.

Neil called Myra to let her know Tiffany had accepted their offer. Myra was so overjoyed that her whooping boomed through the phone.

♫ Chapter Thirty-seven

Darnell's palms were sweating, and it wasn't because of the warm spring weather. He sat in his car, parked outside Tiffany's house, filled with apprehension. He had considered calling, but he did not want Karlie blocking his call. She gave him mean looks whenever he passed her in the hallways, and Darnell felt two feet high. Walking out on a sick woman in the hospital was abominable. His mother had chewed his ears off when she heard how he had handled things with Tiffany. Darnell heard a sharp rap and pressed the automatic button to lower his window.

Karlie had spotted him. "What're you doing here?" She dispensed with any formalities and pretense of being polite.

"I am here to see your mother," Darnell answered.

"Why? You just up and left her in the hospital." Karlie's fiery eyes scared him. "She did not deserve that."

Darnell pressed the button to roll the window up and got out of the car. His tone was apologetic when he said, "I know, Karlie, and that is why I am here."

Karlie crossed her arms defiantly, feeling torn. A huge part of her wanted to insult him and send him on his way, but she knew that her mother would probably never forgive her if she did that.

Darnell noticed Karlie's offensive stance and decided to wait it out. He could be just as tough and stubborn.

But if he had Karlie pegged right, Darnell knew that her impeccable upbringing would win out against her rebellion.

He was right. Darnell silently observed Karlie as she turned around and stomped to the gate. She opened it with a wide swoosh and then opened the front door with one huge swoop, making her displeasure known. She ventured into the house, then disappeared to her room.

Darnell wasn't bothered by Karlie's antics. He was just grateful that she had let him in. From where he stood, Darnell could see that Tiffany was in the living room. What could he say to make things right? Saying a silent prayer, Darnell walked forward and entered the house.

"Hello, Tiffany," he called, but she did not answer. He repeated his greeting as he strolled into the living room but still received no response.

Tiffany hadn't turned around, so Darnell walked around to look her in the face, determined that she was not going to ignore him.

"Tiffany," he said again. "I'm sorry, baby. I'm sorry for walking out on you like that, and I know it's been a couple weeks, but I was scared. It seems dumb, I know, but it is the truth. I could not bear to see you like that, because I am in love with you, Tiffany. I did not plan to feel that way, so I retreated. I do not know what I could ever say to mend things between us." Darnell stopped. He did not know how else to say he was sorry.

"Actually, it's been three weeks, and you could start by telling me that again," Tiffany answered.

"What?" Darnell scrunched his face. She'd lost him with that comment.

"Repeat the part about how you love me," Tiffany reiterated with a huge smile.

"I love you, Tiffany." Darnell rushed over to her and got on his knees. "I know we had an agreement that we would not fall in love, but I did fall in love with you. I am miserable without you, and I want to spend whatever time you have left with you."

Tiffany cried. "I love you too, Darnell. And I do understand why you left the way you did." She reached over and hugged Darnell before kissing him passionately.

"I am so glad you could find it in your heart to forgive me," Darnell said, trailing kisses all over her face.

"I just knew all you really needed was time. Time to find your way back to me."

Ryan and Thomas both went in to take the paternity test. It was over in a matter of minutes. Both men returned home for the weekend, pondering how their lives would change with a teenage daughter. The results would be in that Tuesday.

That same Saturday, Tiffany took a turn for the worse. She had a fever from pneumonia, which racked her body. She spat up so much mucus and blood that it had to weigh a good six ounces. Myra drove her to the doctor's. Dr. Layton took one look at her and hospitalized her instantly.

Her condition was so dire that Dr. Layton proposed moving ahead with the risky surgical procedure to remove the tumor from her lung.

Tiffany discussed the proposal with Karlie. "What do you think, Karlie? Do you think I should do it? I will do it for you if you want."

Karlie scrunched her lips and thought for several minutes. "Mom, I don't think you should take the risk. Not with a fifty-fifty percent chance."

"Okay. I understand," Tiffany agreed. She had blockage in her airways and was in tremendous pain, and the doctor promised to increase her medication.

Karlie spent the entire weekend filled with worry. Neil and Myra opened their heart and home. She would stay with them when she was not by her mother's bedside. With Myra's help, Karlie made some chicken soup and tenderly spoon-fed her mother the broth. Karlie became frightened when she saw how much of an effort it took Tiffany for to swallow and keep down the soup.

Karlie was in Neil's kitchen, eating some ice cream but mostly staring into space, when Neil walked in the room to check on her.

"Karlie, what're you doing up at this hour?" Neil asked. It was almost three o'clock in the morning.

"Just thinking."

"Speak what's on your mind," Neil commanded and took a seat next to her.

"I don't want to burden you anymore, Neil," Karlie said. "You have done enough."

Neil rested his hand across Karlie's back to comfort her. "Karlie, you can never be a burden to me."

"I hate this disease with every fiber of my being. I hate what it is doing to Mom physically and emotionally. I'm trying to remain hopeful, but Mom is not going to make it to my sixteenth birthday."

"That's right!" Neil slapped his head. "I didn't even realize your birthday is almost a month away. I tell you, March drags on and on." He patted Karlie on the shoulder. "No matter what, Karlie, you'll always have me."

"Yeah, until the tests reveal my father's identity," Karlie replied.

"No, Karlie. I won't stop caring even then," Neil promised.

"The thing that bothers me is that either way it goes, my father won't really know anything about me," Karlie confessed. "Thomas will have a heads-up, of course, but still. . . ."

Neil understood her dilemma. He put his hands up in a silent command to wait a minute before he left the room. A few minutes later, he returned with a lockbox.

Karlie looked at him curiously.

Before Neil opened the box, he swore Karlie to secrecy. "What I am about to share with you, nobody knows about. I am showing you only because I want you to believe that I do care about you."

Neil opened the old box and took out several pictures and letters.

Karlie gasped. They were pictures of her in all stages of her life. "How did you get these?"

"Tiffany and I kept in touch over the years," Neil admitted. "She sent me pictures and kept me abreast of how you were doing. To Tiffany, you were so precious, and she shared her most valuable treasure with me. Anyway, I will give these letters to your father so that he'll get a chance to know you a little better. How does that sound?"

Karlie had tears in her eyes when she blurted, "Why can't you be my father?"

Neil's heart swelled at her outburst. "I wish I were. I may not be your biological father, Karlie. But I have loved you from the start."

"I know, Neil," Karlie said. "Thank you for always being there for us. We couldn't do it without you."

Before going to the hospital later that Monday morning, Darnell stopped by Neil's house to see Karlie.

"Hey, Neil. I came by to check on Karlie before I head over to see Tiffany," he announced.

"She's asleep," Neil told him. "Actually, she was up pretty late last night and was real upset that Tiffany might not make it to her sixteenth birthday."

"Who says she has to wait to celebrate her birthday?"

Neil creased his eyebrows at Darnell's question until understanding dawned. "I like the way you think."

Darnell became excited. "Leave everything to me. I will call when it's time."

Neil and Darnell gave each other a high five.

"Wait out here a minute," Neil told Karlie before entering Tiffany's hospital room.

Karlie's heart skipped a beat. *Why does he want me to wait out here?* Suddenly, Karlie was afraid to see her mother. Afraid of what she might see.

Neil opened the door a crack and peered out. He gave a barely perceptible nod before closing the door.

Karlie walked forward as if she were going to an execution. Her feet dragged, and her heart pounded mercilessly. Taking a huge gulp, Karlie opened the door.

"Surprise!"

Karlie was so shocked, she almost tripped over her feet. Everybody was there. There were balloons and all sorts of decorations.

The small crowd sang, "Happy Birthday to you."

Touched, Karlie started laughing and crying. She looked over at her mother, who was also smiling.

"Happy Sweet Sixteen, Karlie," Tiffany said. Her gaunt, pale face radiated.

Karlie ran over to her mother with elation and gave her a hug. "Thanks, Mom."

"You're welcome, but who you really need to thank is Darnell. It was his idea."

Spontaneously, she went over to Darnell and gave him a hug. "Thank you so much. You have no idea how much this means to me."

Pleased, Darnell grinned. "No thanks necessary. I did it for both of you."

Karlie looked over at Neil. "And you were in on this?"

Neil raised both hands. "Guilty as charged."

Jamaal and Brian had gotten permission from Dr. Layton to put music on for an hour. Jamaal plugged in the simple boom box, and soon Mary J. Blige began singing, "Let's get this party started."

Myra came in with a huge birthday cake with sixteen candles burning.

Karlie laughed with glee. "This is the best birthday ever."

Karlie blew out the candles, and her mother helped her cut the cake. Ryan and Patricia came in during the cake sharing. Ryan had hired a professional photographer to take pictures and make Karlie a video.

Everyone had a chance to say something.

Tiffany recorded a special message for her daughter to hear on her actual birthday. Her voice was so hoarse that she had to whisper to get the words out.

Neil left the room when he heard the poignant message. It tore his heart that death was inevitable. If there was anything in his power to bind the chilling hands of death, Neil would do it in a heartbeat. But death answered to God.

Neil peered back inside the room when he saw the photographer leave. Tiffany crooked her finger at him. Neil gladly went inside the room.

"Neil, you are such a good friend to me . . . more than a friend," Tiffany began. "I don't deserve you."

"Please," Neil said. "You would do the same for me."

Tiffany patted a spot on the bed, and Neil obliged. "Neil, I am tired. I don't know if I will make it past next week. Even though the paternity test results come in tomorrow, I want to officially make you Karlie's guardian and the trustee over her estate. My manager and friend, Winona Franks, oversees it now and will continue to do so, but you will have the final say. I know I'm springing this on you, but I need to die knowing Karlie will always be okay and that her needs will be met. I know you will put her welfare above everything else."

Neil felt honored at her request. "Tiffany, are you sure? What about Karlie's biological father?"

"I'm positive. Ryan or Thomas will be well set for life—I made sure of that—but Karlie's estate is massive and needs the right person," Tiffany stated firmly. "Neil, in these past months, you've been more of a father to Karlie than any of these men. You are the only one I really trust."

Neil leaned in and rested his head on Tiffany's stomach. "Okay, Tiffany. You know there is nothing I wouldn't do for you. I could never refuse you anything."

Tiffany shifted. "I know, Neil. Just take care of my daughter. That is all I ask."

♫ Chapter Thirty-eight

Would I lie for her? Neil asked himself. Tuesday morning was so glum and full of clouds. Rain threatened to burst through the clouds at any moment. Neil pulled into the center to get the paternity test results. Tiffany had also signed the papers making him her health and legal proxy. So he was able to claim the results without any hassle. He selfishly chose not to call Ryan or Thomas until he had seen the results himself.

Neil looked at the small slip of paper that would decide Karlie's fate. His eyes widened. Just to make sure, he read the results again. *No, it cannot be.* Neil clenched his jaw in anger and disbelief. He now had his answer. Yes, he would lie for her and to her.

Neil sped home to tell Myra the results. She clutched her chest in dismay. "No, Neil, you're lying."

"Myra, you know what this means." Neil gave her a pointed stare.

"Yes, but I am not sure I feel the same way anymore . . . about . . . you know . . . the offer."

"What do you mean, you're not sure?" Neil demanded.

"Neil, you have been so busy with Tiffany that you haven't seen any of the subtle clues I have been leaving you."

"Myra, what on earth are you talking about?" He was not in the mood for any riddles. "If you have something to say, I wish you would just spit it out."

"Haven't you looked at the calendar lately? Haven't you seen the blue lines I drew through the red stars?" Myra quizzed. Her excitement was palpable.

Neil looked at Myra and calculated. Her eyes sparkled, and she hummed with barely concealed joy. "You are pregnant." Neil's mouth hung open.

"Yes," Myra shouted with glee. "We're going to have a baby. I didn't realize it, because I lost weight instead of gaining. Because of everything going on with Tiffany, I just didn't put two and two together, but—"

"But I don't get it. Shouldn't you be gaining weight and not losing?"

"Yes, but since I've been helping Tiffany, I haven't been eating as much sweets. . . ."

"Oh . . . thank you, Lord. Thank you." Neil grabbed Myra off her feet and swung her around with elation. He showered her face with tiny kisses and placed his hands across her stomach. "Myra, this is great news. Karlie is going to love having a little sister or brother to play with."

The room suddenly became quiet, and Neil's smile faltered as understanding dawned. "Myra, no, do not do this. We agreed. Karlie is mine, and I love her."

"Neil, Karlie is not your child." She patted her stomach. "This one is. I know we agreed to take her in, but now things : . . have . . . changed. I only suggested we take her in the first place because I never thought I would have a child of my own."

"Oh, so your reasons for taking Karlie in were purely selfish, and now she is expendable. Is that what you are telling me, Myra?"

"Well, no." Myra shook her head and took a small step back to think. She did not know how to explain her conflicting emotions. "It's just that neither of us has ever been a parent before, and I want just the two of us to experience it together. That is all."

"And how would Karlie interfere with that?" Neil seethed, truly seeing Myra for the thoughtless woman she really was. His eyes filled. "Please, Myra, don't do this. You see, Karlie is my daughter. I have always loved her, and, Myra, I want her here with me."

"I do not want to take her anymore," Myra finally spat out, poking him in the chest. Her nostrils flared, and her voice escalated. Neil had pushed her hand, and now she was ready to come back swinging.

"This is a human being you are talking about," Neil said with amazement. "My daughter."

"No," Myra cried. Broken, she said, "Karlie does not have your blood flowing through her veins. She is not your child."

"She's mine, Myra," Neil whispered as the tears rolled down his face. "In my heart I adopted her, and she is mine."

No matter what he said, Myra refused to budge. Silently and filled with hurt, Neil put on his coat. "I am glad you finally have the child you so badly wanted, Myra. But at what price?"

The question hung in the air as the door closed behind him. Myra covered her mouth in shock as the full implications of his question sunk in. *No,* her heart screamed. This could not be happening. How could Neil think to desert his own child for another? "I don't believe it," she whispered. "Neil would not do this. He's only trying to make me feel guilty." Then Myra stiffened her spine. Neil was not going anywhere. He was not about to turn his back on her. Not now. Neil couldn't even hurt a fly. He would not do this to her. Protectively, she placed her hands over her stomach. "Don't worry, baby. Daddy didn't mean what he said."

Myra's conscience had been pricked, but she vehemently shook her head, refusing to heed what it was telling her. "No, Karlie doesn't need Neil. She's practically an adult already, and she has four other men she can choose from. She's sixteen. She can even plead as an adult in any court. Karlie can take care of herself. She was practically born with a silver spoon in her mouth. She'll be fine."

Myra's resolve strengthened; she was absolutely convinced that Neil would come around. He always did. "Blood is thicker than water. This is his blood growing inside me. I have the upper hand. Neil will see things my way." Myra didn't know how inaccurate her prediction was, but she would find out the hard way.

Neil barely had time to cool down before Ryan and Thomas arrived at Tiffany's house. He had called both men while walking down the block to Tiffany's house. They pulled up within minutes of each other.

As soon as the men were settled, in the living room Neil set his face like a flint and injected a brisk, no-nonsense tone in his voice. "Gentlemen, we all know why you are here, so let's get right to it."

Both men looked at Neil with anticipation. "Ryan, you are not Karlie's father."

Ryan put both hands on his head with visible relief. He turned to Thomas and shook his hand. "Congratulations, Thomas. You have a prize for a daughter." He looked at his watch, ready to depart. Typical for him, he was already on other business.

As soon as Ryan departed, Thomas looked at Neil expectantly. Neil merely shook his head.

"No," Thomas murmured. The truth pierced his heart. "My heart literally aches. I didn't expect to feel this way." He gave Neil a piercing, accusatory stare. "But you sat there and let Ryan congratulate me."

"I let Ryan believe what he wanted to believe," Neil said without rancor.

"Why?" Thomas needed to know. What kind of sick game was Neil playing? He was two seconds away from decking him.

"Because I need you to agree to do something," Neil said. Seeing that he had Thomas's undivided attention, Neil continued. "Simply put, I cannot allow Tiffany to ever know the truth. It's too much for her to bear in her condition."

"But what about Karlie?" Thomas asked. "She deserves to know the truth."

"I will tell Karlie the entire sordid truth," Neil said, "then persuade her that it's necessary to keep up the pretense."

"Do you think lying to Tiffany is a good idea?" Thomas was extremely doubtful. What Neil was asking him to do was to betray Tiffany's trust.

"C'mon, man. Your name is already on Karlie's birth papers. So, what's the difference, now? You love Karlie, don't you?"

"Yes." Thomas hesitated. He loved Karlie immensely.

Neil could see that he was getting through to him and pushed on. "Thomas, you have got to do this for everybody's sake. Karlie needs a father, and Tiffany needs that reassurance before she dies. For Pete's sake, Tiffany is on her deathbed. Do you know what the truth would do to her? Can you live with that on your conscience?"

"All right, Neil," Thomas said, acquiescing. "If you think this is the best course to take, I will do it."

Neil relaxed his shoulders with relief. For a split second, he thought Thomas would insist on telling Tiffany the truth. But thankfully, the other man had seen the rationale behind his actions.

This was a lie of compassion. A necessary lie. God would understand and forgive. At least that was what Neil assured himself of as he watched Thomas depart to give Tiffany the "wonderful" news. Neil walked home. He would wait for Karlie to get in from school. Then he was going to convince her to lie to her mother as well.

He heard her enter the living room and watched as she came over to him.

"Hi, Neil."

"Karlie, let's have a talk." He led her over to the couch.

Karlie's hands shook. "I don't know what it is, but I'm already nervous," she confessed.

Seeing her shudder, Neil got right to the point. "Karlie, the paternity test results came in today."

"Oh," Karlie said. She remained pensive for a few minutes before asking, "Who is my father?"

Neil's throat suddenly felt parched. "Karlie, neither Ryan nor Thomas is your father."

"Then who is?"

Neil didn't answer. Instead, he waited for the awful truth to hit her.

Karlie's face appeared frozen, until her mouth slowly opened and she exhaled loudly. "I think I'm going to be sick." Karlie covered her mouth with her hands as the bile rose to the surface. She raced to the bathroom and spilled her guts for what felt like an eternity. Spent, Karlie sat on the toilet. In her haste, she had left the door ajar. Karlie looked up and saw Neil standing there.

He walked into the bathroom, went to the sink, and turned on the faucet. He grabbed a washcloth, wet it, and washed Karlie's face. He gave her a firm hug. "Karlie, it doesn't matter how you got here. God wanted you here, and that's what matters. Tiffany loves you. I love you, and it doesn't matter to me one bit who your father is. As far as I'm concerned, he was just a means to an end."

"Though Mom told me that her stepfather raped her, I just never once considered the possibility that he could be my father. I'll never look at myself the same again. I'm so mortified. I just can't believe it. Clifford Peterson is my, my . . ." Karlie couldn't bring herself to say it. She looked at Neil. "Does Mom know yet?"

"No, I haven't told her. But, Karlie, you're still you," Neil assured her. "Clifford Peterson does not determine your character. When I look at you, I see a beautiful young woman." Neil lifted her chin with his index finger until Karlie looked at him. "Karlie, it would kill your mother to hear this, so I convinced Thomas to tell Tiffany he is the father."

"But why? You told me the truth. My mother deserves to know," Karlie said.

"Karlie, you're not a child. You're mature enough to understand and handle the truth. Your mother is too ill. She's not ready for this. Believe me, I know it."

Karlie retreated to her bedroom to cry and think. She called Jamaal, but his grandmother said that he was not home. Karlie wondered where he could be when she needed him now so badly.

The doorbell rang. Karlie cracked her door open. She heard Jamaal's voice. *Thank God.* Karlie grabbed her coat, raced down the stairs, and catapulted into Jamaal's arms. She tugged his hands and led him over to her own house to talk.

Jamaal followed Karlie into her bedroom. Curious, Jamaal looked around her private sanctuary. It was neat and organized and filled with all kinds of girly stuff.

Karlie sat Jamaal down and told him everything. To her surprise, Jamaal agreed with Neil.

"But how can I lie to my mother about something this important?" Karlie asked, tortured.

"Because in this instance your mother's welfare is more important," Jamaal said matter-of-factly.

"I want to tell her the truth," Karlie responded with sheer stubbornness. "I want to tell her because then I get to ask her why she even kept me. I want to know why she didn't abort me. She must have known that Clifford Peterson could be my father."

"Karlie." Jamaal was shocked at her statement. "How can you even say such words? You're here because in spite of everything, your mother loved you."

"But . . ." Karlie faltered and began to cry.

"Karlie, you'll be sixteen soon," Jamaal stated. "And you're old enough to know that these things happen, and it does not make any sense to even ask why. You just have to accept it and move on."

"I don't know," Karlie said, feeling confused. "This is just all too much for one person to handle."

"Grow up, Karlie," Jamaal told her with a sudden firmness. "Somewhere out there is someone else with even bigger problems than what you have. You have a mother who loved and doted on you. You have financial security, which some of us can only dream of."

"You sound so grown up," Karlie said with a little voice.

"That is because I had to," Jamaal said. "My neighborhood grows you up quick, and I have learned how to fend for myself. It's time you do the same, Karlie."

"All right," Karlie said, acquiescing. She lowered her head, but her resolve strengthened. "I'll do it. Both you and Neil are right. My mother cannot handle the truth right now." She lifted her head and declared, "I would rather lie to her and have her live a day longer than lose a day because of my own selfishness."

"I think Neil believes it's for the best." Jamaal comforted her. "That is the only reason why he would ask you to go along with it."

"I know Neil loves me and my mother. He means the best for us," Karlie said. "He would not suggest it if he did not think this was the only way."

"You really value his opinion, don't you?" Jamaal asked.

"Yeah," Karlie confessed. "I wish he were my father or that he would offer to take me in. I'd live with him in a heartbeat."

"That's life, though. We don't get what we want, but we have to live with what we get."

Neil drove Karlie to the hospital to meet Thomas. Together, Thomas and Karlie went into Tiffany's room to break the "news."

Outside her room, Neil paced and anxiously waited for Thomas and Karlie to come back out. Neil did not know that he had it in him to orchestrate such a scheme, but there was no black or white in life. Life seemed generously sprinkled with patches of gray. Sometimes people had to do things that they would not normally do if the occasion called for it.

Though shall not bear false witness.

"Forgive me, Lord. Forgive me," Neil prayed.

Thomas came out first with unshed tears in his eyes. "Tiffany was so relieved when I told her that I was Tiffany's father that she started crying real hard till she coughed up blood. I think you were right. Tiffany could not have handled the truth."

"Thanks," Neil said and shook the other man's hand. "So what happens now?"

"I guess Karlie will be coming to live with me," Thomas answered happily. "I am thinking about moving her back to Tiffany's house in L.A. A change might be good for her. I will take good care of her, I promise."

"You'd better," Neil replied. He good-naturedly patted Thomas on the back and watched him leave. He did not have any time to reflect on Thomas's decision, because Karlie exited the room. "How did everything go?" Neil asked gently.

"It was surprisingly easy to do. I even promised to help her finish some song she's working on," Karlie informed him with a jaded tone.

Neil examined Karlie. Her eyes had a new, cynical look to them, which was not there before. Neil was sorry to see the youthful innocence gone from her eyes, and he knew he'd help put the cynicism there.

"You, Thomas, Myra, and I are the only people who know the truth," Neil said.

"Now we have to live with it. Thomas told you he wants us to move back to L.A.?"

"Yeah," Neil said and injected a pleasant tone in his voice. "I am sure you'll be glad to be back once everything's settled." Neil could have kicked himself for that insensitive comment when what he really wanted was to take Karlie home with him.

"You mean once my mother dies," Karlie said, correcting him. She shook her head before walking toward the elevator. Neil's glib comment had hurt her. She knew he did not mean anything by it, but it still hurt. Karlie loved Neil, foolishly hoping that he would insist that she come live with him, especially now that he knew the truth. But that had not happened. Instead, Neil seemed happy to hoist her into another man's hands.

♫ Chapter Thirty-nine

Darnell kissed his daughters good night and whispered a silent thank-you to his mother before leaving for the hospital. She had agreed to watch April and Amber, and Darnell had promised that he would be home in time to pick them up from school.

Darnell would spend the night with Tiffany. He had already called the substitute line to take a personal day. Darnell intended to camp out at the hospital until Dr. Layton kicked him out.

He entered Tiffany's room quietly, in case she was asleep. He needed not to have bothered, because Tiffany was alert. Darnell could see her eyes light up when he entered the room.

"How're you?" Darnell asked.

"I am still here," was Tiffany's half attempt at a joke. "I'm actually writing a song. As you can see, it's a messy, creative process." She pointed to the papers strewn all over her bed and tossed on the floor.

To Darnell, her voice sounded weak and lifeless. He tried to remain unaffected and went over to sit next to her. She looked so pale and fragile.

Darnell reached over to the side table and picked up a brush to straighten her hair. Tiffany had a bad case of hospital hair. Darnell repositioned Tiffany so that he cradled her from behind. He pulled the brush through her hair with gentle strokes. Darnell was slightly alarmed to see threads of hair come out in the brush.

He almost gave a cry of alarm but caught himself in time. He extracted the small clumps of hair and hid them in his pocket.

"That feels so good," Tiffany said.

Darnell stopped when he saw another clump come out into the brush. He had not expected this to happen. So he gently pinned her hair in a small bun and repositioned her on the bed. Darnell rushed over to the bathroom to put the pieces of her hair in the trash can. The last piece of hair, he put in his pocket as a keepsake. Darnell tried to be strong, but still the sobs came.

Tiffany heard low sobs coming from behind the bathroom door. It took every ounce of energy she had left to call out, "Darnell, are you okay?"

"Yes," Darnell answered. "I am fine. I will be right out." He composed himself before reentering the room.

Tiffany peered into his handsome face. "I know you're not okay. What's the matter?"

"It's just that I am not ready to see you go," Darnell cried out. "I just reconnected with you. Why is God taking you away?"

"Darnell, do not be angry with God," Tiffany pleaded. "I have had a full life, even though I am still young. I had a wonderful career, a beautiful daughter, and now you. I cannot complain."

Darnell did not know how Tiffany could be so optimistic with her life ebbing away from her. He did not think he would be so grateful if he were in her shoes. "I do not know how you do it, Tiffany."

"I just face one day at a time. My biggest fear was that I would not find out who Karlie's real father was, but I did, and I am quite happy with the outcome."

"How's Thomas handling the news?"

"Pretty well," Tiffany sighed. Her breathing was labored.

Darnell could see the effort it took for her to stay awake. "Go to sleep, my love. I will be here when you awaken. I will be here all day."

As he watched her sleep, Darnell thought about how much Tiffany had come to mean to him in such a ridiculously short amount of time. He truly loved and cherished this woman and knew his life was that much better because of her. She turned to get comfortable, and Darnell smiled. He honestly could sit and watch her and not get tired.

He had forgotten the beauty of genuine love. Tiffany looked so angelic that he felt his heart expand at the mere sight of her. Darnell closed his eyes and envisioned what could have been. Darnell opened his eyes and looked at Tiffany. He touched her hair and admitted, "Tiffany, as sure as I know God is real, I would've married you. I can see it clearly."

What was stopping him from marrying her now? Once the thought entered his head, it grew like wildfire. He could still marry her. She was still here, and Darnell couldn't think of a better way of expressing his love for her than by making her his wife.

Suddenly energized, Darnell looked at his watch. He could make it to the jewelry store, Zales, if he jumped on the highway. He was a man on a mission and drove like it. God cleared the path, and he made it to store in record time and without a speeding ticket. Darnell went to look at both wedding and engagement rings. His eyes scanned the rings until they rested on what he knew was the perfect set. Darnell made his purchase and returned to Tiffany's room.

She awakened when he entered. Darnell watched as she slowly opened her eyes to smile at him. Then he watched them focus on the glistening diamond before her.

"Tiffany Knightly, I love you with all my heart. I never expected I would find someone to fill the gap left by my first wife's death. But my life is complete because of you. I know without a doubt that God led you to me because I was drifting along, until you came and settled me. Tiffany Knightly, will you do me the honor of becoming my wife?"

Tiffany held her answer back. She looked at Darnell with an intent expression. "Darnell, are you sure this is wise?" she croaked.

"Yes, I am." Darnell nodded quickly.

"You do not have to do this for me because I am dying," Tiffany said. "I do not need a mercy wedding."

Darnell immediately took offense. "I know what I can or cannot do, Tiffany. I want to do this because I love you. That is the only reason, and I want to declare my love for you before man and God." Darnell took her hands and held eye contact.

Tiffany looked away. "I don't know."

"Well, I do." Darnell spoke confidently. "You added a new sparkle to my dull existence, Tiffany. You made me love again, and I do not regret it one bit. I would rather love you and then lose you than continue living my life in a bubble."

"We could just exchange vows without getting legal," Tiffany suggested before going through a brief coughing spell.

"No." Darnell remained adamant. "We are going to make this good and legal."

"Still . . ." Tiffany thought about it. "Do not tell your daughters. It would be too confusing for them, I think, and they already lost their mother."

"If that is what you want," Darnell agreed without hesitation.

"Then my answer is yes," Tiffany quietly replied.

Darnell reached over and sealed their commitment with a searing kiss. "We'll get married tomorrow."

"I need a little more time than that." Tiffany smiled.

"Okay, one week. We'll get married next Friday morning."

Neil entered his house and went to check on Karlie, who was already asleep in bed. He then entered the master bedroom and saw that Myra was also asleep. He looked at her sleeping frame and felt a huge anger engulf him. Clenching his fists, he turned away, before he gave into the impulse and hit her hard.

Neil could never have imagined Myra would be so callous toward an innocent girl. He could not have imagined that Myra would try to use emotional black-mail against him. He wanted to comfort and protect Karlie through her grief and the rest of her growing pains. She was a beautiful young woman who, with the proper guidance, would go places. Neil feared Thom-as's head was too much in the clouds to be of much use to Karlie.

But what could he do? His hands were tied. He al-most hated Myra for making him choose between his child and Karlie. That was not a fair choice, for he al-ready loved them both.

Then Neil thought for a moment. This was not the Stone Age. It was the twenty-first century. He was more than capable of caring for his child without shar-ing the same roof. At least his son or daughter would have a full-time mother. In a matter of days, or even sooner, Karlie would lose the only real parent she had ever known.

Neil walked to the door, opened it, and then stopped. But who was he really kidding? He wanted to be there for his unborn child. He wanted to be there for every single experience. Feeling trapped, Neil silently closed the door

"Only you, Tiffany Knightly. Only you."

Tiffany grinned and turned her head toward the voice she knew so well. "Winona! What are you doing here? I told you not to come until tomorrow. I didn't want you to see me like this."

Winona waved her hands dismissively. "As if I would listen to you. I am here with goodies for your wedding night. Tiffany, you should know me better than that. What I cannot believe is how you still manage to be on your deathbed and snag a husband. Evidently, I taught you well." Winona patted the sleeves of her red business suit with a self-satisfied smile.

Tiffany cracked up at her friend's good-natured ribbing. "Winona Franks, you are hilarious."

Winona smiled along, but the smile slowly dwindled. Her face broke. "Tiffany, I . . ."

"No," Tiffany warned. "We are not going down that road called 'Feel sorry for yourself.' Winona, I am getting married. Can you believe it? I met the most wonderful man. Well, I met him again, and Darnell knows my past and still wants to marry me."

Winona hugged her chest and spoke tenderly. "Tiffany, Darnell is a smart man. He knows better than to let a diamond slip through his fingers."

Tears came to her eyes. Tiffany looked at her friend. "For the first time in my life, Winona, I have felt the love of a man who truly loves me."

"Hi, Tiffany."

Tiffany looked at her door. She breathed, "Hi. Come in here and meet Winona."

Winona looked at the gorgeous man who entered the room, and gave Tiffany a wink. "Tiffany, you did good," she said, flirtatiously giving him the once-over.

Tiffany gave her friend a firm look. "Winona, I would like you to meet my married friend Neil Jameson."

"Oh." Winona plopped her hand over her mouth before saying, "I am so sorry. Talk about foot in mouth."

Neil extended his hand. "Winona, it is good to finally meet you. I have heard so many good things about you." He looked at Tiffany and smiled. "I'll leave you two to catch up, and I will see you tomorrow morning."

"Okay, see you then." Tiffany remained silent until he left. "Winona, I don't believe you. That was so embarrassing."

"What! I didn't know." Winona lifted her shoulders. "Besides, you didn't see the way he looked at you, Tiffany."

"What do you mean?" Tiffany creased her brow.

"He looked at you like a man in love."

"Winona, you're a mess. Stop it." Tiffany laughed.

"I know men, Tiffany, and I love when I see it," Winona retorted. "Take it from me. Neil Jameson is head over heels in love."

♫ Chapter Forty

"I have been dying to see your face," Tiffany remarked weakly when she saw Neil at her door the next morning.

Neil did not like her wisecrack and told her so. "Not funny." He perched on her bed.

It was Friday morning, and her wedding day. "What are you doing here so early? You should be home, getting dressed."

"I just felt like seeing you."

"Tell me what's on your mind," Tiffany said, prodding him before succumbing to a fit of coughing. He grabbed a piece of tissue to wipe the slobber off her face.

Tiffany did not look good at all. She had lost even more weight, and her eyes seemed to be bulging from the sockets. Dr. Layton had told him that Tiffany was no longer able to hold down any food. She was medicated and fed intravenously through an IV tube.

"Myra's pregnant."

"That's great news, Neil. I am so happy for you." Tiffany's lackluster tone was a major indication that she was in decline.

Neil observed what a huge effort it was for her to take a breath. He saw Tiffany close her eyes and became concerned. "Tiffany."

Tiffany stirred and strove to speak, but her voice was a mere whisper. "Neil, I am so tired. I think I held on this long only so I could see you. Neil, promise me you'll still . . . look out . . . for Karlie."

"Yes, I will. I'll take care of our daughter," Neil quickly promised in an effort to get Tiffany to stop talking, but she had more to say. Tiffany was too far gone to catch the significance of his words. That was as close to the truth as he would chance telling her.

"Tell Darnell I love him."

What was she saying? Neil's heart rate sped faster than lightning once he realized that Tiffany was actually saying her good-byes.

"No," he cried out in denial. "Tiffany. No. Just hold on. Please."

Neil grabbed her hand and felt how cold it was to the touch. He started rubbing her palms.

"I am . . . just . . . so . . . tired." Tiffany barely got the words out before closing her eyes.

"Tiffany." He got off the chair, sat on the bed, and moved his face close to hers. "Open your eyes."

Neil kissed Tiffany on the lips. They felt chapped and cool. Valiantly, he tried to keep from panicking and felt her wrist for a pulse.

He could feel a small heartbeat under his finger and collapsed with relief. Tiffany must have just drifted off.

Neil felt a wall of tears break lose within him. He could hardly breathe, trying to contain it. His nose started running, and his eyelids released the flow of tears. Neil grabbed a tissue and clenched his lips.

Tiffany could not leave like this. She was supposed to be getting married to Darnell in four hours. He saw the designer gown hanging by the door, and his heart wrenched.

Neil reached for the bucket of ice and the towel by her bedside. The nurse made sure these were available and constantly replenished. He dipped the towel into the bucket before squeezing it dry. Neil tenderly placed the cool cloth across Tiffany's forehead.

That seemed to revive her, and Tiffany opened her eyes to look at Neil. She smiled. To Neil, she looked like an angel, which made his fear increase.

"Tiffany, do not go. Please!" Neil begged.

She made a move to comfort him, but her hands fell to her side. "Neil . . . take care of Karlie . . . please."

"I promise," Neil reiterated. He would have given her the world at that moment if he thought it would prolong her life for one second.

"Good-bye . . . Neil."

"No!" Neil yelled. He rushed out of her room and spotted one of the nurses in the hallway. "Help! Help! She's . . . I don't know!"

He rushed back into the room and grabbed Tiffany and held her in his arms. He literally felt the last air leave her body.

"No." Neil cried and cried, but it was of no avail. The wind took Tiffany's last breath away on a solitary ride, and she was gone. The air had captured her essence to take it away to parts unknown.

Just like that. The best friend he had ever had in the world was gone.

Neil curled into the bed with Tiffany. He lost his composure and cried and cried. He cried for Karlie, who had inexplicably just lost her mother. He cried for Darnell, who obviously loved Tiffany and had lost his second chance at love.

Then Neil cried because he had loved her too. Neil had loved Tiffany from the moment they had bonded underneath their special tree. He had loved her with a depth that he had never given himself the opportunity to express and had contented himself with being the best friend that she could ever need.

Neil cried because death was a war he could not win. It was not a battle worth fighting. Everyone lost against death, eventually.

Darnell entered the hospital with the wedding rings in one hand and a huge bouquet of roses in the other. He knew he had hours to go until he tied the knot, but he was already dressed. He had dropped his girls off at his mom's home but had left his cell phone in the car, so he'd missed Neil's frantic calls. Darnell was in such a jovial mood that he smiled at everyone he passed. But as he neared Tiffany's room, Darnell noticed a sudden urgency around him.

He heard a man's wail and felt a shiver creep up his spine. Darnell rushed on even faster, willing his feet to move forward. Then he saw a group of people exit Tiffany's room, and his heart dropped. Darnell saw Neil leave the room with tears streaming down his face. Darnell stopped mid-stride as Neil's eyes focused on him. *No!* he screamed inside.

"Darnell." Neil uttered his name with a sense of devastation.

"No." Darnell dropped the flowers and the rings and pushed past Neil. He had to see her himself to believe it. She could not be gone.

Neil stood to block him.

In a fit of anger, Darnell shoved Neil out of the way. His grief made him strong enough to move the much larger man. "Tiffany!" Darnell exclaimed as he entered the room.

"She's gone."

Darnell shook his head, refusing to accept what was right before his eyes. "Tiffany," Darnell cried. "Wake up, baby. We're getting married in a few hours. I've got everything arranged."

Of course, Darnell got no response. His body slumped over, and Darnell began to cry, finally accepting the truth. He allowed the tears to fall. They trailed from his eyes down his cheeks, unheeded. No amount of love was going to bring her back to him now. Tiffany was gone just as quickly as she had entered his life. "Why couldn't you just hold on for one more day?" Darnell moaned.

"Darnell."

Darnell looked up to see Neil standing by the door. "What?"

"They're waiting to . . ." Neil trailed off. Then he tried again. "They're waiting to take her body away."

Darnell nodded his head and slowly stood up. He closed his eyes and turned his head as he saw the nurses enter. He could not leave her just yet, but he could not watch, either.

As they took Tiffany away on the gurney, Darnell looked out the window. People were going about their business as if nothing had happened, as if he had not just lost the woman of his dreams. Darnell put his hands over his face and wept.

♫ Chapter Forty-one

The day of the funeral was sunny and bright. Everybody marveled at the beautiful weather they were given.

Tiffany was as gorgeous as a bride on her wedding day. She was dressed in what would have been her wedding dress, and her hair and make-up were done to perfection.

Karlie clutched Neil's hand and looked around at the crowd. "I don't believe it. Even the press is here."

"Do not concern yourself about them," Neil assured her. "They're not important. Concentrate on your nucleus of friends who are here for you."

Neil crooked his head in Jamaal's direction. Jamaal sat on her right, and Neil on her left. Jamaal looked superfine in his black suit. His grandmother had bought it for him, and he was rocking it like nobody's business.

"Karlie, you look like a beautiful angel," Jamaal whispered. "I love you, and I'm right here for you."

His words gave her the courage to last through the ceremony. Karlie tried to concentrate as Darnell read the obituary and Neil read the scripture. She barely heard Pastor Johnston's eulogy. She struggled with the fact that her mother was truly gone.

Then she heard her name called. Karlie bravely marched forward, placing one foot in front of the other until she was behind the podium. She didn't know how she was going to do this. But she was going to sing her mother's last song.

"I'm going to sing a new song. My mother wrote it just before she passed, and it meant a lot to her. So, I hope it blesses you too." Then Karlie opened her mouth. Her voice stopped everyone in the audience and they listened in disbelief. No one knew that Karlie had inherited her mother's talent.

"Wow."

"Listen to that voice."

"She sounds like an angel."

"I think I've found another client!" Winona exclaimed to her husband.

Neil's heart expanded, seeing her continue her mother's legacy. Tiffany lived on still in her words, and in Karlie.

Her voice rang loud and clear as Karlie belted out the words:

My old life was just a song
That everybody played.
A tune that everybody heard
But no one really knew the words.
Then the lyrics of true love
Hit my heart with a resounding note
And now I live to sing this song
Of grace and hope—and you.

I am singing a brand-new song
I sway to a different beat
I hear a mesmerizing tune
Echoing back at me
For He rewrote my pain—with everlasting peace.

I sing this song so free
His love gave that to me
His tears washed away past sorrows

As I lay cradled in His arms
There's no place else that I could feel
This balm that soothes my soul
And now I live to sing this song,
Of grace and hope—and you.

When Karlie finished singing, everyone was in tears. She had done her mother proud and had honored her with the song.

Neil found Karlie's voice enthralling. The church prompted her to sing the refrain again, and he had to excuse himself to keep from bursting into tears. The song was just so . . . Tiffany. Neil went into the back of the parlor to check on everything. He stopped short when he recognized who was standing there. "Mrs. Peterson?"

Merle jumped with surprise. She certainly had not counted on being recognized.

Neil clamped his mouth shut to keep from causing a scene, knowing the press was there to report it. He firmly grabbed Merle by her shoulders and escorted her outside.

"You are not welcomed here," he spat out viciously.

"She was my daughter." Merle was flabbergasted.

"A fact you have completely ignored for the past sixteen years."

"I just came to pay my last respects," Merle said.

"Please spare the drama for someone who'll believe you," Neil snarled. "Your only reason for showing face is to find out about the money."

Merle held her heart with obvious shock. "I loved my daughter."

"You did not give two cents about her. Tiffany begged me to call you when she was in the hospital, and you did not even deign to visit her. Not even *once*. Tiffany was willing to forgive you. I, on the other hand, am not. You are a cold, heartless excuse for a woman."

"She was my blood," Merle shouted. Any pretense of dignity was long gone.

"Get out," Neil commanded angrily. "Your daughter died thinking she was a whore because of you and what your sick husband did to her."

"I j-just wanted to s-say good-bye and t-tell her that I am sorry I didn't come to see her at the hospital," Merle stammered.

"Spare me the fake regret," Neil bellowed. "Your sorrow means nothing now that she is dead." He moved toward the older woman as anger shot through his spine. He was going to wrap his hands around her neck and strangle the life out of her. Merle Peterson did not deserve to be alive while her daughter lay in the grave.

Merle backed away from Neil in shock. Her eyes were pinned on something behind him.

Neil turned his head to see Karlie standing by the door. She was obviously looking for him. He was relieved that Karlie was still far enough away not to have heard the exchange.

"His eyes," Merle said with stunned disbelief.

"Go," Neil commanded with desperation. Karlie was coming closer.

Merle turned and almost fell in a mass at his feet. She walked away, whispering, "She has Clifford's eyes."

Merle did not know how she had even made it home in one piece. She did not know how to handle the guilt that now consumed her entire being. She opened a bottle of scotch and drank the entire bottle, attempting to get those piercing eyes out of her mind.

In a drunken fit, Merle took all of Clifford's pictures and belongings and threw them in the middle of her living room floor. She cursed him and called him all kinds of names while she was doing it.

Not that it would do any good now. Her daughter was gone. Merle could not right the wrong that she had done. She went into her cabinet and opened another bottle of liquor. She drank it straight from the bottle.

Swaying, Merle got a match from her kitchen. She was going to burn everything that had belonged to him. She held the bottle at a tilt so half of it emptied as she walked.

In one huge motion, Merle swung the match into the pile of pictures and clothes. She hadn't tracked just how much liquor she had poured. The flame and the liquor made contact, and the fire quickly spread, greedily lapping up everything in its path. Then the fire raged out of control, spreading to the curtains, the carpet, the staircase . . . all around . . . everywhere.

Merle instantly sobered when she saw what was happening. She flailed her arms as if that could stop the fiery monster now eating away at her legs . . . her dress . . . her face. Flames engulfed her body as she stopped, dropped, and rolled. Merle could not escape and screamed as the fire devoured her greedily.

The three-alarm fire was the headline on the ten o'clock news.

Neil listened as the news anchor stated that the woman being rushed to the hospital was none other than Merle Peterson, mother of the late Tiffany Knightly. She was now fighting for her life.

Good, Neil thought. *Let her fight as her daughter fought for hers. Knowing, the old bat, she will probably survive.*

Neil listened with half an ear as the anchor sensationalized the two tragedies within the same family, which had occurred in such a brief span of time. He sat back with relief and smiled. Merle would never be the same after that. The pain Tiffany had felt on the inside, Merle would wear on the outside. Neil did not feel any remorse at his terrible thoughts. Vengeance was indeed the Lord's, and He had repaid in full.

♫ Chapter Forty-two

Karlie was all packed and ready to go. Jamaal, Brian, and Tanya were all there to help her. She expected Thomas to pull up at any minute outside Neil's house.

It had already been two weeks since her mother's death, and Karlie could not have imagined that time would fly by so quickly. She had thought for sure that time would stand still, but it seemed to keep on moving. Life was still going on.

The attorney had read her mother's will, which left almost all her assets to Karlie and a hefty portion to Thomas. Tiffany had declared Neil the head of her estate until Karlie reached twenty-one. But Tiffany had generously bequeathed a full scholarship for Jamaal and a hefty monthly allowance. Karlie had been pleasantly surprised. Jamaal's grandmother had fainted when she heard the news, but he'd taken it in stride. Karlie saw him wiping tears from the corners of his eyes, though, when he thought no one was looking.

Inheriting her mother's generous nature, Karlie had insisted Neil foot Merle's hospital's bills. It was the Christian thing to do, and Karlie knew her mother would approve. Neil had bitterly stated that Merle Peterson would live with that lie Clifford had told her to the grave. Karlie had then countered that she, Neil, and Thomas would take their truth to theirs.

The only thing left for Karlie to do was to say goodbye to her friends and Neil. It was a sad and teary farewell among the friends. Everybody hugged and promised to keep in touch. She was going to miss them all.

Gathering her courage, Karlie walked over to where Neil and Myra stood. "I guess this is good-bye." She valiantly refused to cry.

"I wish you all the best, Karlie," Myra said before going into her house.

Neil noticed Myra's quick exit and bit his lip. He gave Karlie a big hug. He did not want her to go but knew he could not say the words aloud. "I have those pictures and letters if you still want them."

"No," Karlie said. "Keep them. I want you to have something to remember me with."

"Karlie," Neil chided, "I won't forget you. I could never forget you. To me, you're my . . . I love you."

Karlie sniffed. "I won't forget you, either, Neil. You have been more of a father to me than anybody else, and I thank you for that."

They heard a horn toot and looked to see Thomas waving at them. He had already packed her carry-on bags and their luggage in the car. Karlie stepped away from Neil and ran over to the car. She jumped in, and the car sped off.

Neil stood at the door for several minutes. He watched Karlie speed out of his life as quickly as she had entered. He immediately felt sorry that he had not stepped up to the plate and done the right thing. Neil slammed the door with a bang and entered his house.

Losing Tiffany to cancer and then Karlie because of Myra's selfishness ate at Neil's heart. He stewed in his bitterness for another couple of weeks before he finally exploded. He pulled into his driveway one evening after work and went in search of Myra. She was talking on the telephone as if everything was all right. As if she had not driven a knife through his heart.

Neil took the phone out of her hands and slammed it into the cradle. "Myra, I am leaving you. I am going to get Karlie. She is my daughter and she needs me and I promised her mother I would look out for her."

Angry, Myra snidely remarked, "What? You got a thing for the daughter like you did the mother?"

Neil instinctively raised his hands and stepped toward Myra. Then his anger dissipated, and he stepped away from her. He could never lay a hand on her, not even now.

"You have got to be the most selfish woman on the face of this earth. What kind of heart do you have, Myra? Your best friend died and her daughter has no real home, but you can only think of yourself. I have to wonder what kind of woman I have really shackled myself to. You are thoughtless and insensitive beyond belief."

Myra's mouth popped open like a fish's. "You have no right to address me in that way, Neil," she sputtered. "I was only being honest with how I feel. That is not selfish."

"It is selfish," Neil argued. "And it leaves a bad taste in my mouth. Myra, you are making me regret that you bear my last name."

"Oh!" Myra exclaimed. "Why are you being so nasty and vile toward me? Karlie isn't even your child."

"Not biologically, no. But Karlie deserves to be with someone who knows and loves her, Myra. She just lost the only family she had in the world, and for all intents and purposes, she is my child."

Myra purposely tightened her fists, refusing to concede.

Neil shook his head with incredulity. "Myra, won't you even consider it for me?" Neil pleaded with her one last time.

Myra shook her head. "This is our first chance to be parents, Neil. We do not need a teenager in the way."

"I see," Neil said sadly. "So the only reason you wanted her was because you did not think you would ever get pregnant. Is that it?"

Myra nodded her head in the affirmative. She felt free to tell the truth because she knew Neil would not leave her now, not when she was pregnant with his first and possibly only child. A child was a gift more precious than gold.

Neil knew that there was no need for any more words, because Myra had made up her mind. Nonetheless, he persisted. "Myra, please."

"My mind is made up, so I suggest you accept it, Neil. I did not want it to come to this, but now I see that it must. I am giving you a choice, Neil. It is either me and your child, or Karlie. You cannot have both."

"I do not work well with ultimatums, Myra," Neil warned.

"Take it or leave it," Myra replied. She made the rash comment, confident that Neil would back down.

"Then I guess this is good-bye, Myra," Neil said firmly. "And as for my child, I will see you in court when the time comes." He left Myra standing there after that comment.

She cringed when she heard the door slam. A searing pain shot through her body. Myra clutched her stomach and fell to the floor.

Neil booked his flight for California. He would leave in two days. He could not wait to see Karlie. Neil had called Thomas, who said that Karlie was not happy. Thomas loved her enough to let her go with Neil. Hearing that cemented Neil's decision. Karlie was his, and she belonged with him.

Thomas didn't tell Karlie that Neil was coming, knowing she would love the surprise.

After he had walked out on Myra last night, Neil had headed to the office, intent on bunking out there, until he remembered that Tiffany had given him a key to her place. So tonight he intended to sleep there.

When he parked in front of Tiffany's house later that day, an older woman came through her gate and ran over to him. Neil recognized Ms. Brown almost immediately.

"Thank God you are back. I saw an ambulance transporting Myra to the hospital. I do not know what was wrong. The paramedics would not tell me anything."

"Do you know which hospital?" he asked with alarm.

"No." Ms. Brown shook her head over and over again to emphasize her point. "I don't have a clue where they took her."

Neil thanked the older woman and rushed in the house to get out the phone book. He punched in the numbers to Long Island Jewish first. If Myra was not there, he would call Winthrop next.

Lucky for him, Myra was at Long Island Jewish. Neil thanked the operator and raced over to the hospital as fast as he could. On the way there, he prayed countless times that Myra would be okay. He was upset at her, but he did not think he would be able to live with himself if anything happened to her or the baby.

Neil entered the obstetrics ward and asked a nurse for Myra's room. He walked up to the door and opened it slowly. He could not help but shiver at the memory of what had happened the last time that he was inside a hospital. Tiffany had died.

Myra turned her head and exhaled with relief when she saw her husband standing there. She opened her arms, and Neil hugged her. "Thank God, you are all right," he said. "I do not know what I would have done without you."

"No, Neil," Myra said. "You have it all wrong. I cannot imagine my life without you."

Neil shifted before placing his hand over her midsection. He looked at his wife with the question in his eyes.

"Our baby is fine. But Dr. Friedrick warned that he might put me on bed rest if the contractions return. He is concerned because since I am thirty-four, I may be at risk for placenta previa, which is when the placenta is attached low in the uterus. He told me, though, that ninety percent of the time it goes away on its own, but he'd know more when I come back for the ultrasound in three weeks. In the meantime, I'm not going to worry. God will see me through," Myra stated confidently.

"I am so sorry I wasn't here, Myra," Neil said and released a heart-wrenching sigh.

"Do not apologize, Neil," Myra interjected quickly. "Please do not say you are sorry, because you are only going to make me feel worse than I already do."

Neil sat on the bed next to his wife to hear her out.

"Once you walked through that door, I knew that I had lost you for good over something that was so stupid. Neil, I was just jealous."

"Of what?" Neil asked.

"I was jealous of the way that you were with Tiffany, and I transposed all those feelings onto Karlie," Myra confessed. "I also stupidly thought that with Karlie there, that would take something away from the baby."

"Myra, I already love this baby more than you can imagine. You have no need to worry where that is concerned," Neil answered matter-of-factly.

"Neil." Myra hiccupped. "I was incredibly selfish. Please, baby, forgive me. Give me a second chance."

"Consider it forgotten, Myra. Because I do love you, and it was wrong on my part to walk out on you like that in your condition."

"But I gave you an ultimatum," Myra said. "You had every right to do what you did. I deserved it."

"Yes, you did," Neil joked.

The two shared a laugh. Then Myra spoke. "Neil, lying here in this hospital gave me time to think and reflect. I want Karlie to come live with us, because even though I was not acting like it, I do love her."

"Are you sure?" Neil could not disguise the happiness and hope in his voice.

"I'm positive," Myra answered. "I am glad that God did not punish me and take away this little gift that He gave us. I promised Him that if He let this baby live, I would do everything in my power to make it up to you and Karlie."

Neil caressed Myra on her stomach. "Thank you, Myra. Karlie is going to be so happy because she really likes you."

"Does she?"

"Yes, she does," Neil confirmed.

"Then go get her," Myra commanded. "Go get our daughter."

♪ Epilogue

Karlie had just completed her studies when she heard the doorbell. Thomas had declined to send her to school and had hired a full-time tutor for her instead. Karlie hadn't put up too much of a fight, but she still could not get used to the fact that Thomas was now her guardian. He was nice to her, and Karlie could see that he was really trying to be the father he had never been. She admitted that she was the hindrance. She barely spoke to him and contented herself with her music or television.

Karlie missed New York, and she missed Jamaal. It was not the same between them with this huge distance. Their conversations were already becoming stilted and sparse.

Karlie got up when she heard a distinct voice that sounded suspiciously like Neil's. It could not be. Walking into the foyer, Karlie could not believe her eyes. It was Neil.

"Karlie."

Karlie ran toward him as if she was five years old and pounced into his arms.

"Neil. What're you doing here in California?"

"I came to see you."

"You flew all this way to see me?" Karlie was amazed.

"Yes," Neil said. "I want to make you an offer."

"What?" Karlie became excited and hopeful.

"I want to know if you want to come back to New York and live with me," Neil said.

"I'd love to." Karlie beamed. "But what about Thomas?"

"I already spoke to him about it. He says that you're not happy here, and he is willing to relinquish all his rights as your father. He did not feel good about the lie, anyway."

Karlie squealed even louder. She felt as carefree as a kid again. "I had hoped and dreamed for this moment. I prayed and prayed, and when I didn't see it happen, I was, like, well, God didn't answer my prayers. But He heard me. He just took His own time answering."

Neil laughed at her enthusiasm.

"How does Myra feel about all this?" Karlie asked.

Neil wavered for an instant before deciding to tell Karlie the truth. "Well, Myra is coming around. She just has to get used to the idea of having a teenager."

Neil quickly gave her a brief version of what had transpired between himself and his wife. To his utter surprise, Karlie defended Myra.

"Neil, I can understand how Myra felt. I mean, why would she want me around when she is going to have your child? She probably fears that I would replace her child."

Neil looked at Karlie, amazed that one so young could be so astute and perceptive. "Does this mean you are not coming with me?" Neil asked.

"I am definitely coming," Karlie affirmed. "But I have always wanted a little sister or brother, and Myra is going to need my help. I will be your live-in babysitter."

"No," Neil corrected. "You'll be a big sister and daughter."

Karlie hurriedly called Jamaal and Tanya to tell them that she was coming back to Hempstead.

***

The day after Neil's arrival, Karlie packed enough of her clothes to fill one suitcase. She saw Thomas standing by her door.

"Hi," she said shyly. Karlie watched Thomas enter her room to sit on her bed.

"I love you, you know," he said.

Karlie nodded. "I know," she said quietly.

"I knew you weren't happy," Thomas said.

"I love you, but . . ." Karlie didn't know what to say without seeming insensitive.

Thomas held up his hands and smiled. "It's fine. I, on the other hand, love it here. I guess I should go house hunting soon."

"No." Karlie shook her head. "Stay here. Mom would have liked that."

Thomas nodded, and after moments of awkward silence, he got to his feet. "Karlie, I wish you the best. Neil loves you, and if I thought for one minute . . ."

A horn tooted. Karlie and Thomas smiled before he picked up her suitcase. The two went out the front door, and Thomas placed her case in the trunk of the car. Suddenly, Karlie remembered something. She ran up to her bedroom to retrieve two items she would never leave behind. Karlie gently placed the blanket inside her suitcase and carried the painting Thomas had given her.

Karlie walked out of the house, ready to continue her life with Neil and Myra.

Before they pulled off, Neil asked her, "Are you sure you have everything?"

"Yes, *Dad*. I have everything I need."

Reader's Guide Questions

1. Tiffany faced sexual assault from her stepfather. She reacted by sleeping with four different boys. Do you think her reaction is typical of victims of sexual abuse? How could her mother have helped? What resources for victims of abuse are provided by your church or by your community?

2. Discuss Tiffany and her mother's tumultuous mother-daughter relationship. Do you agree/disagree with Merle's decision to put Clifford above her daughter? Do you agree with Tiffany's decision to support Merle financially?

3. Neil and Tiffany shared a lifetime friendship and a special bond. Do you think that men and women can truly be platonic friends?

4. Why do you think Neil and Tiffany kept their friendship a secret from Myra? Do you agree with their rationale? Do you think that Neil should keep his friendship with another woman a secret from his wife?

5. Myra desperately wanted a child, so much so that it consumed her. She ate to fill that void. What are some behaviors we engage in to fill a void in our lives?

6. Neil wondered if Myra battled depression. Do you believe that she was depressed? Share your opinion(s) about whether or not you think it is possible for a Christian to face depression. Should Christians seek professional help, or should God be the only medium used?

7. Neil became highly involved in church activities as a means of escaping his home life. Should God reward his efforts even if his motives were not truly pure?

8. Tiffany discovered God's redemption and forgiveness. Darnell rediscovered his relationship with God. Describe how both Tiffany's and Darnell's attitude about God and church changed from the beginning to the end of the story.

9. Darnell and Tiffany struggled with keeping their relationship pure. What advice can we give for adult Christian singles that are dating?

10. When Karlie found out the truth about her father, she disrespected her mother and called her a whore. Why do you suppose Karlie wasn't as angry with Thomas, who abandoned her as a child?

11. Neil purposely lied to Tiffany about the results of the paternity tests. He also invited Karlie and Thomas in on his scheme to withhold the truth. Is there ever a good reason or time to lie? Is lying ever a necessity?

12. Darnell struggled with Tiffany's impending death and disappeared for a brief period. Do you think

his behavior was understandable or reprehensible? Give your rationale to support your position.

13. Discuss everyone's reaction to Tiffany's death. Do you agree with Neil kicking Merle out of her daughter's funeral?

14. At the end of the story, when Thomas agreed to let Karlie leave with Neil, was he shirking his duty? Do you think he did the right thing?

About the Author

Michelle Lindo-Rice graduated from Argosy University with an education specialist degree in education leadership. A pastor's kid, Michelle upholds the faith through preaching, teaching, and ministering through praise and worship. As a young teen, Michelle discovered a passion for reading and writing and feels blessed to use this talent to bring God glory. She currently lives in Port Charlotte, Florida with her two sons and works as a reading specialist for elementary special education students. *Sing A New Song* is her first published work.

UC HIS GLORY BOOK CLUB!

www.uchisglorybookclub.net

UC His Glory Book Club is the spirit-inspired brain-child of Joylynn Jossel, author and acquisitions editor of Urban Christian, and Kendra Norman-Bellamy, author for Urban Christian. This is an online book club that hosts authors of Urban Christian. We welcome as members all men and women who have a passion for reading Christian-based fiction.

UC His Glory Book Club pledges our commitment to provide support, positive feedback, encouragement, and a forum whereby members can openly discuss and review the literary works of Urban Christian authors.

There is no membership fee associated with UC His Glory Book Club; however, we do ask that you support the authors through purchasing works, offering encouragement, and providing book reviews, and of course, through your prayers. We also ask that you respect our beliefs and follow the guidelines of the book club. We hope to receive your valuable input, opinions, and reviews that build up, rather than tear down, our authors.

WHAT WE BELIEVE:

— We believe that Jesus is the Christ, Son of the Living God.

— We believe the Bible is the true, living Word of God.

Urban Christian His Glory Book Club

— We believe all Urban Christian authors should use their God-given writing abilities to honor God and to share the message of the written word that God has given to each of them uniquely.

— We believe in supporting Urban Christian authors in their literary endeavors by reading, purchasing, and sharing their titles with our online community.

— We believe that everything we do in our literary arena should be done in a manner that will lead to God being glorified and honored.

We look forward to the online fellowship with you. Please visit us often at www.uchisglorybookclub.net.

Many Blessing to You!
Shelia E. Lipsey,
President, UC His Glory Book Club

ORDER FORM
URBAN BOOKS, LLC
78 E. Industry Ct
Deer Park, NY 11729

Name: (please print):_____

Address: _____

City/State: _____

Zip: _____

QTY	TITLES	PRICE
	3:57 A.M Timing Is Everything	$14.95
	A Man's Worth	$14.95
	A Woman's Worth	$14.95
	Abundant Rain	$14.95
	After The Feeling	$14.95
	Amaryllis	$14.95
	An Inconvenient Friend	$14.95
	Battle of Jericho	$14.95
	Be Careful What You Pray For	$14.95
	Beautiful Ugly	$14.95
	Been There Prayed That:	$14.95
	Before Redemption	$14.95

Shipping and handling-add $3.50 for 1st book, then $1.75 for each additional book.
Please send a check payable to:
Urban Books, LLC
Please allow 4-6 weeks for delivery

ORDER FORM
URBAN BOOKS, LLC
78 E. Industry Ct
Deer Park, NY 11729

Name:(please print):_____

Address: _____

City/State: _____

Zip: _____

QTY	TITLES	PRICE
	By the Grace of God	$14.95
	Confessions Of A preachers Wife	$14.95
	Dance Into Destiny	$14.95
	Deliver Me From My Enemies	$14.95
	Desperate Decisions	$14.95
	Divorcing the Devil	$14.95
	Faith	$14.95
	First Comes Love	$14.95
	Flaws and All	$14.95
	Forgiven	$14.95
	Former Rain	$14.95
	Forsaken	$14.95

Shipping and handling-add $3.50 for 1st book, then $1.75 for each additional book.
Please send a check payable to:
Urban Books, LLC
Please allow 4-6 weeks for delivery

ORDER FORM
URBAN BOOKS, LLC
78 E. Industry Ct
Deer Park, NY 11729

Name: (please print): _____

Address: _____

City/State: _____

Zip: _____

QTY	TITLES	PRICE
	From Sinner To Saint	$14.95
	From The Extreme	$14.95
	God Is In Love With You	$14.95
	God Speaks To Me	$14.95
	Grace And Mercy	$14.95
	Guilty Of Love	$14.95
	Happily Ever Now	$14.95
	Heaven Bound	$14.95
	His Grace His Mercy	$14.95
	His Woman His Wife His Widow	$14.95
	Illusions	$14.95
	In Green Pastures	$14.95

Shipping and handling-add $3.50 for 1st book, then $1.75 for each additional book.

Please send a check payable to:

Urban Books, LLC

Please allow 4-6 weeks for delivery

ORDER FORM
URBAN BOOKS, LLC
78 E. Industry Ct
Deer Park, NY 11729

Name: (please print): _____

Address: _____

City/State: _____

Zip: _____

QTY	TITLES	PRICE
	Into Each Life	$14.95
	Keep Your enemies Closer	$14.95
	Keeping Misery Company	$14.95
	Latter Rain	$14.95
	Living Consequences	$14.95
	Living Right On Wrong Street	$14.95
	Losing It	$14.95
	Love Honor Stray	$14.95
	Marriage Mayhem	$14.95
	Me, Myself and Him	$14.95
	Murder Through The Grapevine	$14.95
	My Father's House	$14.95

Shipping and handling-add $3.50 for 1st book, then $1.75 for each additional book.

Please send a check payable to:

Urban Books, LLC

Please allow 4-6 weeks for delivery